MW01089095

WHERE
THE
LOCKWOOD
GROWS

BY OLIVIA A. COLE

Cloud Parliament
Dear Medusa
The Truth About White Lies
Time to Roar

FALOIV
A Conspiracy of Stars
An Anatomy of Beasts

THE TASHA TRILOGY
Panther in the Hive
The Rooster's Garden

WHERE
THE
LOCKWOOD
GROWS

OLIVIA A. COLE

Little, Brown and Company

New York Boston

Interior art: Tree shadow copyright © merrymuuu/Shutterstock.com. Vine border copyright © Olga Illi/Shutterstock.com. Interior design by Vivian Jones and Jenny Kimura.

Cover art copyright © 2023 by Erwin Madrid. Cover design by Jenny Kimura. Cover copyright © 2023 by Hachette Book Group, Inc.

Little, Brown and Company
Hachette Book Group
1290 Avenue of the Americas, New York, NY 10104
Visit us at LBYR.com

First Edition: August 2023

Little, Brown and Company is a division of Hachette Book Group, Inc. The Little, Brown name and logo are trademarks of Hachette Book Group, Inc.

The publisher is not responsible for websites (or their content) that are not owned by the publisher.

Little, Brown and Company books may be purchased in bulk for business, educational, or promotional use. For information, please contact your local bookseller or the Hachette Book Group Special Markets Department at special.markets@hbgusa.com.

Library of Congress Cataloging-in-Publication Data
Names: Cole, Olivia A., author.
Title: Where the lockwood grows / Olivia A. Cole.
Description: First edition. | New York : Little, Brown and Company, 2023. |
Audience: Ages 8–12. | Summary: "In this dystopian tale, young Erie and her older sister, Hurona, leave the only home they've ever known and discover that the world is much larger and more complicated than they'd ever imagined."
—Provided by publisher.
Identifiers: LCCN 2022032152 | ISBN 9780316449120 (hardcover) |
ISBN 9780316449328 (ebook)
Subjects: CYAC: Secrets—Fiction. | Sisters—Fiction. | Family life—Fiction. |
LGBTQ+ people—Fiction. | LCGFT: Dystopian fiction. | Novels.
Classification: LCC PZ7.1.C6429 Wh 2023 | DDC [Fic]—dc23
LC record available at https://lccn.loc.gov/2022032152

ISBNs: 978-0-316-44912-0 (hardcover), 978-0-316-44932-8 (ebook)

Printed in the United States of America

LSC-C

Printing 1, 2023

*For everyone who believes
we still have time*

In the lockwood we have a formidable enemy and a powerful friend. It can't be cut by any ordinary axe; it can't be burned. It grows to a towering height overnight. But like a loyal friend, it is dependable. It does what we need when we most need it. The oxygen it provides is equivalent to a rainforest; it stops wildfire in its tracks. The lockwood's trimmings can be used to make toilet paper, brick, packaging. And then the pods! What a gift of science and nature. There were some mistakes in the early execution of the lockwood's power—but we have learned from those mistakes. To dwell on them is to take our eye off the shimmering promise of our future.

—GOVERNOR MAVELON WILE

BEFORE I WAS called into the trees, I would daydream. Before tree shoes, I was barefoot. Me and my sister, running through the tangle once the light broke through. Hurona flapped her arms big and slow. She was a dragon.

What are you?

Whatever she was, I was too. Two dragons. Two flying elephants. Two griffins. Flying through the almost-dark.

She's older, so the lockwood trees called her first.

When it was my turn, I gave up bare feet for tree shoes.

Do you remember what I told you?

Yes.

Stay small. Move slow.

We weren't dragons anymore.

1

I'M NOT AFRAID of the dark.

If you think about the darkness the wrong way, it might seem like it's hiding something from you. A spider, or a monster, or a ghost. But it helps if you make friends with the dark. Like I have.

The old folks need headlamps to get dressed, but when I wake up, my hands and feet find their way. Cave dark. Belly dark, like our entire town of Prine has been swallowed. But we haven't been swallowed, because I hear the tiny, sticky steps of a beetle on my window's screen. I imagine it's saying good morning, and I answer under my breath. Then I press my ear against the wall beside my bed, where I hear my sister, Hurona, murmuring, and I smile. She says I'm always talking to myself, but she does too. Especially lately. I think it's something about the dark—it makes you want to whisper, just to fill the space.

The gloom is thickest in the morning—we haven't cut the lockwood back yet. The lockwood...I've seen things like it in old, old comic books. A plant that grows like it wants to choke out the sun. Maybe it would if the kids in Prine didn't climb up every morning to cut the vines and let the light in. Until then, it's dark. And this is the time when the dark keeps my secret for me.

It's hidden under my mattress, and I find it easily. The old phone fits in my hand like a flat pink brick. I duck under my covers, fully dressed, and a moment later have it pressed against my ear, listening to Aunt Josie's voice.

I never met Aunt Josie, but these are the voice messages she left Mom before she died. I found the phone one day when I was looking for socks and Hurona's drawer was empty. In my mom's dresser, it was tucked into the back behind flannel pajamas. Nothing saved on it but the voice messages.

Mom didn't notice I had it until the day I asked her, *What conservancy did Aunt Josie work for?* and Mom's eyes jerked up. She knew I could only have learned about it from one place, and told me to put the phone back. And I did. For a while. But the recordings of my aunt's voice were like listening to a ghost whisper in my ear, and I've never been scared of ghosts: I'd welcome them if they came— Aunt Josie, my dad, Gran'Ida. I've even *asked* them to come before. They take up enough invisible space in our house. They might as well come inside. But they never do.

What's gone stays gone, my mom always says. She's not interested in memories unless there's something she thinks she can learn from them. Like when she figured out our great-uncle, who was dead, used to go to fascist rallies. *That kind of thing is like a mutant octopus,* she says. *Just cut off its tentacles and it will grow ten more until you actually deal with the problem of a mutant octopus.* But it's not like that with Aunt Josie. Just that the fires took her, and that keeping our eyes on the future is how we prevent more loss. Mom doesn't think there's anything to learn from just missing people.

And I don't know if there is either. But I sit and listen to Aunt Josie's voice under my blanket anyway. So many voice messages, some short, some long. Dozens of them. I have a rule: If it's thirty seconds or less, I can listen to two. Otherwise I only listen to one each morning. Today is a two-message day.

> 1. Hi, it's me, just returning your call. I'm at the zoo until four. I'll call you after. Later.

> 2. You left just before they brought the falcon out! You really missed out. Only nineteen left in the world. I know it depresses you. Maybe I shouldn't have invited you. Are you going on a date with the guy you met in Kincade? I wish you'd let me meet him. You don't have to be so secretive all the time! Well, thanks for coming anyway. I hope it wasn't too much for you. Next time invite me to your lab! Or is that a secret too? Gotta run. Love you! Later.

All her messages end with that one word: *later*. I whisper it under the blanket, wondering if my voice sounds like hers, since it doesn't sound like Mom's; wondering what secrets my mom kept from Aunt Josie, wondering if they're the same ones she keeps from me.

Then the phone goes back under my mattress, and I take a

deep breath. In the familiar dark, I reach for the place I know my doorknob will be, but before I turn it, I whisper one more thing to myself:

"Stay small. Move slow."

The orb in the kitchen is illuminated—Mom is awake, and the smell of eggs and bread drifts down the hall. The light gets brighter with every step, like I'm rising from the bottom of a pond. And there she is: bent over her microscope, hair piled on top of her head and out of the way, hands flying between its dials and her notes. Her projects are spread over every part of what used to be the dining room. Mom doesn't really do small or slow.

"Good morning, Erie," she says, without taking her eyes from the scope. "Eat."

"Good morning." I sit down at the wobbly folding table. I feel my eyes get big. "You made bread."

She looks up then, a brief glance. Her smile is like a quick bird.

There are two kinds of bread: soft bread and hard bread. The hard stuff is what you buy in the general store, the kind they ship in from Petrichor. The soft stuff is what my mom makes when we've gotten a little bit of money. The bread tastes good, but that's not what makes me smile. It's what the bread *means*. She only makes it when she's feeling hopeful. It makes me feel guilty for having her phone under my mattress.

"Enjoy," she says. "Sorry about the mess."

She always says that, like we're not used to it. The "mess" is overflow from the shed behind our small, square house—the shed is where all her *real* projects are. It's spring now, the ground and air thawing. She'll be back out there soon. Until then, the sprawl of all her work stuff looks strange compared to the bareness of the rest of our house. Mom grew up in the fires. She says it only takes losing everything once or twice before you stop wanting to own anything at all. *Including memories*, I think. I know she had to have lived somewhere outside these trees at one point—they've only existed for so long. But it's like she never kept the memories, or they burned in the fires too.

"I don't mind," I reply. And I don't. I like the cold months, when she's still in here before I go to the trees. I like watching her. She's still staring at something through the microscope, adjusting a dial here and there. Her soldering iron sends up the faintest plume of gray smoke. I try to imagine myself the same way. Warm. Ready. I place my lockwood knife on the table and sit down to eat.

I'm only two bites in when Hurona's door opens. My stomach twitches. Sometimes I think I'm hungrier for my sister than the eggs. She enters the kitchen with the smooth expression she always wears. Unlike me, she wakes up wide awake, no lag time. Part of why she was so good in the lockwood before she sized out.

"Hi," I say, and she waves a little wave. She hears the little sister in my voice the same way I do. We're like the two lakes we were named for—close, made of the same stuff, but just far enough to be different. Of the five Great Lakes, only Huron and Erie haven't dried up. It makes no sense, because the other ones were bigger and should've lasted longer. *You're survivors, like them*, our mother says when she talks about naming us. I always wonder: *What will we be when those lakes dry up too?* I could ask. I know she'd have an answer. But I don't really want to know.

"Thanks for the eggs," Hurona says. She will only eat a few bites. It reminds me to slow down.

"I could use a few more." Mom doesn't look up. The buzz of soldering makes her sound far away. "Mind grabbing some before you go to work?"

"They overcharge at the general store," my sister says. Her face tightens. I stop chewing.

Our mother looks up.

"And what would you suggest?"

"I hear they're half the cost in Petrichor," Hurona says.

"I'll wait here while you walk fifty miles for eggs," Mom says. Her eyes flash.

Hurona and Mom look at each other. As usual, I feel like a moon that can't decide which planet to orbit. Sisters are supposed to always be on the same side, but sometimes it feels like Hurona can track down a fight like a hound tracks blood.

I want to say, *Don't you see the soft bread? Don't you know what that means? Why do you want to ruin it?* But like so many other things, I swallow the words. Maybe she finally notices the bread, because Hurona's prickled face smooths out again. She turns her eyes to me.

"Walk with you?" she asks.

"Okay," I say quickly, before she can change her mind. I take one more tiny bite. If Hurona notices how tiny, she doesn't say.

"Hatchet?" Hurona says when we get to the door.

I freeze, then pat my hip. My knife is still sitting on the table, and my face heats up. My sister has been out of the trees for as long as I've been in them. Two years, and I still sometimes skip the important stuff.

"Headlamps," Mom reminds us, as if we could forget. You can forget a blade, but you can't forget the dark. It won't let you.

2

MOST MORNINGS, WHEN I leave the house by myself, I switch on my headlamp before I step out into the black. It's so dark that if the ground had disappeared overnight I wouldn't know until I was falling. And though I'm not afraid of the dark, I *am*—like every kid in Prine—afraid of falling.

Today, though, with my big sister by my side, I do as she does, and that means putting on our headlamps but not turning them on until the door closes behind us. And for a moment we don't exist. Belly dark. But if you've been up top, then you know better than to think the lockwood is a beast. It's just a plant. Even if it is a very hungry one. Still, for the few heartbeats before we switch on our headlamps, it does feel like we've been swallowed.

"Ready?" Hurona says softly, and even though she can't see me, I nod.

My fingers find the switch the way they could find my ear, or my navel. Then light: an orange pool ahead. Then a second pool joins it. Hurona's.

"Let's do it," she says, and even though I walk this path alone every morning, now I follow just half a pace behind her as we make our way through the black streets of Prine.

Once we get to the Spine, we can actually see without head-lamps, but leave them on anyway. The Spine is the avenue down the middle of our tiny town, one thing lit up with Prine's precious solar power. From somewhere in the dark beyond the Spine I hear a few of the little kids' voices raised in song:

> *The Spine of Prine is glowing;*
> *it's the only thing that will*
> *until they beat the lockwood back,*
> *which grows tomorrow still.*

I glance at Hurona, see the tight smile lift one corner of her mouth.

"Remember singing that?" I ask. It makes me feel older, thinking about kids' songs as something of the past.

"Yes," she says.

"They're up early."

"Probably have siblings going to the lockwood. Whole house awake," she says.

I eye her sideways.

"Do you ever miss going to the top?" I ask.

"For the first year, they had to climb," she says. "Before they brought the cranes. Did you know that? I did it too once. Climbed all the way up without the crane just to see if I could."

This isn't an answer, but I hadn't really expected one. She folds her smile up. I don't say anything else until we get to the corner where we will go on our separate paths: she toward the general store for eggs, and me toward the cranes.

"See you," I say. "I'll try to drop you some pods if I see them."

"You're not supposed to do that," she says, already half gone. "Focus on the trimming. Let the pod kids take care of the pods."

"I was just kidding," I call, but she's far enough away now where she can pretend not to have heard me.

"Thank you for your service!" someone calls from one of the black streets off the Spine, and even after two years in the lockwood, I still think they're talking to someone else. I wave at the face I can't see and nod my head. The light from my headlamp swims around.

My mom invented the type of headlamp that we all use—her one success. I used to want to be an inventor too. Daydreams from before I went into the lockwood. My very first invention was an ant trap that didn't hurt the ants. I've always loved bugs—so tiny, so strong. Even now as I walk, I search the glow of my headlamp for lines of black ants.

"Don't be late!" another voice calls to me from the dark. "I'd like to see the sun before noon today!"

If Hurona was here she would mutter, *Then let's see you go up.* I'm too afraid they'd hear me. I look up into the knot over Prine, but my headlamp is like a feather trying to pierce stone. I keep my eyes on the ants. We all march to work.

"Erie Neaux, good morning," says Mx. Amur, standing at the entrance. Here is one place where Prine allows plenty of solar in the early hours. Mx. Amur is short and muscular and walks with a cane. She has eyes the color of wet grass and is the only (I think) one besides my mom who has ever lived somewhere other than Prine—Sacramento, before the Arborklept, the last really big fire. Mx. Amur talks about it sometimes, what it was like to live outside this place. She moved here with her wife, but then her wife died. Mx. Amur had stayed. I asked her why once and she said, *I'm just like everyone else here: I can't afford to leave.* But Hurona had been there too, and when Mx. Amur had turned away, my sister whispered, *Even if she had money, she'd stay. People stay because they're scared of being in the world outside the lockwood.* And I think she must have been right, because Mx. Amur is one of the few people with a car, even if it hasn't run since I learned to walk. It's a teal van and may have been shiny at some point. But now it's as scuffed up as an old shoe, sitting behind her house, covered in leaves.

"Good morning, Mx. Amur," I reply, and scan the faces already here. Dezbah. Saola. Hector. Curie. A couple of new kids who must have just had birthdays. All I see of their faces is their chins—new kids are always looking up. Here, with the solar torches in a ring around us, you can see what a headlamp alone can't show you. Here you can make out the tangle.

"Think they know what they're in for?" Banneker says.

They appeared by my side while I was studying Prine's version of the sky.

"If they've been paying attention to Mr. Ovitt they do," I say.

"Yeah, but who does that?" They snicker, and we both giggle before their eyes go back down to the notebook they're always carrying. I don't bother trying to see. It's all numbers. They write a few more—math equations. I hate math.

"Can you even see?" I say.

Banneker nods. One long loc slips out of the bundle at the back of their head. Banneker's thin brown hands rise to tuck it back. But a minute later they're putting the notebook away. We're going up soon. Banneker's eyes skitter over the new kids' faces, then up at the tangle. I always think their brain is filled with their own kind of math. Banneker is the best pod kid in Prine, and it's because of those eyes. Never missing a thing. Seeing how things fit together. And also, of course, because they're skinny. Small enough to get between all the knots of the lockwood, with eyes sharp enough to find every pod.

"My mom said you used to be able to see the mountains from Prine," they say. "But the lockwood swallowed it up."

I feel myself frown. I hadn't expected them to say that, and it makes me feel a little lost. Everyone is always talking about the lockwood swallowing Prine, but I'd never thought of it as the rest of the world being swallowed instead.

"Where's Darah?" I ask. Prine is small enough to where we pretty much know everyone. And that means knowing who's missing. But I didn't really need to ask. I already know the answer.

"Too big," Banneker says. Two heavy words. Too. Big. We all will be one day. The lockwood swallows then spits out kids who get too big to fit between the branches. Spits us out like peanut shells or fish bones. Small kids cut back the lockwood, and all the young people too big for the branches work on the ground, like my sister, gathering fallen pods and clearing away the lockwood vines that those of us in the trees throw down. Then everyone else in Prine scrambles to do what needs to be done in the short window of sunlight. Adults take the lockwood we cut and feed it into the pulping machine. It buzzes all day long and into the evening. And then we do it all over again the next day, the lockwood springing back overnight. It's hard to think about the mountains. It's hard to think about anything except: *Stay small, move slow.*

"Anyone with a faulty hatchet?" Mx. Amur calls. She motions us all closer and we cluster around, holding our blades up for her to see. The one I clutch used to be Hurona's, which is lucky, because the hatchets cost a lot of money. I don't know how much, but Hurona made a big deal of telling me not to lose it. The blades are made of some special stuff they make fifty miles away in Petrichor; it's the only thing that will cut through lockwood. Quickly, anyway. You could sit up there with a saw and eventually you'd cut through. It would take forever, and nobody has forever when the sun is waiting.

Hurona says it's a scam—that most of the money people in Prine get for selling pods has to pay for new hatchets, but how can we complain? Without them, we'd be crushed. If only given the chance, the lockwood would do what Dr. Lunata Elemneiri, its inventor, had designed it to do: keep everything out. Fire. Smoke.

Wind. I think it would keep out the air if we let it go. There would be no wildfires—which is why Dr. Elemnieri invented lockwood to begin with—but there would be no Prine either.

Mx. Amur checks my blade, waves me toward the crane. I'm not one of the ones she has to worry about. Kids with no legacy, kids who are the first in their families to go up. Those kids don't know right away. This is what me and Banneker mean: *Think they know what they're in for?* Not just the danger. The dread. When your pants are suddenly too short, knowing what it means. When your sweater starts to show your belly. I'd always wanted to be tall like Mom, strong. But Prine needs me to be small—its survival depends on my smallness.

And so every day after my shift in the lockwood, when I'm allowed to go to school for a few hours, I stare at the lessons I'm supposed to be learning, and rather than learning them, I think small thoughts. Goldfinch. Spring toad. Small and narrow. When I sleep in the early evening, I try to dream small dreams—a doll's teacup, a single screw from my mom's shop. But if I ever dream at all, I never remember them.

"Up we go," shouts Mx. Amur when everyone's hatchet is sharp and ready.

Up we go.

3

EVERY TUESDAY THE trucks from Petrichor rumble through the tunnel of lockwood toward Prine. The people who come on the trucks all wear white uniforms with reflective strips down their arms and spines, and their shoulders and chests all read FOLROY—the company that buys the pods and clippings, who sells us the hatchets. They also bring us medical supplies, and sometimes mail. Some days they arrive just as me and the other lockwood kids are coming out of the trees; sometimes they're waiting for us, ready to weigh the collected pods and pay the mayor. Either way, they always smile and wave at us: *There they are! The little birds! Birds in the lockwood!*

They've never been up in the tangle before. We're not birds.

The crane lifts us high up, the lights from the ground like staring moons. Everyone's headlamps twinkle like fireflies. The newer kids chatter, but me and Banneker stare silently up at the lockwood, closer every second. When the crane grinds to a halt, Mx. Amur extends the ladders, then she says one word:

"Climb."

We climb. The ladders sway, but I'm strong. Most of the time the lockwood feels like an enemy, but this is the one time it's a comfort, when you step from the shaking ladder into the iron tangle. From there, you're on your own. You balance. Your blade is still clipped so your hands can find a grip. I remember the first time I touched the branches, how surprised I was at the warmth of the wood, if you can really call it wood. The way it feels rough and smooth at the same time. It's like reaching into the ocean and instead of wet, finding dry. I monkey-walk along the thickest branch I can find: hands down, butt up. Banneker goes ahead of me. They're a pod kid, so they need to cut out all the pods they can find before I start taking out the branches. We make our way along the thick branch, as far as we can until it's time to squeeze.

The lockwood branches are like a ball of yarn, like someone crumpled up a silver necklace and flung it in a corner, all the links in a ball. My mom showed me how to take a needle and untangle tiny things like that. The lockwood is far from tiny, but me and Banneker are the needles. I slink and squeeze, under and over. I move away from the group, following Banneker. They've already begun to fill their sack with pods. Their headlamp is a yellow wash ahead in the dark. The rest of the group spreads out. No one speaks now. There's no sound except the hiss and shuffle of our shoes on the strange bark. Breath, grunts, and eventually the sigh of the hatchets. We're not birds. Birds would sing.

"All yours," Banneker says softly when they've finished with a branch. I set in after them with the hatchet. It's not really a hatchet—it's more like a steak knife. Whatever metal FOLROY made to fight

16

the lockwood, it's good. It slides through the branches like butter, and the moisture inside the lockwood oozes out. I've learned to avoid touching it. It won't hurt you, but it feels gross and it's hard to wipe off. That's part of what makes the lockwood fireproof: The outer part of the plant won't catch, and the inside is too wet to burn.

Before I drop the first branch, I look down to make sure Mx. Amur has readied the net. Like the FOLROY uniforms, every thread of it is illuminated. It's like a glowing spiderweb underneath us. I let the first winding branch go. When I first started, I would watch it all the way down. Now I just keep cutting.

"What's your mom working on lately?" Banneker says when we've been at it for an hour or two. I think we're getting close—after a couple of years in the lockwood, you start to sense the sun.

"Dunno," I say. I drop a branch—it falls down the tunnel Banneker and I have hacked through the vines. All around us the other kids do the same, everybody snaking through the tightly knitted branches. We don't have to cut it *all*—that would be impossible. But it has to be thinned and untangled enough to let the light through. It's like a math problem, and I picture it in Mr. Ovitt's voice:

If the mayor estimates that the lockwood grows seven feet overnight, and it takes two shifts of thirty kids to break through to the sun, about how many feet does each kid cut?

Every time I'm feeling sarcastic, I imagine Hurona answering. Her imaginary answer: *Who cares? Just cut it. The sun is waiting.*

"Come on," Banneker says, and I snap out of it. They glance back at me as they store a handful of pods. "You live with an *inventor*. Aren't you interested in what she's *invented*?"

17

"She hasn't invented anything since the headlamps," I say. "Otherwise we wouldn't live in Prine. We'd move to Petrichor. Maybe somewhere even farther."

"She's working on other things," Banneker insists. They like talking about my mom's tinkering because they're a tinkerer too. I had imagined being an inventor when I was little, but Banneker really could be one. My mom once told them being good at math helped with making stuff, and now whenever they're not in the lockwood they're studying equations. "Just because the world doesn't know what they *are* yet doesn't mean anything."

"Okay fine," I say. "She's working on sparrows."

"Sparrows?" Banneker says, and they're really alarmed, because they pause picking pods and gaze down at me. "Like experimenting on them?"

"No," I gasp. "No way! Not *real* sparrows. Little robots. They're tiny and look kind of like sparrows. I don't know what they do. They give off a frequency. Like a signal maybe. She made them small so they can fit through pipes, or even through the lockwood, I guess."

"I wanna do something like that," Banneker says longingly. "I have an idea for this invention. You wanna hear?"

"Of course." I nod. I love hearing about Banneker's inventions.

"Can I have a spotlight?" they say quietly, teasing.

I look around to make sure we're far enough from everyone else to where they won't notice. Not because we'll get in trouble, but because it's our thing. I lock my legs around the lockwood branch I'm on and aim my headlamp at the area right beside Banneker.

They pull off one glove and plunge their hand into the circle of light, moving their fingers like a mouth, like their hand is a scientist giving an interview.

"The arborlaser," Banneker's hand announces. For some reason the hand has an accent. Like maybe British. "It has the power to detect trees that need to be cut down and trees that don't. It fits on your headlamp next to the light and, once switched on, can travel up to five hundred yards! It passes through good trees and cuts right through bad trees! The best part: You don't even have to leave the ground!"

I clap a tiny clap, making whispered cheering sounds. They grin.

"Wait," I say, addressing the hand. "Is the lockwood a good tree or a bad tree?"

"It depends on the day," Banneker's hand answers, and we both laugh quietly. They put their glove back on and return to picking, chuckling. After a long time they glance at me again. I already know what they're going to ask.

"How's Hurona?"

"She's fine," I say, because it's what Hurona would want me to say.

"Good," they answer.

I gaze down before I drop another branch of lockwood. The ground lamps make it hard to see anything but their glow, but somewhere down there on the ground is Hurona, a girl like Darah who, after years in the lockwood, was suddenly "too big." Mx. Amur had called Hurona "a golden weasel" when she was eleven, the highest of compliments. Hurona, tall as our mother, Nadine Neaux, but thin as a wire. She could slip through the knots of the lockwood and then cling to a branch and cut faraway vines without once having to move.

But then she grew.

Hips at first, the vines squeezing tighter than before. Then breasts. I was nine then, and I remember how when our mother made stew, Hurona only used the ladle once before dropping it back into the blue pot. Once she started on the road to "too big," she tried to shrink. There are some girls who shrink so much they get sick. Others just get sick of trying, and end up where Hurona ended up—on the ground beneath the nets, harvesting pods that the pickers missed. But I've seen the way the older girls walk around Prine. Something in their eyes is still shrinking. Many of them only last on the ground for a few years and then they disappear. Hurona says they go to Petrichor to look for real work, a real life. A life that has more daylight than Prine can give. This is what makes the adults shake their heads. Because Petrichor might have light, but it's a city. Cities are huge, strange, anonymous. No one knows anyone, and no one cares to take care of each other. This, Mr. Ovitt says, is why once people are gone from Prine, they stay gone. They forget what home means. He talks about Petrichor like it's a nest of spiders, and everyone who goes there becomes a fly stuck in its web.

Twenty feet away, one of the newer girls slips. We haven't broken through to the top layer yet, where sun starts to creep through. Everything is still dark, and I can hear her hands slapping at the gnarled and tangled branches, looking for a hold. I know right

20

away that she hadn't anchored herself properly. It's easy to forget in the dark, moving from branch to branch.

I hear her screaming the whole way down.

It's better to fall in the beginning, before the net is full of branches. I know the sound of the crunch by now. I stare at Banneker and they stare back, our headlamps making each other squint in the short silence that follows. I lower my eyes when the girl starts screaming again. The sound rises up into the tangle. I focus on the path of a green beetle, trundling along the vines. I let it crawl onto my finger, then relocate it down to a vine I've already cut. The girl's cries are quieter now. A broken arm or leg probably. From below comes the red flash-flash of Mx. Amur's emergency unit. I should be getting back to cutting, but my knife feels so heavy in my hand. I stare down and down, even when the ground lights fill my eyes with spots. From somewhere up here in the trees, I hear someone start to cry.

The lockwood kids aren't birds. Birds would fly.

4

DAWN IS STARTING to peek through now, but I'm back on the ground. Sometimes Banneker and I stand and watch the second shift for a while before going to the schoolhouse. My mom says I've seen sunrises—when I was two, before the lockwood was planted—but I don't remember them. Watching the limbs fall and the tongue of sun creep through are the closest thing.

"I think I'm going to skip," Banneker says when we turn away. "I'm tired, and I don't feel like hearing Mr. Ovitt go on and on."

I just nod. Mr. Ovitt does go on and on, but that's not even what bothers me. He's always lecturing. My mom once said that he sits on a high horse. I don't know about that, but in class he always perches on the corner of the desk with his arms crossed and tells stories about his life. And in the stories about his life, he always has it harder than we do.

"When I was your age, I went to school for eight *hours a day."* I make my voice like a toad to sound like our teacher. *"And you can't even stay awake for* two.*"*

Banneker snorts.

"Ovitt never had to wake up at four," they say. "*And* he didn't have to go into the lockwood before school."

"No, but he probably did see the fires," I say, and we're both quiet then. Yes, the lockwood chokes the sun, but Prine was one of the last old towns left after the Arborklept. They had sheltered Prine with the lockwood just a couple of years before the Arborklept. So much had to be rebuilt after that. But not Prine. The lockwood is like a guard dog that takes its job a little too far. But I guess we still need the guard dog.

"Well, I hope it's fun," Banneker says. They pat my back, all sarcasm. Then they pause. "Wait, are you wearing…a bra?"

I freeze. I don't know how they felt it—although I guess if I can feel it as much as I do, it's probably easy to tell through my shirt. I'd found it last week in Hurona's room when I was snagging a pair of socks. I don't need it yet, not like Hurona does. Or says she does. But it feels cool to put it on…even if I had almost ripped it trying to figure out how to wear it. At the same time, it feels kind of like standing too close to the edge of a cliff. When I actually need a bra, it will probably also mean I'm too big for the lockwood.

"Um, maybe," I say. I've never been embarrassed in front of Banneker before. Not about anything real. I can't tell if it's because I'm wearing a bra I don't need, or because they noticed.

"Don't be weird," they say with a laugh, and move off down the Spine. I watch them go. Even after hours in the trees, they walk with a bop in their step. Part of me wants to go home too. Take off the stupid bra and sleep. But I can imagine my mom looking up at the clock and then looking at me, her eyes made huge by her goggles. She would just send me back.

The schoolhouse is three rooms, and the smallest room is for kids my age. Rows of old wobbly desks. A smudged whiteboard. Mr. Ovitt's desk, just as old and wobbly. He has a bulletin board behind it, and most of the stuff on it, he says, was from whoever the teacher was before him. Sometimes I think about who the teacher will be after him—sometimes I picture it being me. I don't know anything to teach anyone. Maybe that's why teaching sounds cool—because to do it, I'd have to learn from someone who's seen more of the world, someone who could tell me all the things I'd teach—all those things I really want to know.

Also on the bulletin board are a few old magazine covers, one from when polar bears officially went extinct. There's also a map of Petrichor, faded and folded. It's pinned up with everything else, and it's been there as long as I can remember. Through the wall I can hear the little kids singing one of their factoid songs.

> *Solar power makes us run;*
> *it gives us heat and light.*
> *It gives us electricity;*
> *it makes our world work right.*
> *When the sun can reach our panels,*
> *it gives us what we lack.*

24

But first it has to reach us,
so we cut the lockwood back.

I sit rolling a pencil back and forth under my hand—it's bumpy and doesn't roll smoothly because it's made of lockwood. It makes a rhythm when I roll it over my desktop. I sit at the same desk every day—by the window, even if there's not much to see yet except the Spine, figures making their way through the little-bit-less-dark. In the world outside Prine, the sun has been up for three hours. But we'll have our sunshine soon. The sky looks calico—the second shift is starting to break through. On the windowsill, a beetle is wandering. I'm tired, but I perk up. Mr. Ovitt hasn't started yet, so I lean over to get a closer look.

It's small and reddish brown and wanders back and forth along the crack of the window.

"What are you looking for?" I whisper. But I already know. Some people see bugs and the only thing that comes to mind is *eww*. But bugs have a language just like us that you can see if you watch long enough. This bug is called a dustnose beetle and it's sensing the light that's starting to break through. Like the people of Prine, dustnose beetles work in the dark, but they're attracted to the light. I hold my pencil out, just in front of its chompers. Not to scare it, just to see. Its antennae seem to consider. Then it latches on. I stare for what feels like a long time, and eventually see dust forming. It's munching on my pencil. I laugh quietly to myself. At least I have an excuse not to do my schoolwork now. *A beetle ate my pencil, sorry.*

Mr. Ovitt turns on the screen at the front of the room, and

everyone who chose to come to class today looks up with interest. Mondays are usually science days, but the screen coming to life means he has something different planned.

"Most of you know the name Dr. Lunata Elemnieri," Ovitt says. He doesn't need to call the class to order. We're all usually too tired to chat. I leave my pencil to the beetle and turn to listen. "The inventor of lockwood. Today she's appearing on the Newscast for a special interview, and I thought we might all enjoy hearing a scientist talk about the creation we all know so well."

Everyone sort of murmurs. Most of us will probably sleep. I imagine Hurona: *Oh, great, more lockwood, just what I want to hear about, thanks.* I slip my hands inside my desk, where I'd stowed my book. There are stacks of books that have ended up in the schoolhouse—I'm not even sure where they came from—and many of them are falling apart. We're supposed to read them, but no one ever has time, and every time I start to, I fall asleep, or I go into the lockwood, or I think about my sister and wonder if she's still shrinking. Books just can't keep my focus. Except for one.

The Encyclopedia of Entomology.

The illustration of a bee on the cover had called to me from the first time I saw it. When I opened it up, I learned that *entomology* means *bugs*. I was seven that first time, and I borrowed it from school so many times that I eventually just kept it. Nobody noticed. Definitely not Mr. Ovitt, who's telling us about what screens looked like when he was our age while he plugs things in. The book is three hundred pages long, and I don't care that some of the pages are torn and stained—some of the tears and stains are from me. I open it, and suddenly my muscles don't feel so tired. My head doesn't hum from the sound of the pulper outside. I get lost in maggots and wasps while Mr. Ovitt waits for the screen to find a signal. If we hadn't spent the morning cutting the lockwood back, there would be no signal. I look up when Mr. Ovitt turns up the volume of the screen.

"Welcome to Newscast," the voice on the screen says, and I finally look up. "We're so glad you could join us, Dr. Elemnieri."

The camera pans to the famous scientist, and I've seen her before, of course—Mr. Ovitt worships her. But I'm always surprised by how glamorous she is. She wears a fuchsia suit and matching satin tie in her hair. Her skin is deep brown, her eyelashes so black it's like a ring around her eyes. Diamonds sparkle at her earlobes. Her smile is like its own precious stone.

"I'm glad to be here," she says. She has a faint accent. "Thank you."

"You are the inventor of the lockwood and the scientist known fondly as the Vine Mother," the host says, "and today is the anniversary of your first big botanical invention. How does that feel?"

"Well, it feels a little odd, to be honest!" Dr. Elemnieri's laugh tinkles. "It was such a rushed process. We needed a solution to protect people from the fires, and I had developed a fast-growing, fireproof little plant. The governor asked if I could modify my creation for large-scale use, and I said I would do my best. And, well, the rest is history."

"What a success," the host says, beaming. "From what I understand, lockwood is planted in stripes now, yes? As speed bumps, essentially, for wildfires that crop up?"

"Yes." Dr. Elemnieri nods. "That's the general idea. We found that was more successful than early experiments with the plant, in which it was used as a sort of fence around towns."

Up by the screen, Mr. Ovitt is watching with a half smile on his face. My stomach feels kind of sour. I've heard my mom talk about this: how if they had learned to plant stripes sooner, maybe Prine would have a normal sunrise. I glance out the window. The sun is breaking through in chunks now. They'll have finished clearing it all by ten thirty. Not bad. Plenty of time for the solar panels to soak up the energy.

"Erie Neaux," Mr. Ovitt calls. I look back to the screen. "Pay attention."

This is why Banneker skipped. Now I'm thinking of what they had said—how Mr. Ovitt has never gone up into the lockwood before but acts like we're brats when we're tired or bored. The sourness in my stomach gets sourer. I wonder if this is part of why my sister's face is always so pinched.

A man has joined Dr. Elemnieri on the screen now—he's white and his face is shaved clean, and he has a messy head of brown hair. He sits with his hand resting on her knee.

"Now to pry into your personal life just a tad." The Newscast host smiles. "What a love story! The inventor of the lockwood marrying a small-town man. How did that happen?"

I roll my eyes. Who cares.

"I met Arlo at the Imaginarium Festival of Science a year after the first lockwood groves were planted," Dr. Elemnieri says, grinning. "Eight years or so ago now. As you know, I'm a woman of science, and didn't much believe in love at first sight. But when Arlo approached me at the festival, I was...well. The evidence speaks for itself."

The fingers on her left hand flutter like the wind stirred them up. A ring the size of a lockwood pod. I can't help but think having a ring like that would be like stepping onto a catapult aimed out of Prine.

"Mr. Kylak," the host says, leaning forward, eyes locked on the handsome man, "what did you say to Dr. Elemnieri that day to get her attention?"

Arlo Kylak has the kind of face you see on toothpaste advertisements—the kind of face my mother would say is digitally enhanced, so symmetrical it's almost boring. But his voice isn't boring: when he speaks it sounds like wind through a hollow tree. Like a lullaby.

"Oh, that's for just us two," he says. His hand clasps over hers.

Mr. Ovitt turns the screen volume down, frowning.

"I think we've heard what we need to hear," he says, and he casts a glance around the room. His eyes land on me last. I think he's checking to see if any of us have noticed that he has a crush on Lunata Elemnieri. How could we not? So obvious. He looks away, folding the screen back into the wall. Then he goes on: "But that's what I wanted you all to hear: that sometimes one discovery can lead to another discovery. Dr. Elemnieri didn't know that her lockwood would also produce a replacement material for plastic. There is nothing new under the sun...until there is!"

He dives into a lesson about the periodic table and elements, but outside, sunshine has broken through the lockwood. It's hard not to stare as the ground in Prine becomes gold. Mx. Amur always says we should be proud of the work we do to keep the town running, but after seeing Dr. Elemnieri on the screen, the only thing that feels like it's really running is my imagination, taking me away from Prine and its tangle. So many hours of my life belong to the lockwood. What would I do if they belonged to me instead?

5

I'M IGNORING MR. OVITT. The butterflies in my book are more interesting. I learn that after they crawl out of their cocoons, they're not quite complete. They have to assemble their own proboscis first. They come into the world for the first time, and the first thing they have to do is put themselves together. I feel a little like that when I leave for the lockwood every morning, and I wonder if Hurona does too. What does she have to assemble before she's ready to face the world?

"Erie Neaux," Mr. Ovitt calls, and I jerk my head up. He's standing at the front of the class with my sister, like she stepped right out of my daydream. She's still dirty, so she hasn't been home to shower. Hurona doesn't go to school anymore, and I've never asked what she does with her scarce free time. Mr. Ovitt cups his hand and wiggles his fingers, beckoning. "You have a family situation. Go ahead."

I slowly slip *The Encyclopedia of Entomology* into my bag and meet Hurona at the front of the class.

"Mom needs us," she says simply. She doesn't have to explain.

I already know what it means. We walk quickly down the Spine, stepping through patches of sunlight. She glances at me after a minute. "Are you wearing a bra?"

"No," I lie, and my face feels hot, like the sun breaking through the lockwood is shining only on my cheeks.

Inside our house, the storm of my mom's workshop has become a hurricane. The first thing I notice is that the screen built into our old refrigerator is cracked, a screwdriver on the floor beneath it. I can tell it's at the end of a thrown trajectory. All the chaos that was Mom's workbench before I left for the lockwood is now a chaos scattered around the house. Screws in the kitchen sink, a hammer through the wall. Mom is nowhere.

This hasn't happened in a while.

"Ma?" I call. Everything is quiet except for the dripping faucet. "Are you here?"

But I already know she is. So does Hurona. We've done all this before. Hurona walks slowly to the pantry door, which is closed firmly. She takes a deep breath, and I watch from a distance, holding mine. Then Hurona cracks open the door, and there's Mom. She sits with her back against the shelves, knees curled to her chest. The door widens, and light spills across her shoes. She blinks at the stripe of sunshine.

"You're home early," Mom says.

"Yeah," Hurona says. She's always the one who helps Mom when she gets like this. The oldest daughter. I never feel like more of a little sister than days like today, when what Mom needs is something only Hurona can give.

"The sun's through," Mom says.

"Yeah, for a little while."

"Help me up, Hurona."

When Mom is on her feet, the three of us move silently through the kitchen, cleaning up everything she sent spinning. I'm in charge of broken glass—I have an eye for the sparkle. I find shards even when they've disguised themselves in dust or shadows. I do that while Hurona and Mom make sense of screws and the soldering iron, which had melted a bit of carpet where it landed, still hot.

"Could have been a fire," Hurona says softly.

"I was watching," Mom says.

I want to say, *But the pantry door was closed*. But I don't. I catch Hurona looking at me, warning me. She should know by now that whatever I'm thinking will stay in my head. But my head feels full. I've never seen a fire. But I think of Aunt Josie's voice left over from this morning. I know how she died. I know about the Arborklept. What if a fire started right here? *Inside* the lockwood? What if Mom started it?

"You were watching the Newscast," Hurona says. She's staring at the smashed screen.

Mom only nods. She's stacked everything back at her workbench now and stands looking down at the old screwdriver, the one that smashed the screen. She has newer, better tools, and she never uses this one. I've asked her why and she always says it's for good luck, not for good work.

"You should just throw it away," Hurona says. She sees Mom staring too.

Mom raises her face to look at us—everyone says Hurona looks like her, and when she wears this expression I see why. Her long face, the half-moons under brown eyes.

"How can I throw it away?" Mom says. Her voice sounds closer to normal now. *No crying in the Neaux house*, she always says, but we all have our own version: Our throats get tight and growly. Things get silent. Things get broken. "It's the thing that keeps me going."

"Don't give up, Ma," I say, to say something. "You'll figure it out."

She looks at me like there's something she wishes she could say, or maybe like she wishes I said something else. But in the end she just says:

"Are you girls hungry?"

She goes from tinkering in the dining room turned workshop to tinkering in the kitchen, the smell of soft bread and boxed soup turning our house into a warm, quiet den. We all settle in. That's the thing about working in the lockwood—you start the day for everyone else, but by the time you free the sun, you're too tired to enjoy it. Still, having us all in the same room feels like a small miracle. Hurona here eating and not barricaded behind her door. Even when my eyes close, I'm listening for the sound of my sister's breath.

6

I WAKE UP in the dark. I sort of remember Hurona pulling a blanket up to my shoulders, but she's gone now. The glowing clock on the wall says midnight, but I can hear the hiss of one of my mom's contraptions. I pop my head over the top of the couch. She's crouched low over her worktable, a dim blue light illuminating whatever she's working on. She and the light are both quiet, trying to let me sleep, but I get up and drift over. It's rare that I have her to myself.

"You fell asleep in the middle of eating," she says without looking up. "We didn't want to move you."

A feeling I don't like flashes through me—a dull thrill that I hadn't finished dinner. I tried to dream I was a tiny lizard, skittering between leaves. My stomach growls. Mom raises her eyes then.

"Go eat," she says, an order.

So I eat. Tiny bites, watching her work.

"Are you working on the sparrows?" I ask.

"Yes. Although I don't know why."

"What do you mean?" I say, nibbling a piece of potato.

"It's not the sort of thing FOLROY wants."

"They wanted your headlamps," I remind her. I'm trying to be like Hurona—not a kid, but a person she can rely on. "Maybe you can make something else like that."

"I'm tired of making things that keep my daughters in the trees," she says sharply. "I want to make something that gets them out."

She looks up, like she remembered that it's her daughter she's talking to. I see a glint of the thing that had made her throw the old screwdriver through the refrigerator screen.

"A girl died today," she says. "Did you know that?"

The potato in my mouth suddenly tastes like sandpaper. I swallow it slowly.

"I thought she just got hurt."

"No," my mother says. "She's dead. She was eleven. And she'll be replaced by tomorrow. And Dr. Lunata Elemnieri...well. She doesn't care what her creation has created. She gets to go on television and live her diamond life and dance under the stars with her boring husband, and she doesn't care that a whole town of children has never seen those stars."

The news about the girl who fell makes me feel cold. I remember the sound of her screaming. It sounds different in my memory now. Now that I know. For some reason I think about the butterflies in the encyclopedia. How they come out of their cocoons and put themselves together, but their wings are still like paper. I don't like to think about it. Instead I think about how Mom says Arlo

Kylak is boring. I was right. It makes me feel closer to her, knowing I know her at least this well.

"Look out there," she says, pointing at our black window. I'd fallen asleep but the lockwood had not. Everything I spent my morning cutting back has knitted together again. No moon. No stars.

"There's nothing to see," I say, because there isn't.

"Exactly," she says. "I want more for you than nothing. Is more than nothing so much to ask?"

"I don't mind going up," I say, even though I do, because the circles under her eyes look deeper than ever and I want her to rest. "I don't need stars to live."

"No," she says. "But you need stars to dream. And so did that girl."

I swallow nothing.

"Well, tomorrow is Tuesday," I say. "And FOLROY will be here. Maybe tomorrow they'll see your sparrows and want to buy them. That's your dream, right?"

"That's one of my dreams," she says. "The others are a little more complicated. Some of them make me feel guilty. But guilt is useless unless you change something with it."

Then she's curled back over the blue light, and it's like we'd been two people standing on a frozen river. Each of us is perched on an iceberg. The icy water drifts her away, and eventually I flow into my room to keep sleeping. But not until I pull the old phone out from under my mattress, hold Aunt Josie's voice close to my ear. Usually I would wait until tomorrow to listen to a new message, but tonight I break my rule.

Nadine, you can hold a grudge like no other. You must have gotten that from Dad. I didn't mean to hurt your feelings, and we could talk about it if you'd answer your phone. Sisters are supposed to be honest, I thought? Maybe my honesty is a little clumsy. I'm on my way to Petrichor to pick up a specimen. Call me back. Later?

Later. Later. Later. She always thought there would be a later. Had they been able to see each other before the fires took her? I feel myself falling asleep, slow and heavy, but before I do I roll closer to the wall and press my face against it. On the other side, I can just make out the sound of Hurona whispering in her room—I don't know if she's cursing or praying, but buried in the blur of words I hear her say my name.

7

THE AIR IS warmer than yesterday. Just overnight spring has gotten bolder. Once we get to the top and there's some light, I'm going to look closely at the trees to see if any buds have started to appear. Because of the lockwood, sometimes I forget to pay attention to the alder and the box elder. I used to climb them—I used to play all afternoon in the sun without really thinking about what needed to happen for the sun to shine. The lockwood has a way of both widening and narrowing your eyes.

"Erie!" someone calls, and I turn back, hoping it's Hurona. But it's Banneker, trotting out onto the Spine from the dark alley that leads to their house. I'm just as happy it's them. Their house is a lot like mine—a one-level cube with two square windows like eyes—but with newer paint. Not because their family makes any more money than mine does—none of us own our houses anyway. But Banneker's mom cares about things like painting, and smiling in public. Neither Banneker nor I have dads—mine is dead and theirs, like so many others, left for Petrichor in search of work and never came back. Banneker told me once that they thought their dad was actually dead too. They also have a brother—Carver. He worked in the lockwood for a while before going to Petrichor. Banneker says he sends money sometimes. When it comes to dads, I'm not bitter: Mine died when I was two, and I don't remember him. But if Banneker is, they never say so.

"Hey," I say when they catch up. "Did you hear?"

"Yeah." They nod, still rubbing sleep from their eyes. "Mx. Amur came around to tell us after dinner."

"I was asleep when the news came," I say. "What was her name?"

"Helia," they say, and that's all. I know her name. Younger than me. The friends you make before the lockwood sort of drift away once you're old enough to go up.

"Mourning in shifts today," they say after a few minutes. "We'll go to the funeral instead of school."

"Busy," I say. "Lockwood, funeral, FOLROY."

"I forgot about FOLROY."

I never forget about FOLROY. FOLROY visits are the only day Mom actually leaves the house, marching to the Spine with a new invention. She's never embarrassed that they say *no* every time, but I am. Even if I feel guilty about it.

Mx. Amur is waiting for all of us in the corral by the crane, as always. She doesn't say much this morning, and neither does anyone else. Everyone is thinking about Helia. I stand near Banneker and look up into the tangled ceiling over Prine. I wonder how many other little towns like Prine there are, how if we weren't so tiny, it would take even longer to clear the way for sunlight. Banneker used to talk about leaving, going to Petrichor and finding their brother and maybe even their dad. But their mom says the same thing as my mom when Hurona talks about leaving: "With what money?"

I stand listening to the squeaking song of crickets while we wait. I learned in the encyclopedia that they don't actually rub their legs to sing the way people think. They scrape their wings together to make noise. I think small thoughts—imagining myself small like a cricket. But no matter how tiny I feel in my mind, I can still almost feel myself growing. Eventually I'll be too big. When that day comes, will there be time for books besides the encyclopedia? Can I become a teacher, or an inventor? Or will I be like Hurona, walking around half empty like she left part of herself in the trees?

"Up we go," Mx. Amur calls. Her voice sounds a little pale.

I think when I get back on the ground, I will ask her about Sacramento.

Was it small like this?

Was it brighter?

Did you feel afraid when you were there?

Did you know people there who answered your questions?

Will you answer mine?

INSTEAD OF LOOKING at Helia's body, I spent the mourning period staring at the blister between my thumb and fore-
finger. They will leave Helia on the flowered table for viewing before
they bury her in the town plot behind the general store. We haven't
had a funeral in over a year—lots of broken bodies, but no dead
ones—so no one knows what to do with their hands or their eyes.
At some point Hurona showed up behind me, finished with her
shift of ground work, and she squeezed my shoulder. I can't remember the last time she touched me. We stood close together until the
prayer finished, and then everyone wandered off, watching the sun
break through, and listening to the swoosh and crash of the vines
falling into the nets, the buzz of the pulper. These are the sounds
of Prine.

But today there's also the sound of Helia's mother crying, and
Prine is so tiny that it feels like I can hear her sobs from everywhere.
When the rumble of the FOLROY trucks echoes up from the
lockwood tunnel, I'm almost relieved. Everyone stops what they're
doing except the kids in the trees—they're finishing up, the cranes

bringing them down, the nets being lowered. I'm standing at the top of the Spine when the first trucks roll in.

There's usually a dozen. Shiny white, their beds yawning empty, ready to swallow the lockwood clippings me and the other kids have spent the last week bringing down, the bags of pulp and pods. The mayor will be here any minute, ready to handle the exchange. This part is boring—adults weighing and counting while the ground workers help load everything gathered since the last FOLROY visit. They'll be here for the rest of the day—it takes forever to load all the sacks. I can hear the pulping machine roaring, still chewing up everything from today so it can go on the trucks too. Between the lockwood cutting and the pulper, there isn't a moment of the day where Prine doesn't buzz like the inside of a beehive.

Banneker is already at our spot, the steps of the general store. Mr. Lunder runs it, and I can hear him humming at the counter inside the open door. He doesn't mind when we sit outside, and sometimes he comes out and chats. He usually mistakes me for Hurona, but he has interesting stories sometimes.

Other kids from our shift have already gone home, but this is why me and Banneker have stayed friends. Neither of us like to talk much—but both of us like to watch. We sit shoulder to shoulder on the steps, and after a while they offer me a piece of brownish-red fruit leather. We chew silently, watching.

I'm always a little stunned by the people in FOLROY uniforms—they live only fifty miles away, Petrichor just an hour or so's travel. But they look like they're from a different planet. Their glowing uniforms. Solar, Banneker tells me: Once the country figured out that solar was the future, they put the gathering patches on everything.

But it's not just the uniforms. It's their skin. The under-eye circles that I inherited from my mom are specific to the Neaux family but also to Prine. The FOLROY workers look so...rested. Their eyes are bright, they laugh while they work. They have phones that they check, which always makes me feel envious. New devices, with the signals that reach two hundred miles. I don't know anyone in Prine who could afford one, not even the mayor. All the old devices don't work until the lockwood is beaten back, and what, my mom always asks, is really the point then anyway? That's part of why I've been able to keep Aunt Josie's messages to myself. That, and Mom doesn't like thinking about the past.

"I thought Hurona already worked this morning," Banneker says, and my eyes follow their finger, where my sister stands at the rear of a truck, helping heft the sacks of pulped lockwood inside. Her muscles stand out from her arms, and my stomach twinges with admiration before it's swallowed by a sad blue tide. If Hurona saw what I saw from my vantage point, the thickness of her arms, I know her face would close the way it always does. She doesn't work in the trees anymore, but it's like needing to be small is a scar that hasn't healed.

But right now Hurona's smiling and chatting with the girl standing inside the truck bed, grasping the sacks Hurona passes up to her.

"Yeah, she should be done for the day," I answer, raising an eyebrow at my sister. "She must have just wanted to help out."

All my usual watching of FOLROY is set aside now as I watch Hurona. The mouth that is usually lemon tight is relaxed and easy. Her eyes are open windows. The FOLROY girl is her age, maybe a little older. She's white like me and Hurona, and even has the same yellow undertones like us. But she's tinged with gold. Like the other FOLROY people, she looks healthy and full of light. The girl's smile aimed at Hurona is brighter than the sun that trickles down over Prine. But then her eyes lift away from my sister, fastening on something down the Spine, and they cloud a little. She says something to Hurona, who turns to look.

It's my mother. She walks quickly down the middle of the Spine, and I know from the way her arms don't swing that she's already ready to be told "no." Her eyes are the same amber-brown as mine, her hair the same dusty gold, but cut close to her head, longer in the front like a unicorn horn that never fully formed. She swipes it out of her way as she approaches the woman in charge of the FOLROY caravan, Miss Jinnah. I've been seeing Miss Jinnah's face every Tuesday for as long as I can remember. She's been weighing lockwood for as many years as there has *been* lockwood.

"Good morning, Neaux," Miss Jinnah calls from her wheelchair, raising the clipboard in salute.

"Jinnah, hello," my mother answers. She passes by the general store stoop, and I know she knows I'm there, but doesn't look my way. I imagine the icebergs again, her floating on past. "Now, before you tell me no, I want you to hear me out."

And it begins. My mother presents the sparrow that I know she's been working on nonstop for weeks. The circles under her

45

eyes are almost purple. She talks a mile a minute, explaining to Miss Jinnah why FOLROY needs to consider it, why she should take this prototype back to her boss in Petrichor. Miss Jinnah listens politely, but I know in the end she'll shake her head. I know it the way I know that by midnight, the lockwood will already have gnarled over Prine and choked out the moon.

A pair of kids wanders past me and Banneker, arms linked. They're not old enough to go up yet, so they must have been allowed out of school to grieve for Helia. They wander the edge of the FOLROY trucks, and one of them darts their eyes up at me. Under their breath, but loud enough to hear, they sing a little song:

> *The Lakes cut back the lockwood;*
> *the vines they break and bend.*
> *Their mother talks to screwdrivers*
> *because they're her only friends.*

Banneker shouts at them, and they scuttle away, but my cheeks are already burning. Mom has started gesticulating in her conversation with Miss Jinnah. I think of the screwdriver she put through the fridge screen yesterday, and I know I'm too old to be bothered by what a couple of kids say, but the shame is like the lockwood: a slow, dark creep. I wonder what their song would say if they knew Mom's soldering iron melted the carpet yesterday. That it could've been a fire that the lockwood would keep in, not out. I don't like to think about that, so I think about the part of the song I don't mind. The part about the Lakes. Some people call me and Hurona this—two girls, named after two living lakes. But with our names collapsed into one word—"Lakes"—it makes me feel that, as different as we are, me and my sister are the same kind of something.

My eyes move back to Hurona, to see if she's embarrassed by Mom, by her public loneliness. By the fact that this is the only day Mom comes out of our house, and everyone knows it. But maybe we're not the same kind of anything. Hurona doesn't look embarrassed, she just looks sad, and so does the FOLROY girl, whose hand rests on Hurona's shoulder.

9

THEY BURIED HELIA before sunset, but I couldn't bear to watch the ceremony. When I close my eyes, all I see is the dirt closing over the lid of her simple coffin like the knuckles of the lockwood and, once hidden from view, her body shrinking and shrinking until she's no longer a girl but a small, cold bird. So I stood at the edge of the crowd, and I faded farther and farther backward until I was alone on the Spine.

Now I wander down the alleys that are too dark in the morning to see properly. I almost wish I could go back for Banneker, but we'd probably just be silent anyway. So I walk by myself, and I think about how every day is the same. The only difference is when someone gets hurt.

Maybe that's why I don't want to go home, why my feet take me away from the alley that leads to my house. I should be going to bed, to get ready to do it all over again tomorrow. But it's like going back home will be the first domino falling. After that they'll all fall: *bed, darkness, wake up, dress, into the trees.*

Then I see the ants. Except they're not ants, and that's why they catch my eye. Lined up like ants, but too big—beetles. A crusade of them, heading off into the lockwood. They do this sometimes, I'd learned—going back to their hatching ground to lay eggs before they die. They're one of the few bugs that don't seem to mind the cold. They're some of the coolest ones I get to see in person and not in the pages of a book, so I follow them, my headlamp, still buckled at my belt from this morning's shift, bumping my hip with every step.

I've spent so much time in the tops of the lockwood since I turned ten that sometimes I forget what life had been like before. The only thing I used to know about the forest clutched around Prine was how it smelled. Now as I go on following the long line of beetles, I take a deep sniff—almost cedar, but not exactly. It's like there's something musky inside it. The trunks of the lockwood aren't the knots of yarn that I squeeze through at the top. Down here they look almost like normal trees. But there aren't any normal trees in this part anymore. In the circle we carve out around Prine there are alder and box elder, but they're the only ones left. They get enough sun with our help. Almost enough, anyway. Some of their leaves have yellowed.

The beetles wind through the trees, the dim light sparkling off their backs. I remember I used to call them jewel bugs. It makes me look around, searching for more memories. I used to play here with Hurona, when Hurona still played. She was nine and I was four, and most of my memories are of her helping me up. Hurona leaping over a log, and me trying to do the same. Falling. Hurona climbing a lockwood trunk, and me trying to follow. Falling. I was always falling, and Hurona was always there in a flash, her hands gripping mine, pulling me to a stand. Eventually she taught me how to fall safely. How to curl my body and stay bent, how to turn my face. How to land on muscle. *It's okay to fall. You just have to know how. And then get back up.*

But Helia can't get back up.

I pause in trailing the shimmering green stream of beetles, looking up and all around. I'm surrounded by the trees they planted to save Prine, the trees that we have to save ourselves from every morning. I thought coming out here would make me feel better. But now all I can think about is Helia. There's no getting away from the lockwood.

The beetles fade from my mind as I scan the part of the woods I've ended up in. I haven't been this far since I was little, and I see the hill Hurona and I used to climb, pretending it was a mountain. The trail is more grown over here—the other kids play closer to Prine. I never would have come this far without Hurona when I was little. She was always with me, and part of me still wishes she was. She's older now. But so am I.

So I climb, panting as it gets steeper, and eventually I have to stop. The higher I go, the thicker the lockwood gets, the vines turning into branches, some of them growing into each other. I have my hatchet in my work satchel, bumping along beside my headlamp, and I could take it out and cut a path if I wanted to. But there's no point down here. For now, enough light cracks through to see, even if it wouldn't be enough to charge a solar panel.

Up here at the top of the small hill is the clearing that Hurona and I found once—snug as a closet, dotted with smooth flat rocks. I choose one for a seat, leaning my back against the lockwood. I know I should go home. I should wait up for Hurona and ask her if Helia's mother had stopped crying, if she was going to leave for Petrichor now that she was losing the money of a pod picker. Maybe she could survive on the pulp work. Better than she would survive in the city, the way Mr. Ovitt and the other adults tell it.

I realize suddenly that Mr. Ovitt has no children. Hurona told me last year that FOLROY paid Mr. Ovitt, and I don't know why, but maybe, I think, I could get paid to be a teacher too, instead of harvesting pods and pulping vines. One day. When I'm too big.

I slip *The Encyclopedia of Entomology* out of my bag. Its cover is a paler green than anything you'd find in the lockwood, but it's pretty. Are there teachers who only teach about bugs? Where will I fit, once I'm too big?

10

"ERIE!"

I wake up staring into the sun. So bright and searing I can't open my eyes.

"Erie, what were you thinking?"

Hurona. She takes off her headlamp and places it on a log next to me. The sun shrinks to a glow, almost swallowed by perfect dark. I know this dark.

I fell asleep in the lockwood.

Panic skitters through me like beetles. It takes me a second to remember how I got here. I'm on the flat smooth rocks, not up in the trees. I remember closing my eyes, listening to the distant buzzing of the pulper. How did I let myself fall asleep?

"What are you doing here?" I say, scrambling to stand.

"What else?" she snaps. "You didn't come home! I told Mom you were staying with Banneker, and when she went to sleep I came looking for you. What are *you* doing out here?"

I can't believe this. I've never fallen asleep anywhere but my bed or the couch. (And maybe Hurona's floor a few times when I was little.) In the glow of the headlamp, my eye falls on the encyclopedia I'd been flipping through, and I go to shove it back into my bag before Hurona can see. She doesn't say anything—just stands looking at me in the dark, dark silence.

Except, it isn't silent.

"Why would you come out here alone, Erie?" Hurona says, but I'm not listening to her. "Do you—"

"Hurona, shh," I say, listening.

"Erie—"

"Shh!"

At first I think it's the headlamp, and that I never noticed the hum while walking down the Spine. But it's not. The sound isn't in my ears, but above my head, a gentle rumble like the FOLROY trucks before you can see them on the road. It sounds blurry, like an impossibly big hummingbird. And then I hear something else: the rustle of the wood and vine. I've only ever heard it when I go to the top, when I monkey-walk along the branches to find a place to sit and cut. This is like that, but different. Almost too soft to hear from down here. There's a creak and a groan, and then the sound of wind whistling between new spaces.

And that's when it hits me.

"The lockwood is growing," I whisper.

She looks around.

"Not down here," I say. "Up there."

Down here, the roots and trunks stay whole and solid. But up there, growth. Up there, where in just a few hours I will be climbing and cutting back everything that keeps Prine in the dark. I don't know how long I was asleep, but I'm suddenly tired again. Dominos. Helia died Monday and they buried her Tuesday, and Wednesday I'll be in the trees again and again and again. At least, until I'm too big, like Hurona, my body growing like the lockwood.

In the light of Hurona's headlamp, I reach for mine and put it on. And just like that, I'm climbing.

"What are you doing?" Hurona hisses, grabbing at my shirt.

"I want to see."

"Get down here!"

"I want to see it growing."

I leave my bag on the rocks. Just me and my headlamp going up. I don't know why I need to see it for myself. I pull away even harder when Hurona grabs me again, but she has a good grip this time. I glare down at her—this time it's her blinking in the light of my lamp.

"Stop, Erie," she demands. Big sister voice. "There's no crane, no net."

"You did it once," I reply. "You told me. You did it without a crane, just to see if you could."

Right now, I need to do what Hurona has done. She always feels so far away. *She would rather whisper to herself in her room than talk to me*, I think. I see the distance on her face even now, staring right at me. I jerk away, and she lets me, and even though it's what I said I wanted, it makes me sad.

I climb.

I hold the vines tight as I go up and up, trying not to look down and see my sister either looking or not looking. I also try not to think of what would happen if I fell. Would I die like Helia? Would my mother cry? Would she stay at my graveside for more than five minutes, or would she just go back to her shed?

The vines are warm under my hands, as strange and dry as always. As I get higher, it gets tighter. I think small thoughts, the way I always do, the way Mx. Amur says is best. I try not to think about the height, or how there's no net under me. But the wind I hear whispering through the new growth above seems to whisper it: *No net, no net, no net.*

But still I climb. After a while it feels like I'm climbing to the moon, on and on, leaving Prine behind. I remember what Mom said, about how we need stars to dream. I'm suddenly determined to see them.

I can feel the breeze cutting through the vines. They thin out as I get closer to the sky. My heart starts to hammer, but my palms don't sweat. Prine only gives you one thing to be good at, and I'm very good. My hands find holds and my feet settle into crevices. Up and up, until the next time I push off with my foot, my head breaks through. Clean, cold, open air.

The lockwood kids aren't birds, so what am I, up here in the sky? I'm standing at the top of the world looking at the moon.

And the stars.

They're so bright. And there's more than I ever could have imagined. They spread across the sky like someone crushed marble into dust and blew it from their palm. Around me, the lockwood rocks a little, but I'm not afraid. I'm planted like my own kind of tree, my feet wedged into the tight spaces between boughs. I feel like I've traveled a hundred miles, like Prine is somewhere so far I couldn't even fly there.

Beside me is the rustling of the vines—Hurona breaking through next to me. I can't remember ever seeing my sister's face white with moonlight.

"You did it," she says quietly. I feel like crying and I don't know why so I say nothing. I feel stubborn. On the horizon there's a big blur of light.

"That's Petrichor," she says.

Fifty miles, I think. Fifty miles to a different world. Somewhere nearby I hear an owl call.

And then the buzzing again.

The stars and my sister almost made me forget why I climbed up here in the first place. I turn toward the humming sound, louder now that I'm at the top. As I turn, the stars shine directly into my eyes, and I blink hard at the sudden brightness.

Wait. Not stars.

Lights.

The hum is even louder now—nothing like a truck. But still like a gentle rumble. Whirring, I realize. Like a hummingbird, yes, but if its wings were metal.

And then I see that they are.

"It's a drone," Hurona says, shocked.

The light beams from a machine that reminds me of a tiny comet. Round and black, with silver wings that catch moonlight. It seems to travel on an axis I can't see, circling and circling, a path so large that when it flies away from me, I lose sight of it. I can barely hear the buzz. But then it completes its circle and hums back where I can see. When it's closest, I hear the machine hissing. I watch it, stunned, and a little scared. What if it changes course and runs into us? I'm about to duck back down when I notice what's causing the hissing sound.

"It's spraying something," I say. From the corner of my eye, I can see Hurona's mouth hanging open.

There's a liquid misting from the round black machine that shines in the moonlight. It's not water. I've seen rain on lockwood—it beads and slides off like oil. But whatever the machine is spraying makes the lockwood shudder.

First they shudder . . . and then they grow.

It's like watching a snake wake up from brumation. All the coils are stirring. I realize a moment too late, and I stare down in horror, waiting for the vines around us to tighten and squeeze. Helia fell, but we would be crushed. Except the machine isn't spraying any of the liquid on the place where I stand.

It's only circling the area above Prine.

And the lockwood is growing. I hear it creak and groan, louder here than on the ground. I watch the vines nearby reach and curl, twisting around each other. Before my eyes, within arm's reach, the pods that Banneker picks appear, round and black. The hole that we carved out at dawn fills in, inch by inch. The flying black machine's circle grows smaller and smaller, until the hissing stops. Prine is covered again.

My mind buzzes like the machine, a thousand questions humming. And as always, I try to ask my sister.

"Hurona, what…?"

But the words won't come. In Prine, we all know that the lock-wood grows overnight. I don't dream anymore, but when I did, it was about the vines as snakes. The snakes would eat the sky until they were fat and monstrous. But these aren't snakes. They're plants. And someone has given them something stronger than water.

I try again. "Who…?"

"I think I have a pretty good idea," she says. Her mouth isn't hanging open anymore. It's the grim line I know so well.

The black machine has widened its orbit again. It rotates slowly outward, like it's checking its work. It's almost hard to keep an eye on it, the metal blending with the night. It's circling higher. I try to be like Banneker and keep my eye fixed on it like a pod. It circles over one more time, just low enough for me to see the red type on each of its silver wings. Big bold letters cut through moonlight, and Hurona reads them out loud:

"FOLROY."

Even when the machine spins higher and higher, eventually setting off on a straight course under the stars, I can see where it's headed.

It hums through the night straight toward Petrichor.

11

AS SOON AS our feet touch the ground, Hurona is marching back toward Prine. Her silence, the silence all around us, feels like a squeezing python. I don't even want to look up. The vines feel more alive than ever.

"Hurona," I call after her when she gets too far ahead. She moves fast and with purpose, the light from her headlamp unwavering.

"Keep moving," she says. "We need to get home."

I make my wobbly legs run to catch up.

"But what are we—"

She stops abruptly, so suddenly that I almost run into her back. I hear a buzzing again, and I cringe, looking up at the vine ceiling. But this buzzing is closer. Hurona is buzzing. She reaches into her pocket, pulling out a slice of moonlight.

But there's no moonlight in Prine. Not now.

It's a phone.

Except Hurona doesn't have a phone. Neither of us do. And definitely not one like this, with a display the size of her hand, the glow from it crystal blue.

"Hurona?" I say, my voice squeaking. "What's...?"

She mumbles something, but she's not talking to me. She's talking to whoever's on the phone. *Her* phone. In the dark of the lockwood, the screen lights up and a face appears, looking confused, then shocked. Tan skin, hair in brown waves around her face. It's the girl from the FOLROY truck. My sister has a secret phone, and she's talking to a girl who works for FOLROY. Someone who doesn't live in Prine.

I feel dizzy, like lockwood is squeezing part of my brain. My first day going up, I was nervous, but everyone thought I was brave because I didn't cry, because I didn't sway when I looked down and saw how high I was. I just pretended that the ground followed me up. But right now I feel like the ground has dropped from under my feet. First the flying black machine like a circling comet in the night. Now this. I sway. I'm going to fall.

Hurona catches me. Like she always does in the lockwood. Her hand around my wrist feels like gravity.

"Not a good time, Iva," my sister says to the girl.

"I just need to know if you're still coming," Iva says quickly. "If you're not actually going to leave Prine, I need to know now."

"Leave Prine?" I say. It feels like I'm talking underwater.

"Not a good time, Iva," Hurona repeats, growling. She ends the call at the same time I jerk my arm out of her grasp.

"Erie," she says softly, a different version of the big sister voice. She doesn't touch me again, but her tone feels like a hand on my back. "I need to tell you something."

"Who was that?" I interrupt. "How do you have a phone? *That* kind of phone?"

"Keep your voice down," she whispers.

We're in the lockwood. Deep enough to where I can't make out the lights of the Spine. Everyone in our town is asleep. That's when it really sinks in. My sister has a secret—a big one. I think back to this morning when I walked past her door—her voice had murmured my name, and I thought she'd been blaming me for borrowing socks. Had she actually been on the phone talking to that girl? I don't want to be a snoopy little sister. But right now I wish I could put my sister's whole life under Mom's microscope.

"You're hiding stuff," I say. "From Mom. From . . . me."

I wish I hadn't said the last part. I can still hear the squeak in my voice.

"We all hide things, Erie," she sighs. "Including you."

"I don't hide anything," I say.

She gives me an exasperated look in the glow of my headlamp.

"Like I don't know you have Mom's old phone," she says.

I pull back, shocked.

"Well, I'm not *talking* to anyone!"

"No. You listen to Aunt Josie's voice messages. Why?" Before I can answer, she waves her hands, like she's clearing the question from the air. She takes a deep breath. "Erie, do you know what we saw tonight?"

"That's not what I want to talk about," I cry. "I want to talk about what that girl said! You leaving Prine. What did she mean?"

I'm used to my sister's silence. Between she and my mother, the Neaux household is full of it. And I guess my silence too. But the silence that sits between us now is as thick as the lockwood. I can't read her face. Her eyes are looking somewhere outside the glow of the headlamps. A factory is whirring inside her. She reaches up and switches off her headlamp.

"Yours too," she says.

We haven't done this in a long time. Talked in the dark. We used to. There's so much darkness in Prine—we used to be allies inside it, sharing secrets. I switch off my headlamp, and the gloom is immediate. Total. If I was out here alone, I might be afraid. But I can hear my sister breathing.

"I'm leaving," she says in the safety of the blackness. "I can't keep working on the ground picking pods. There's no future here."

"What about me?" I squeak. I clear my throat. "What about Mom?"

"Iva is going to find me a job in Petrichor. I'll send money back. I'll save enough so that you and Mom can move too."

"Iva."

"My girlfriend."

"You have a girlfriend?" But of course she does. I think back to the FOLROY trucks, Hurona helping load sacks when she didn't have to. The girl's hand on her shoulder. The girl's face on her phone. I repeat her name: "Iva."

"We're going to get an apartment together."

"You're only seventeen!"

"Yeah," Hurona sighs. "But I'm from Prine. And I hear that

people from Prine don't have trouble finding work because everyone knows we've been working for so long."

"You're always saying that," I say. I feel kind of mean. Or like I want to be. The dizzy feeling comes back. "You're always saying what you *hear*. You *hear* eggs cost less in Petrichor—"

"They do," she interrupts. "They overcharge for everything here because they know we have no choice and don't get paid enough to go anywhere else."

But I press on. I feel the way my mom must sometimes feel— like the pressure inside is rising. I feel like a shaken bottle of soda.

"You hear that eggs cost less, you hear that Prine workers can get work in Petrichor. What else do you hear? That you're not telling me?"

It's easier to say these things in the dark. But her silence feels heavy without being able to see her face. Is she thinking? Is she angry? Am I right? That she's holding more secrets just behind her tongue?

"I already knew that FOLROY is cheating us," she says, her voice low. "But now we've seen what we saw, and it's worse than I thought."

We used to hold hands in this kind of dark, but not now. I grip my own palms together.

"How?" I whisper.

"Think about it, Erie," she says. "Think about what it means. If FOLROY is making the lockwood grow, it means they're lying to the whole town. It means they took an invention that was supposed to help people and are using it to hurt people."

"Like Helia," I say.

"Yes, and no. Helia fell. But there would be nothing to fall from if it wasn't for FOLROY."

Between us, the phone lights up. It's Iva calling back—I see her name and a photo of her face. She's pretty, dark eyes under dark eyebrows. Part of me doesn't want Hurona to answer—I want it to be just us two in this tangle, sharing secrets. But I also *do* want her to answer. I want to be part of whatever secret world they're building. I don't want to be on the outside of it.

Hurona answers.

"I told her," Hurona says when she connects. It's not a video call this time, and only Iva's voice answers.

"And?"

"And slight change of plans. When I get to Petrichor, I'm going to go see Lunata Elemnieri," Hurona says.

"What?" I say, at the same time that Iva makes a sound of surprise.

"Whoa," Iva says. "Um. Why? And how do you plan on doing that?"

"I'll tell you everything later," Hurona says. Her face is lit blue again, and she stares hard at me. "I don't know how yet, but I'll figure it out. Enough is enough."

Years back, a huge storm blew over Prine, only a few hours after we had cut back the lockwood. It ripped shingles from our roof and we had jars and bottles on the floor, catching all the leaks. Some of them brimmed, the water trembling. I think both my sister and my mother are like those jars, brimming. Maybe I am too. Full with Helia. The callouses on my palms. FOLROY and its humming black bird. You can pour out rainwater. But what does a *person* do when enough's enough?

"I'm coming too," I say. It's like a rabbit darting out of my mouth.

"What did she say?" Iva says.

"Nothing," Hurona tells her, squinting at me in the blue light.

"I said I'm coming too," I repeat, louder.

"Keep your voice down," my sister hisses. "And no. You are staying here."

"I won't let you go without me," I say, and I vaguely hear Iva say she's going to *let Hurona handle this* and she'll talk to her later. I am the *this*. It makes me stubborn.

"I told you I'm going to go and save money," Hurona says. She hasn't even noticed that Iva hung up. "Then I'll come back and get you."

"That's what everybody who leaves for Petrichor says," I say.

"This is different," she says, frowning.

I bite my lip. Everyone talks about the lockwood as a swallowing beast, but the way older folks tell it, Petrichor is another kind, the kind that chews before it swallows. For me, it's more like the purple beetles that sometimes show up in the fall. We call them Backward Bugs, because they crawl backward, eating up the surface of the leaves they walk on. In that way, they never leave footprints, and that's how the lockwood is—it disappears us. And even though it makes me guilty, that also makes me think of my mom, how the past is something she swallows down.

"What's Mom going to do if you leave?" I squeak out.

Hurona's quiet for a long time.

"Mom is an adult," she finally says.

That doesn't answer the question, I think. But I can't make myself say it out loud.

"Why not just take us both now?" I whisper, trying not to plead. "Wouldn't it be better if we were all together?"

"Mom isn't going to leave that easily," Hurona says sharply.

We're both quiet for a minute. I know she's right. She doesn't leave the house, let alone the protective circle of the lockwood. I think the memories of the Arborklept are like a wall me and Hurona can't see.

"Maybe I can make Lunata Elemnieri give me a job," she adds, mostly to herself. "I don't know. I'm going to figure it all out."

"If you're going to see Lunata Elemnieri, I'm going too," I whisper fiercely. "I saw it too. I was there."

The truth of this feels like solid ground. I root myself in it.

"You're staying here, Erie," she says firmly. "Do you even understand what you saw? This might be dangerous."

I don't really see how it could be dangerous, and besides, I've already climbed the lockwood at midnight. Without help. What I do every morning is scarier than a scientist with diamonds in her ears. *And her boring husband*, I add silently.

"I saw what I saw," I answer out loud. "And I'm coming with you. We can go and talk to her and you can find a job and then we'll come back and get Mom."

I hope she doesn't hear how desperate I am. The idea of staying

66

with Mom makes me feel panicked. Not because I'm scared of her. But with Hurona gone, who will open the pantry door after one of Mom's storms? I try to imagine being the one doing it, and my heart starts to hammer. I think of the jars of rainwater again. I feel full to the brim. But I can feel the *no* getting ready on Hurona's lips. I imagine the space between us stretching, then tearing. I imagine watching her disappear down the tunnel that the FOLROY trucks rumble through every Tuesday. Never seeing Hurona again feels scarier than the lockwood.

"Erie...," she begins, but another rabbit shoots out of my mouth.

"If you don't let me go with you, I'm telling Mom."

Hurona taps her phone, waking its blue light, then aims it at my face like a torch. We stare at each other. But looking at her in the light, I also think: *She needs me. She doesn't know it, but she needs me.*

I remember watching Hurona shrink, trying to stay small enough to keep working at the top. She's been on the ground looking up for three years now. When I close my eyes, I can picture my first day in the lockwood, looking down at her as the crane carried me up. The way my big sister's face watched me go with eyes like scraped knees. She's trying to save me by going to Petrichor. But who saves Hurona?

She must see something in my eyes change. Something passes between us, the way it did when we were little. Out in the trees, feeling that Mom's storm had rolled on and it was time to head home. I wonder if Hurona remembers. If she does, she doesn't say. In the light of her secret phone she squints at me, and I can tell she still wants to say no. But just like in the lockwood, I know when I've chosen a branch that will hold.

"Let's go home."

We go, the Spine like a beacon. Our house is still and silent, like we're returning to our sleeping selves from a dream.

In the hall, Hurona whispers: "My room. Your door is too close to Mom's. You'll wake her."

She closes us inside, tosses me a blanket. It's the only place I'd want to be tonight. But once my sister is asleep, my eyes won't close. Time passes long and slow. It feels like the sound of the lockwood growing followed me home. I stand up and search through the dark to Hurona's door. I know how to turn the handle so it's silent. I can hear my sister's slow, deep breaths. I creep back to my room, feeling like a shadow. Hurona doesn't know how quiet I can be. I slip Mom's old phone out from under my mattress. With so many secrets in the air tonight, it feels like the secret of Aunt Josie is the only thing that will help me sleep.

I crawl into bed, select the next message, and press the old black glass against my face.

> *Nadine, are you feeling sad? I'm still in Petrichor if you want to come visit. I want to meet the girls. I can't remember the last time I held a baby—all I hold are birds these days. I know you said you'd never visit the city again. I passed your old apartment last week. Remember that change starts with changing your mind. Later.*

I hold the phone against my chest, my heart beating fast. Aunt Josie was in Petrichor, and once upon a time, Mom went too. Our mother, who never leaves home unless she has to. Imagining her journeying outside Prine feels like imagining a different person entirely. Her own apartment? In Petrichor? Does Hurona know?

I wonder what Mom was sad about—if Petrichor chewed up Aunt Josie before the fires took her. I wonder if Mom listened to her sister's advice. When I think of the way Mom never talks about Aunt Josie, I don't think she did. She keeps the past and its sad memories in a steel box. I'm more determined than ever to go to Petrichor. If I can just get there, maybe I can open that box.

LYING TO MOM is easier than lying to Banneker. When I left
my room, Mom was back to her microscope. I didn't have to avoid
her eyes because hers were already avoiding mine. Avoiding the
whole world. But acting like I'm not leaving Prine in five days while
I trudge down the Spine with my best friend is like trying to ignore
a splinter under my thumbnail.

"Are you okay?" they say, when I have to ask them to repeat
themselves for the third time. "You seem tired."

"I am."

That's the truth, at least. I never went back to sleep even in my
room. I kept listening for the lockwood, and listening for Hurona.
I heard her wake up, heard the muttering start. Now I know she
talks to Iva in the mornings. I wonder what they talk about. If Iva
had been mad when Hurona told her that her little sister was tag-
ging along to Petrichor. Is that what I am? A tagalong? What if
they were coming up with a plan to leave me behind?

"You sure you're going to be okay up there?" Banneker says,
their bushy eyebrows low with concern. They don't need to say

more. We both know what can happen in the lockwood if you're not alert.

"I'm fine," I say, shoving all my thoughts about Hurona to the back of my mind. "What were you saying?"

"I was asking if you heard about the tokens," Banneker says.

"Tokens?"

"My mom says the FOLROY lady, Miss Jinnah, says things are going to be different soon. That instead of paying dollars for the pods we harvest, they're going to start paying in a special FOLROY token. Like their own coins or something?"

"No, I didn't hear about that," I say as we step into the crane corral. I wonder if Hurona has. I'll ask her later. "Is it charity or something? Maybe they don't even need the pods anymore and they're just being nice. Why would they give us tokens instead of money?"

"But why would people want fake money?" Banneker says, making a face. "Nobody could spend it anywhere but with FOL-ROY. That seems kinda messed up."

"That's because it is," Mx. Amur says, and we both jump. I hadn't noticed her in the gloom. The roughness of her voice surprises me just as much.

"Why are they doing that, Mx. Amur?" I ask. "Giving out tokens instead?"

She raises her eyes to the crowd of other lockwood kids. They approach like a flock of ghosts.

"The lockwood makes everyone but Prine rich," she says. And then she's turning away, asking everyone if they need new hatchets. I stare at her so I don't look at Banneker—if I do, I'm going to tell

71

them what I saw at the top of the lockwood. I'm going to tell them about the sound the vines make when they grow. About the humming that's been in my head since I saw the flying black machine. But Banneker doesn't try to catch my eye. They're staring up at the tangle above. I wonder if they're thinking about the mountains we can't see. I can feel their dread like a sore muscle in my own arm. I think Banneker is another brimming jar.

"Do you remember stuff you used to do before you started going up?" I say quietly. Banneker and I had school together when we were little, but they had their brother, Carver, to play with and I had Hurona. It was only when we got into the trees that Banneker and I became friends.

"I used to go on long walks with Carver," they say. "We would just walk and walk once the sun broke through. He had a compass that he said was magic. Said we could never get lost if he had it. And he was right, we never did. He would pack us a snack and we would be gone for hours. My mom would be pulping, you know? We were just running wild. Until he had to go up. Then he didn't have time. Then soon I didn't have time either."

I feel like a bad friend. I feel like I've been walking and climbing next to someone with a finger missing, gushing blood. And I never noticed. Now that I see it, I realize Banneker has been walking around with a different kind of wound. Not missing a finger, but a brother. It makes my chest feel tight.

"Do you ever dream?" I ask, and I wait for them to look at me like I'm weird for such a random question. But they don't take their eyes off the trees.

72

"Not anymore," they say. "It kinda feels like one more thing I don't have space for."

And I know exactly what they mean. Somewhere off in the dark, I hear little kids singing songs on their way to the schoolhouse. My throat tightens even more because I want to yell through the black, *Stop growing, stop growing, stay exactly where you are*, but I know that won't help them either. In Prine, you're either too big or too small, and I just want to be.

HURONA FINDS ME on the way to school on Monday to tell me her plan. Banneker had to talk to their mom before school, so I'm walking alone. Tomorrow is Tuesday. Truck day. The day we leave. Since the night I saw the FOLROY drone, I've been like a rubber band—one minute stretching away from her, the next minute collapsing back to stay close. Thinking about Banneker, the way Carver is like a missing finger, makes me feel achy. I don't want to let her out of my sight, but I also don't want to be too close. She might change her mind, might sneak out with Iva if I look away for one second. So when she tells me her plan, I just listen at first, trying to seem like anything but a tagalong.

"You can only pack one change of clothes," she tells me. "This is going to be a fast trip, Erie. We're going to go, do what we need to do, and then Iva will bring you back."

"What if you can't find a job that fast?" I say.

What I don't say: *I'm not coming back to Prine unless I know you're okay.*

She sighs. I'm glad I didn't say the rest out loud.

"I'll be fine, Erie. Me and Iva have been planning for this."

"For how long?" I say.

She glances at me sideways. "Long enough."

I don't know why she's still sitting on secrets when the biggest one is already out in the open. I still can't believe she was just going to up and leave. I wonder when she was going to tell me. If she was going to tell me at all. But I don't ask that. Instead I ask the question that's been sitting in my throat like a cough.

"And what about Mom? What is she going to think when we're both gone?"

She doesn't answer right away. We walk slowly along the Spine in silence. We pass an alley where a little kid is trying to get their older sister to jump rope with them. The older sister tries, but she's tired from the lockwood. I can see it in the way her shoulders droop like old celery.

"I'm going to leave her a note," Hurona says.

"Saying what?"

"Telling her what she needs to know."

As much as I want to be the big sister, to be the one protecting Hurona, right now I'm glad I'm not. I sink into the little-sister shoes.

"There's something I need you to do, though," she says, and I'm suddenly alert. "Before we go."

"What?"

She glances at me, then hooks my arm with hers and slows down so I slow down too. We're almost to the schoolhouse. I can't remember the last time we walked like this, arm in arm. It makes me feel spongy, like I'm soaking up memories and getting full with them.

"You know the map behind Mr. Ovitt's desk?" she says.

"The map?"

"Yes. On the bulletin board. It's a tourist map of Petrichor."

"I didn't know it was a tourist map," I say, thinking.

"I need you to get it."

"Get it? You mean take it?"

She nods and I frown. The spongy feeling turns jittery instead. Take the map? Go behind Mr. Ovitt's desk and take it?

"How am I supposed to do that?" I whisper, because we're almost to school, and Mr. Ovitt isn't outside but it feels like he still might hear me.

"I'm going to come in and tell him we're having a family situation," she says, like it's the easiest thing in the world. "Then while he's distracted, you walk by, grab it, and go."

We'd been walking slowly, but now I stop.

"You're going to *lie*?"

"Is it really a lie?" she says, looking straight at me. "We do have a family situation."

"Mom is fine!"

"Right now she is. Who knows if she will be later? But it's not even about her. You and me are a family too. And we do have a situation. A situation that needs that map."

I almost ask why we need a map of Petrichor, but it's pretty obvious, I guess.

76

"Doesn't your girlfriend know her way around?" I push. "Why do we need a map?"

She frowns, then her eyes fly skyward, like she's looking for an answer in the lockwood.

"Look," she says. "Iva doesn't know *everything*. I want to be prepared."

"It's old," I argue. "It's been in there forever. What if the city has changed?"

"Erie," she says, dropping her chin. "If you want to come with me, then you need to get the map."

I bite my lip and glance toward the schoolhouse. I could argue more. I could tell her that I'll tell Mom. But that was the card I played earlier. And besides, this is what Hurona needs. I want to prove I can be part of this plan.

"Here comes Banneker," Hurona says in a low voice, and then her arm unloops from mine. It feels cold where her arm had been.

"Hey," Banneker says, trotting up. "What's up?"

"Nothing," I say. Hurona steps away and waves goodbye, but I know it's not a real goodbye. She's going to come inside and lie to Mr. Ovitt soon. I swallow and turn to Banneker. "Is your mom okay?"

"Yeah, she's fine. I left before she was up this morning, and she wanted to check on me. My allergies are flaring up."

I just nod. A lot of kids in Prine have bad allergies. Banneker's eyes are a little swollen almost every day, and sometimes it just gets to be too much. We always joke that it's the lockwood.

"My grandma always said that the warmer the Earth got, the worse everyone's allergies would get," Banneker says.

"Why?"

"Warmer climate means longer allergy season. More pollen in the air. We already have worse air because of all the fires."

I knew about that. They found smoke from the Arborklept in babies' lungs thousands of miles away. We close the distance between us and the school, Banneker rubbing their eyes, and me dragging my feet. Mr. Ovitt is at the old whiteboard when we walk in and ignores us. I'm glad. I think if he took one look at me, the whole plan would be written on my face in cursive. Me and Banneker sit at our desks by the window, neither of us saying much because we never do.

When Mr. Ovitt starts talking about wildfires, it just makes me feel worse. It's supposed to be a history lesson, but it's like he's writing about my mom when he spells everything out on the board. 5 MILLION ACRES BURNED. 50,000 BUILDINGS DESTROYED. He doesn't talk about the lives lost. One of them was Aunt Josie. By the time Hurona walks through the classroom door, I feel a little sick. The wildfire memories aren't mine, but they feel like it. Hurona was right. Mom would never leave Prine so easily. But in the back of my mind, I hear Aunt Josie's voice message, and a voice whispers: *But Mom did leave Prine once. And she's never mentioned it. Why?*

"Miss Neaux, what is it?" Mr. Ovitt says to Hurona.

My heart starts to pound.

"I hope your mom's okay," Banneker whispers. They already know what it means when Hurona shows up at school. But they must see my face because they stop and squint at me. "What's wrong?"

"I . . . have to do something," I whisper.

I know Banneker's my best friend, because they don't say a word when I stand up. Hurona has moved so Mr. Ovitt has his back to the room, and I know that means I have to do it. Now. I creep toward the front of the room. The shaky ladders we climb from the crane to the lockwood don't tremble as much as my knees. My bag bumps heavy against my hip. It sounds loud enough to shake the walls. I can feel Banneker's eyes on my back like two searchlights. My other classmates are either asleep or looking at Hurona.

I approach Mr. Ovitt's desk. Hurona is talking quickly, but I don't know what she's saying. The desk is right in front of me, the board behind it with the maps and the magazine covers just on the other side. My whole body feels wobbly, and I can't stop thinking: If I can't do this one thing for Hurona, how will I help her in Petrichor?

"Are you going or not?" Mr. Ovitt says in that bored voice he always uses. It's not until he's standing right in front of me that I realize he's talking to me.

"Um . . . ," I say. My mouth feels dry. My eyes dart over his shoulder at Hurona, who has her whole palm over her face. I let her down. My stomach feels heavy. I try to say something. "I . . . I just needed . . ."

"Yes?" he says. He has that face that looks like he's two seconds from a lecture.

"I . . . I wanted to borrow your map," I say. My stomach drops lower. I don't look at Hurona again because I know it will probably melt me where I stand.

"My map?" he says. His eyebrows shoot up. "What map?"

"Um...that...that one," I say. My hand rises by my side like a puppeteer lifted it. He follows my finger with his eyes, then his head. "I just wanted to...look at it," I say.

"Oh," he says. His voice dips a little, like a bird landing on a wire. "That."

He walks behind the desk, moving slowly. When his hands lift to reach for the map, I feel my heart flip-flop. Is he actually going to...?

"This isn't mine, in fact," he says. The rest of the class has their own conversations now, ignoring what's happening. Except Banneker, staring at me. My best friend. Who I'm lying to. Mr. Ovitt unpins the map carefully, and when he turns, he keeps looking at it, not me.

"Oh, um, right. It belonged to the last teacher."

He studies the map for a second before extending it to me.

"I'll bring it back," I say quickly. I don't know if that's true or not.

"That's all right. It should probably be..." He frowns, still not looking at me. "Somewhere else. It's just sitting."

I finally find the courage to glance at Hurona again. Her eyes are narrowed into slits. She looks like the cat that used to come to our porch for scraps.

"Um, thanks," I say. "I'll...check it out."

"Go be with your mother," he says, and then he's quickly

turning back to the whiteboard. He starts talking about wildfires again, and I dart my eyes at Banneker. Unlike everyone else in class, they paid attention to the whole thing with me and Mr. Ovitt, and they raise their eyebrow. They have questions that I can't answer. Not now. Then when?

Outside, Hurona doesn't say anything right away. We're half-way home when she says, "You're a terrible liar."

"Unlike you," I fire back. "And I didn't even have to lie. See? You don't always have to lie."

She makes a sound in her throat, but we don't say anything else on the way home. We don't have any reason to rush—Hurona *is* a good liar. Mom doesn't need us. We'll go home and she won't even notice, lost in her microscope. Looking at everything tiny made huge through the lens.

As we walk, I think Mom does the opposite with everything else: with Aunt Josie, our father, Gran'Ida. All the big things, huge losses, made tiny—so tiny they fit into a matchbox. But not a matchbox. That's too close to fire. And Mom can't handle fire unless she makes it herself. Which is why me and Hurona are leaving her behind. The guilt makes me feel scaly, like a lizard walking down the Spine.

But the guilt has a sparkling tail. Tomorrow I'm going to leave Prine for the first time, and the idea of seeing the lights of the city up close make me feel like a huge round balloon. There's no space for something that big in Prine. But maybe there is in Petrichor.

14

TUESDAY MORNING, MY last normal morning in Prine, the kitchen is dark and empty. And even though I know this means Mom has moved her work back to the shed outside, I stand there for a minute feeling lonely. Is this how she's going to feel when she realizes me and Hurona are gone? Has Hurona already written the note? She says I'm a terrible liar, which I guess is true. The only reason I've been able to keep Aunt Josie's messages a secret is because Mom hasn't asked me. Maybe as long as she doesn't ask me outright—"Are you leaving for Petrichor today?"—I can manage not to ruin everything.

I have my bag packed. Only a few things, like Hurona said. Including Mom's old phone and the map from the schoolhouse. I know the phone won't actually work, even outside Prine; it's basically an antique. But for some reason, having Aunt Josie's messages with me feels like taking a part of Mom that I can't reach. Aunt Josie knew the parts of Mom that I never will. All the stuff she locks away. All the stuff I wish I knew.

I watch Mom's silhouette from the kitchen, a shadow on the

other side of the brown paper she keeps over the shed's glass. I slip the old phone out and hold it to my ear.

> *Nadine, it's me. Are we going to talk about this? You've made your choices, I've made mine. What's a few hundred miles? I'm still here for you. You're still here for me. Aren't you? Call me back. Later.*

I swallow and put the phone away. What if I left without saying goodbye? I could just walk to the Spine. There have been days that I have, knowing she won't even notice. I wonder if she'll notice once we're gone. Maybe when we get back she'll look up from her microscope and say, "Oh, the sun is through." Hurona might be able to leave without a goodbye, but I can't. I slip my feet into my climbing shoes, and they lead me across the grass to her shop.

I don't knock—just slip in, the door closing on its own behind me. Mom's hunched over the table with her back to me.

"Good morning, Erie," she says. "I left bread in the oven."

"Oh," I say. I'm surprised. Not that she knew it was me, because she always does. But that she had put bread in the oven. When Mom bakes bread, she sprinkles the yeast into warm water until the yeast blooms. That's what my guilt feels like. Blooming. She may not always look at us, but I get the feeling that she always sees us. I wonder what Hurona's note will say.

"You're welcome," she says, but she's not serious. She doesn't joke very often, and when she does it means that whatever she's working on is cooperating. She always says that—*cooperating*. Like the metal and the wires are just more children and she's raising them too.

"What are you working on?" I say, coming close.

She shifts sideways on her stool. I can smell the smell that I know is Mom's—the smoky scent of the soldering iron mixed with something warm like the bread.

"I'm not really sure yet," she says, which makes me glance at her. She usually knows the end point before she starts. I always try to be like her when I first climb into the lockwood: planning a path through the branches before I take a single step.

I peer over her shoulder, but all I see is a storm. Screws and metal pieces and microchips. On the windowsill sits a tray with a lockwood pod dissected. It looks like any other nut, with an outer shell and hard white flesh inside. Except at the core is a black orb that, when cracked open, releases a rusty-gold dust. I've seen Mom open them before. I don't know what she's looking for. If there's anything to learn about the pods, FOLROY has to know already, since they buy them from Prine.

FOLROY brings us mail, food, money. Sometimes it feels like we rely on them for everything. I don't know what they even do with the pods, but at least they give us what we need to get by. I think about this while looking at the mess of my mom's table. With the way her inventions are going, we need it. I think of Lunata Elemnieri, her boring husband, Arlo Kylak. I wonder if they have kids, if they know their mom is a famous inventor. If they're proud. My mom sees me looking and sighs.

"I didn't get a good deal on the headlamps," she says, like she read my mind. It makes my guilty feelings bloom bigger. "Since FOLROY already had a headlamp model, they took my creation as an *improvement* and not an *invention*."

"Isn't making something better just as good as making something new?" I say. I know how hard she worked on those headlamps. FOLROY's model was clumsy and the light was never where you needed it.

"Sometimes," she says. "Sometimes what exists can't be made better. It just needs to be wiped clean."

I want to make a joke about how her workshop isn't clean, but she's not looking at the pod anymore. She doesn't seem like she's in the workshop at all. This doesn't feel like one of her storms. Sometimes it's like there's a wind that I can't feel, but it carries her far away. What if her mind is all the way in Petrichor? Aunt Josie's message nags at me. I'm going to the city with my sister, and the message implied that at some point my mom went with hers.

"Can you tell me what conservancy Aunt Josie worked for now?" I blurt.

She keeps looking out the window, but I see her eyes sharpen. Usually this would be enough to make me stop. But not today. Everything I don't know feels like a missing bone in my body. I don't know if I can walk out of this room without knowing.

"Mom?" I whisper when she doesn't answer.

"There were two," she says quietly. "One in Petrichor—the Eccles-Tillery Conservancy. Another one to the south. Josie would travel between them, shuttling injured animals. She was like you. Loved anything that crawled."

All the questions I have feel crowded in my throat. Only one finds its way out.

"Did you ever go see her?"

She finally looks at me, and I can tell right away she's not telling me anything else. Clouds have gathered. She readjusts her eyepiece, and the soldering iron buzzes back to life.

"You're going to be late," she says.

I want to tell her. Tell her that I'll see her in a couple of days, and that when I get back, maybe things will be different. That Hurona has a plan. But her eyebrows are low and I know that her heart is too. Instead I move over and kiss the top of her head. It feels like something Hurona would do. My mother freezes, then reaches her free hand to pat my arm without looking up.

When I get to the door, I look back one more time. She was grown up by the time the lockwood was planted. But even though the fire can't get in here, I see the hunch of her shoulders, and it makes me think Prine is somehow making her smaller too.

On the part of the worktable that extends to the door, Mom's little collection of sparrows rests in three rows. I can't tell which one is the prototype—they're small and white, and when I pick one up, it's smooth and cool. It fits in my palm like a wishing stone. Mom doesn't turn to look at me, but I keep looking at her. My first time away from home. Away from her. And I can't even hug her good-bye. The Neaux household doesn't cry. So I take a deep breath and I slip the sparrow into my bag, just so I can have something of hers to hold.

15

I DON'T KNOW if I'm relieved or distressed when Banneker doesn't show up at the cranes.

"Allergies," Mx. Amur tells me, and pats my shoulder when she sees what she must think is loneliness on my face. She pairs me with Curie, who talks even less than I do, leaving my mind plenty of time to turn over all the ways I'm a bad friend for not telling my best friend I'm leaving. Maybe Banneker not showing up is for the best. Less blatant lying.

As usual, when my shift is over, I hear the FOLROY trucks before I see them. Actually, I feel them. After spending the morning in the lockwood, in the air but not a bird, I always feel a little wobbly back on the ground. And sore. I've just taken off my climbing shoes, and I'm sitting on the general store's front steps, where I usually sit with Banneker, when the ground trembles under my heels. The trucks. On their way here. When they leave, I'll be with them. I still don't know the plan. Hurona says if she tells me too soon I'll overthink it and mess it up. I wish I could say she was wrong.

So I wait, and when I feel someone's hand on my shoulder,

I think it's my sister, but I look up to find Mr. Lunder, the shop-keeper, looking down at me.

"Hurona," he says. "Good morning."

"It's Erie, actually," I say. Hurona and I don't look much alike—not to me—but that's not why he thinks I'm her anyway. Mr. Lunder is old, and after his wife died, his brain changed its mind about what it would let him keep. His eyes are always sort of cloudy. I wonder about that sometimes—if when someone you love dies, part of you dies too. If that's why my mom has her storms. She never talks about Aunt Josie, and never, ever talks about my dad— he was sick, and he died, and that's that. But maybe that's why she doesn't talk about them. Did the part of her that remembers shrink, like everything else in Prine? What if whatever I learn in Petrichor can make it grow again?

"Did you know that some people wrapped their homes in foil before the Arborklept?" he says. "To keep the houses from burning? It worked sometimes. Of course, then they jacked up the price of foil."

He does this sometimes. The past swims all around him so it's easy to dip a toe in.

"How are you, Mr. Lunder?" I ask.

"Oh, I'm just making my way," he says, not caring that I didn't answer about the foil. He stares off toward the tunnel where any minute the FOLROY trucks will appear, stirring up dust. "They told me last week that they'd be bringing me some new stuff this week. Stuff people will be excited to get their hands on in my store. Have you ever had a frozen pancake? I bet you haven't."

"Why would I want a frozen pancake?" I say, confused.

"Well, you don't eat it frozen. You warm it up first. It just comes frozen in a package."

"Okay," I say, raising my eyebrow. "But who said they're bringing you frozen pancakes?"

"FOLROY," he says, gesturing in the direction of the tunnel. "We've always had the same stuff. Sounds like they're gonna shake it up."

"Wait, FOLROY brings the stuff you sell in the store?"

He laughs. It sounds like dry leaves.

"Well, yes, Hurona, where did you think it came from?"

I'd never really thought about it. But now that I do, of course it makes sense. Some stuff for sale in the store is grown by people here—tomatoes and other vegetables Mom calls "easy." But most of it, like flour and grits and oat milk, is in glass jars and burlap sacks. I've seen the boxes unloaded from FOLROY's trucks. It makes sense.

"Are people going to use tokens to buy it?" I ask, thinking of what Mx. Amur had said.

He glances at me, his eyes a little clearer.

"You've heard about the tokens, have you?"

"Yes, I heard."

"They sell us the food, and then we pay for the food, and then we buy more to sell. Only one person ever makes any money. What does that sound like to you?"

I remember what Banneker said.

"It sounds kind of messed up," I repeat.

He pauses, squinting.

"You ever hear of Harlan County? Kentucky?"

"No, sir."

"I'd say look it up." He shakes his head. "But how would you? You've heard of coal? They've tried things like this before. Problem is, I'm so tired. I'll just say this: Nothing good comes out of Petrichor. Remember that, Hurona."

He goes on looking at me and my heart sinks. It's never occurred to me to ask him questions before: Has he been to Petrichor? Can he tell me what it's like? Or would asking him draw attention to my sister's plan? *My* plan. I'm going too.

But before I can even choose a question, the trucks are pulling in.

I count this time. Thirteen trucks. Some are big, with their gaping empty beds, ready to receive the sacks of pods and pulped lockwood. Some beds are covered, carrying sacks and crates. This must be stuff for the general store, I realize. I'd always been so interested in people watching and bug watching that I didn't pay much attention to other stuff.

Part of me wants to sprint to Banneker's house and tell them: *Did you know that FOLROY is the one who gives us money for lockwood, but FOLROY also sells us food for our store? Did you know that the money we spend in the store pays FOLROY?* The only time I really think about money is when Mom tells us what we can't afford. It all feels like knots in my head, twisty and turny as the vines I'd spent the morning cutting. I think of the white envelope my mom gets once a month for inventing the headlamp. That comes from FOLROY too.

Then Mr. Lunder is thumping down the stairs, off to see Miss Jinnah. Any minute, Mom will be marching down the Spine. Won't she? When I'd asked what she was working on this morning, she said she wasn't sure yet. I can't think of a Tuesday she missed the trucks, but before I can give it too much thought, I see Hurona.

She's moving slowly, coming out of the trees with a sack of pods slung over her shoulder. She looks so strong and tall and her hair is pulled back in one loose braid. Hurona. My sister. She has a girl-friend. She has secrets. She has dreams. Then she sees me, catches my eye, and gives me one quick nod. She has plans too.

We're actually doing this.

I feel stuck to the stairs. And my sister, because she's my sister, knows this. She pauses, stares at me across the big circle where all the trucks are parked, and slowly tilts her head sideways. Hurona gets feelings sometimes, hunches. She tilts her head like that when something is giving her a feeling, and right now that something is me. I know the face she's making. She used to look at me like this when I was little and was scared to follow her into the lockwood's shade. I know what she's saying. *Are you coming or not?*

I nod.

I come unstuck.

I see Iva hop out of the truck, greeting my sister with a smile like stars. Then she turns to look at me, and she smiles at me too.

16

THE PLAN IS simple. At least that's what Hurona says.

We sit at the edge of the lockwood. All the times we played in the forest when we were little and I imagined something watching us from the bushes... Now I'm that watching thing.

The trucks are almost full—all the pulp and pods loaded up. Miss Jinnah is distributing money. Tokens too, I guess. It's hard to tell, but the adults who are talking to her look angry. Or maybe just confused. Mom never came. I imagine her in her workshop, alone, crouched over her table with what's left of the daylight. My heart squeezes, but then Hurona squeezes my arm. She's pointing.

"Iva's almost done," she says. "When she gets in the cab of the truck, that's when we make our move."

Iva's job at FOLROY is driving the truck that carries supplies, then carting away empty crates when the trucks leave. This is Hurona's simple plan: Just before the trucks leave, me and Hurona will climb in the back and hide in one of the empty crates. When Hurona first told me, I frowned. When she said we were going to

Petrichor, I had imagined watching the lockwood disappear behind us. But not from inside a dark wooden box that smells like onions.

"There's a window in the back of the truck," Hurona says when I tell her this. She only rolls her eyes a little. She's too busy watching Iva to be really annoyed with me. It gives me a chance to study her, looking for any sign of nervousness. But why would she be nervous, I ask myself. She's been planning this for who knows how long. All her nerves are ironed out. Even though it makes me feel even more like a little sister, I keep thinking about Mom.

"Did you leave Mom the note?" I say. I hope my nerves sound ironed out too.

"Yes," she says. "Right by the coffee pot where she won't miss it."

"What if she does?"

"She won't, Erie."

"What did you say?"

"I told her what she needs to know," she repeats.

I gnaw my lip and press my hand against the bag that carries my lockwood knife, my change of clothes, the map, Aunt Josie's old phone. *The Encyclopedia of Entomology.* And the sparrow I'd slipped out of my mother's workshop.

I could still go back. I could wish Hurona luck. But I think of Banneker's brother, Carver. He's somewhere in Petrichor, occasionally sending money home. I think about their dad, who, like so many other people, faded out of Prine and never came back. I can't let that happen with Hurona. And then, pushed down to the bottom of my thoughts, is my own curiosity about Aunt Josie and what sort of life she left outside of Prine. So, I sit with my lips between my teeth, waiting for Iva to give us the signal.

Miss Jinnah is walking toward her truck, the first one in the FOLROY caravan. She pauses by Mr. Lunder. She says a few words and he nods his head. But he looks sad. He had smiled about the frozen pancakes. Now I wonder if he was pretending.

The rest of the FOLROY workers are climbing into their trucks, and their engines fill the circle with rumbling. Iva strides toward her truck. Its back door is cracked open for us. She shoots a look toward the bushes we crouch in. Everyone from Prine is either in the general store or moving down the Spine toward home. The pulper is quiet for the first time since dawn. Iva opens her car door, then leans down to tie her boot.

That's the signal.

It's time.

This time Hurona doesn't need to squeeze my arm—when she stands up, I'm already standing with her. We move slowly out of the lockwood's edge, not drawing attention to ourselves. When telling me the plan, Hurona said, *Move slow.* So I put one foot carefully in front of the other.

We're three feet from the back of the truck when someone calls my name.

"Erie, have you gone to the store yet or are you just going home?"

Everything freezes except for my heart—there's no way it could be ice, as fast and hard as it's pumping. I only turn my head to look. The rest of my body is stuck.

It's Banneker.

They stand at the edge of the circle, alone. And I can see it all over their face. They're confused about why Hurona and I are standing so near the FOLROY trucks when everyone else is heading home.

"Banneker," I croak. "I . . . I thought you were sick."

"I was," they say. "I slept all day and I feel better. I thought you might want to take a walk. . . ."

They trail off. I wonder if they can see the sweat I can feel like a necklace on my upper lip. Me and Hurona had changed out of work uniforms and wear what pass for regular clothes in Prine—cotton shirts and pants. I feel the sweat seeping through at my underarms too. I feel like a giant flashing light.

"Erie," Banneker says, "what are you doing?"

The first trucks in the FOLROY caravan are pulling off, the dust starting to swirl. The sun is starting to set. From the front of the truck, Iva coughs, and I steal a glance at her. She's got one boot up into the truck and is glaring at us. I look back at Banneker, my heart circling higher and faster like a moth.

"I . . . I . . ."

"Erie, *now*," Hurona says, and she looks at Banneker but says nothing. She hauls herself into the truck the rest of the way. Banneker is the only one watching us. Banneker is the only person I'm watching.

"I . . . have to do something," I stammer. "I'll be back."

"Be back from *where*?" they say, alarmed. I can almost see their big brother, Carver, appearing in their eyes, then shrinking.

"Me and Hurona," I say. "We have to do something. But I swear I'll be back, Banneker. I swear."

"Erie," my sister says, once. Iva has started the truck, and Hurona's hand is cupped around the back door. I know she'll go without me. But what if Petrichor is just a bigger Prine, swallowing everyone who goes in? I can't let her be swallowed alone. But what does that mean for Banneker?

I look in my sister's face. She has her hand out, like she has so many times. Helping me up. I have to be there to help her if she needs me. I take one last look at Banneker and jump into the truck. The door slams before I can say *I'm sorry*.

17

I KNOW WE'RE in the tunnel because the world is black. I could see the window on the back of the truck for a moment before we drove in, and then we did and the square of light faded, flickered, disappeared.

"It's okay," Hurona whispers. And I don't know if she's talking about the dark, or Banneker. I want to say, *I'm not afraid of the dark,* because how can anyone born in Prine be? But there's something else we both don't have to say. This dark is different. We know the dark in Prine. We know that in the morning, I will climb into the trees and let the light in.

But in the tunnel? I don't know what kind of darkness this is, or how long it goes. Banneker and I had thought about walking through one time, just to see. But Mr. Lunder called us back. Too far, he said, to get through and back on foot without running out of light first. I remember how Banneker had looked tiny at the start of the tunnel, like the lockwood was a throat of vines waiting to swallow. We had both been relieved to have an excuse to turn around, and we wondered why the tunnel never needed cutting back. Why the tunnel didn't grow like hungry weeds every single night.

Now I know.

Because a circling drone hasn't been feeding it.

The truck goes over a bump, and me and Hurona jostle into each other. I stay close against her side even though I know she notices and is probably rolling her eyes in the black. Still, her hand finds mine and pats it. Three pats, as if to say, *Be brave, Erie.* I try.

"You guys okay?" Iva shouts through the thin wall of the cab. Hurona reaches up and pounds her fist against it in answer. Iva laughs and calls: "Breaking through in a minute!"

In the dark, Hurona's pat turns into a squeeze. I wish I could see her face. I wonder again how long she's been planning this. I wonder if when she found Iva's smile, it was like finding a golden ticket.

"Ready?" Hurona says.

"I think so," I whisper.

Petrichor can't be this close, just on the other side of the tunnel. There's no way we've already driven fifty miles. Is there? But light breaks through the window at our back, and I think we must be *somewhere.*

"The last of sunset," Iva calls over the chatter of her truck radio. "Take a look before it's gone!"

Hurona jumps up, swaying as the truck moves. She braces herself against the wall, peeking out the small window that looks into the cab. Her face glows orange and pink. It's weird to see her illuminated with something other than the yellow of a headlamp. She smiles out the window.

"Come see, Erie."

I stand and almost fall. The truck seems to be driving in a straight line, but fast. My legs are strong from the lockwood, and I find my balance. I peer out the window beside my sister.

"Whoa," I whisper. Straight ahead on the road is the line of FOLROY trucks—we're at the back. But beyond them is the sunset, and I've seen sunset before, of course. In the hole we cut out of the lockwood, the tips of it sometimes paint the top of the sky. Pink and orange and purple. But there's never a horizon, only the puzzle of tree trunks. And that's why this sunset is so special. Because not only can we see the ground and how the sun is like a melting round candle on the horizon. But we can see how...big the world is.

"Do you see the mountains?" Hurona whispers. She doesn't have to whisper, but she does, and it makes me feel close to her. We're seeing this together for the first time.

"Yes," I whisper back. They're purple, almost gone with the sun. I want to say more. I want to say how it feels like my heart is expanding in my chest. But I don't really have words big enough for how huge the world feels. It's scary and beautiful at the same time. I think of Banneker, how I thought they were thinking about math but they were thinking about mountains. Guilt swims in me again.

We watch until the sun sinks. All that's left is a lick of pink on the horizon. It looks like someone breathed orange breath on glass. I sigh.

"There will be another one tomorrow," Hurona says. I can hear the smile in her voice.

"Might as well sit back down," Iva calls. "We've got a ways to go."

We huddle back behind the onion crate again. There's only a faint glow lighting the back of the truck, and I wish I could read. Instead I'm thinking of Mom. I reach into my bag and pull out her old phone.

Hurona sees it and sighs. "Why did you bring that?"

"Because."

I play the next message and hold it against my face.

> *Dina, it's Jojo. I saw something so beautiful today. We released a family of black bears into the conservancy after they were treated for burns. I wish you had been here to see it with me. Don't give up yet. Later.*

I didn't see Mom as the giving-up type. Aunt Josie didn't know that Mom walked to the trucks almost every Tuesday just to be told no. Maybe Josie was talking about a different kind of giving up. Either way, I wish Mom were here to see this too.

18

"WE HAVE A problem," Iva calls through the cab wall, and Hurona jolts up from where she'd slouched. Her secret phone had been a gift from Iva, I learn, and Hurona has just begun to shine it on my book so I can read about Goliath beetles. But now the back of the truck goes dark again.

"What's going on?" Hurona calls.

"There's...there's a checkpoint." Then Iva curses, long and loud.

I sit up straight. I dart my eyes at Hurona but can't see her face.

"What kind of checkpoint?" Hurona says.

"What's a checkpoint?" I whisper.

"They're searching the trucks," Iva calls, then she curses again. "They're looking for contraband."

"Is this normal?" Hurona demands.

"They...do it sometimes," Iva says.

Hurona bangs the wall, so loudly I jump.

"And this isn't something you thought to tell me?" Hurona shouts.

"They haven't been checking FOLROY trucks lately," Iva wails. "I thought it would be fine. But they're stopping up ahead, I can see the checkers' flashlights....Oh my gosh. This is bad."

"What will happen?" Hurona demands, her face pressed against the window. I peek from behind her, and far ahead I can see the flashlights too.

"They'll fire me," Iva says. "Then...then they'll take you into custody."

"For *what*?"

"I don't know! They've done it before. They always assume people are stealing. Either product or FOLROY secrets."

Now Hurona curses, and my eyes widen. Hurona never curses.

"What do we do?" Hurona says. "Do you have FOLROY uniforms we could put on?"

"No!" Iva says. She's almost shouting. "No, and you'd need a badge anyway! Crap crap crap!"

She has slowed the truck little by little, and we creep along at the end of the FOLROY caravan. Through the small window, I can see her knuckles gripping the steering wheel tight.

"You have to get out," she says, too softly at first. Then louder: "Hurona, you have to get out. You have to get out of the truck."

"What??"

"You have to," Iva says. She takes her eyes off the road to look over her shoulder. Her eyes are big and wet. "I can't let you get locked up. If they charge you with a crime against FOLROY, they could keep you for months while you try to get someone to represent you."

"But we didn't do anything," I cry. "We haven't stolen anything! Can't we just tell them that?"

"They won't believe you," Iva says. "You're in a FOLROY truck and you're not supposed to be. Case closed."

She has stopped the truck.

"You've gotta get out, Hura," she says. I don't recognize the nickname, but it doesn't matter because Hurona does. She glares at Iva through the window. "Quick. Please."

"What are we supposed to do?" Hurona demands. "We're already twenty-five miles from Prine. Walk? At night?"

"Use the phone I gave you," Iva begs. Her radio hums. "There's a bus line on this road. You can use it to get to Petrichor and I'll meet you there."

"This wasn't the *plan*, Iva," Hurona says. I hear the crack in her voice. The Neaux household doesn't cry, but we're not in the Neaux house anymore.

"I know, and I'm so sorry," Iva says. She's turned all the way in her seat now that the truck has stopped, staring at my sister.

"Truck twelve, everything okay?" says a voice through the radio.

"Crap!" Iva scrambles for the radio. She casts Hurona a pleading glance before answering. "Everything's fine, a flock just passed over and left a bunch of droppings on the windshield. Had to clear the window so I could see."

She looks at Hurona.

"Go," she says. "We'll figure it out."

Hurona shakes her head and turns away. The air in the back

of the truck feels tense, the way it does before one of Mom's storms. I wonder if, back in Prine, Mom is storming right now, reading Hurona's note. Whatever it said.

"Come on, Erie," my sister says, and she's shoving the back door open. She's on the ground, pulling me down before I even realize she's grabbed my hand. No sooner do the doors clang shut behind us then Iva is speeding off down the road to catch up with the rest of the FOLROY caravan. We stand in the middle of the road, not dirt like in Prine, but paved hard and smooth. It feels like standing on a stage. Except there's no audience—it's just me and Hurona standing alone in the world that feels huge. Lights line the road, brighter than the Spine. But I know we're not in Prine, because in Prine, my big sister doesn't cry. And here, she does.

19

WE LEAN AGAINST a streetlight, not speaking. Hurona doesn't look at me while she dries her tears. I know she's embarrassed. I'd cried in front of Banneker once, and they didn't understand why I was uncomfortable. *Everybody cries*, they said. And I know that's kind of true. But if I said that to Hurona right now, she'd probably take my head off. So I just stand quietly, waiting for her to be ready. After a while I pull out the map from my backpack. I had it folded inside the encyclopedia.

In the light from above, I study it. The big lopsided circle around Petrichor could be a wall or a fence—I can't tell. The details are small. But I see the streets and the plazas and the parks. There's so much of it. It goes on and on. I feel like I could fit Prine in the palm of my hand. I imagine myself as the tiny ants I love watching, walking along the map in my hands. I know when I get there, I probably will feel that small.

"See anything interesting?" Hurona says quietly.

"Just streets and stuff," I say. "Where does Iva live?"

"Heming Street, maybe? Leming Street?"

I want to say, *You don't know? You've come all this way and you don't even know where she lives?* But she looks like she feels bad enough, staring at the phone Iva gave her. I put the map away.

After a minute Hurona holds up the phone.

"This says that there's a bus stop one mile back."

"Okay," I say. Neither of us has ever ridden a bus, but saying so feels like it would be betraying her somehow.

"This wasn't the plan," she says. She's saying it to me because I'm the only one here, but she's looking up at the stars.

"You can call her later," I say. I want to be for Hurona who Hurona is for Mom. "You can talk about it. Figure things out…"

"She left me and my little sister by the side of a road at night," she says. "I'm not calling her. Ever."

"Okay," I whisper.

"Let's go find the bus stop," she says.

I just nod, and we set off. Footsteps in Prine are silent on dirt roads. Here they sound like slow, heavy raindrops. We'd passed the bus stop while in the back of the FOLROY truck, and it feels weird to be walking back toward Prine when we just left. But it also feels like we've been gone forever. I think about Banneker's face as the truck door closed. Part of me wants to run all the way home, twenty-five miles or not.

The bus stop is like a tiny square house with a long bench inside. The roof is slanted and see-through—it's not raining, but we stand under it anyway, because maybe that's a rule, and maybe the bus won't stop if you're not under it. There's a big blue button with a sign—PRESS TO SIGNAL—and Hurona and I exchange a glance of doubt before she presses it. The little house immediately glows blue, and I sit inside it watching the night insects eventually flock to the light. I stare at them, the way they circle and flutter. Banneker hates bugs. But I love watching them. Some of them fly in hurried zig-zags, others spin slowly, wandering.

Hurona, though, stares down at the phone that Iva had given her. She's waiting for it to ring, but there's no way Iva is already back in Petrichor. She's probably just cleared the checkpoint.

"Does that have the internet?" I ask, nodding at the phone.

"Yeah."

"All the way out here," I breathe. "Wow."

"You know there are some cities that have made it so everyone has the internet?" she says. "For free."

"Not places as far as Prine," I say doubtfully.

"Even places as far as Prine. They bury wires and stuff so people can have it no matter where they are. They realized it's better to have access to information."

"What kind of information?"

"Like what I just told you," she says, smiling faintly. "I wouldn't even have known that some people have this," she holds up the phone, "for free."

"What else have you learned?" I ask. We haven't talked this much in a long time.

"Some really, really important stuff," she says. "Look."

She holds up the phone, and on the screen I watch a baby goat bouncing in circles around a house tinier than this bus stop. It vaults off the roof and into a patch of clover. I look up at her sharply, confused, and find her holding back laughter. When she sees my face, we both crack up.

"Why do you have that?" I ask. "Whose goat is that?"

"This is what Iva sends me all the time." She laughs. "I get home from the lockwood, and I have like ten videos like this waiting for me. No idea whose goat it is. It could be someone in another country."

"She just sends things like this all day?"

"Yeah. She has her phone all day, so she can."

"Wow."

The world isn't just bigger than I could have thought. It's different. I know what the internet is, of course. Every now and then Mr. Ovitt manages to use the FOLROY signal housed in the trucks on Tuesdays, and he downloads stuff for us to see. Other times he waits until the sky has been cleared and can occasionally tap into Newscast. The thing about the lockwood is that you spend so much time thinking about how to beat it back, that you don't have a lot of time to think about much else. Or wonder what you're missing. I sit next to my sister in the blue glow of the bus stop watching video after video of animals playing and running. One is a fluffy white animal sliding on ice. I've seen them before in pictures but don't know their name.

"What's that?" I ask, pointing.

She squints to read the caption under the video.

"A polar bear," she reads. "It says they're extinct now."

"Oh."

And that makes me think of what Mom said right before I left:

how me and Aunt Josie both loved anything that crawled. How it felt like a secret when she told me. It's not much of a secret, but in our family everything feels like that: my dad and my aunt, gone; my mom and my sister, silent. This is why I haven't put the phone back, I think. Because it seems like Aunt Josie is the only one who tells the truth, and she's not even alive. I can't talk to her, but I can listen.

Hurona and I sit like this for hours. I can't help but think that right now the black FOLROY drone might be humming over Prine, the vines snaking up higher and higher. Maybe the little machine has already come and gone. I can almost hear the hum in my ears.

Then I realize that it's not in my memory—I *can* hear something humming.

The bus.

Hurona looks up first, the far-off grumble reaching our ears, headlights growing brighter and louder. Before it's even close, I can tell that it's huge. Two levels, and painted bright green. Its engine is silent. The hum I heard was the sound of the tires against the hard-paved road. When the bus slows to a stop, there's the faint whistle of brakes.

Hurona steps forward and I'm glad—I suddenly feel like I don't know how to do...anything. In Prine, everything is the same every day. I thought new would be exciting. And it is. But in the lock-wood, I feel like I can trust my feet, even high up over the ground. Now every step feels like I'm going to trip.

The door to the bus hisses open and the driver stares down at us. She's brown-skinned with long dark hair in two braids on either side of her face. Her work uniform is pale blue, a hat the same color perched on her head. When neither Hurona nor I move, her deep brown eyes focus on us a little more closely.

"Box is lit," she says, nodding at the stop house. "Are you getting on?"

"Um, maybe," Hurona says. I stay silent. "Is this bus going to Petrichor?"

The driver nods, still studying us. After my mother's storms, when me and Hurona would return home from the woods, Mom would look at us like this. Looking for holes in our clothes, dirt on our faces, signs of where we'd been, what we'd been doing.

Over the driver's shoulder, in the very front seat, sits a girl around my age, with the same dark eyes and round chin. Her hand reaches over the top of the seat to offer the driver a long red stick of licorice, which she snakes through the ventilation holes of the plastic box surrounding the driver's seat. Her daughter, I can tell, by the way the woman waves the offer away.

"Are you going to Petrichor?" the driver asks, when Hurona still hesitates. "If so, this is your bus."

"Yes, ma'am," Hurona answers. "But is this the only one? I mean, will it take us . . . straight there?"

"This is the only bus to Petrichor from the townlands." The driver nods. Her tone isn't exactly kind, but it's patient. I think patience is a sort of kindness.

"Okay," Hurona says, and taps my arm to follow her up the steep stairs. But I already am. The smaller the gap between us, the smaller my doubt feels. Well, not smaller. But quieter.

"Six fifty," the driver says, and from her bag Hurona unfolds bills I didn't know she had. I wonder if Iva gave her these too, or if she'd found some other way.

"No change," the driver warns as Hurona is about to feed a bill into the slot. Hurona freezes, then fishes out coins from her bag and drops them in instead. The driver pushes two tickets out from the slot of her plastic box.

I whisper thank you. She must see my lips move because she nods, then angles her head back toward the many empty seats. Her daughter eyes us as we pass, and I sneak a look at her too. She wears denim on top and on bottom, her hair pulled up in a messy bun. She has red streaks dyed in it, and a beaded necklace that hugs her throat. The shoes on her feet are bright pink, and she has the sole of one pressed against the driver's cube.

"Here," Hurona says. We go midway back. It's the seat I would have chosen too: not the front, not the back. Halfway between. A safe distance, I hope, from...anything. Hurona sits with her back angled against the window and I perch next to her. The streetlights out in the black night are brighter than the inside of the bus. The lights in here are dim and the same bluish tint as the bus stop. It sort of feels like being in a spaceship.

"Are you going to tell Iva we're on the bus?" I ask. I nod at the phone. She never seems to put it in her bag—she holds it in her hand like it could ring any minute.

"No," Hurona says, and nothing else. Her face is a sealed envelope. That doesn't change just because we left Prine.

I look around the half-full bus. People ride alone and in pairs, most of them wearing uniforms, some blue, some beige. Across the aisle, a white woman a little older than my mom sits toying with the rings on her fingers, just gazing around. She catches me looking and smiles wide. But most people sleep, gentle snores from ahead and behind.

The sight of many nodding heads, eyes closed, reminds me how tired I am. The bus is strange, but not exactly scary. It's almost like being inside a traveling house. It makes me feel slightly safe, and I wish Hurona would sit closer so I could lean against her a little. But I won't ask.

Instead, I clutch my arms tight around myself and try not to think of Mom, or Banneker, or Helia and her mother's tear-stained face. Sleep is like falling into a sudden hole, the ground disappearing under my feet. I wish all falling was this gentle.

20

I **WAKE TO** my sister shaking me, hard. My name gusts out of her mouth.

"Erie," she says. "We might have a problem."

When my eyes open, the streetlights are no longer passing in quick bursts. Instead the bus is creeping down the road. Outside pulse beats of orange light. I peek over the seat in front of me to see better: a line of trucks and buses ahead, also moving slowly. Orange caution lights in a line across the road, people in uniforms milling back and forth.

"What is it?" I say, rubbing my eyes.

"They're saying there's a checkpoint ahead."

"The one Iva was talking about?"

"No, we passed that a little bit ago while you were sleeping. That one was for trucks only, I guess. This one is for buses."

"Who cares, then?" I whisper, wondering why she looks so worried. "We paid to get on the bus, right?"

Everyone around us looks unbothered, yawning while they reach into bags and pockets.

"The driver said anyone without paperwork will be removed from the bus," Hurona says.

"Removed?"

"Kicked off," Hurona says. She still hasn't looked at me. She seems rigid, staring straight ahead. "And based on what Iva said, taken into custody."

"What does that even mean?"

"It means that we need to figure something out," Hurona says. "Or we may not be going to Petrichor *or* Prine."

"No papers?" someone whispers, and we both jerk our heads to find the woman across the aisle peering in our direction. "If you don't have papers at the checkpoint, they'll be taking you off the bus, yes. Last time I saw them take somebody off, it was a girl around your age. They put her in cuffs."

"Why?" I breathe. My eyes dart between her face and the orange lights flashing closer up ahead.

"Petrichor is crowded," she says. "They don't want people coming in unless they're authorized to be there. Work papers or medical papers. If you don't have 'em, they'll keep you for a few days while they figure out what you're doing in the city and if there's somewhere else you need to be instead."

"Somewhere else like where?"

"Like back in the townlands." The woman shrugs. "With parents, if you're a runaway. Or your home country, if you're not American. Things like that."

"We're not runaways," I say, even if we sort of are. Are you a runaway if you're running away but plan to come back?

"But do you have papers?" the woman says. She wears glasses on a gold chain around her neck and places them on her nose. When she peers at us, she looks like an old turtle. Neither of us answer. Hurona doesn't move but I can feel her energy crackling like static.

"We'll have to talk to them," Hurona says a second later. "Let them know we have family in the city…"

Hearing Hurona think of Iva as family makes me wince. It makes me think, again, that maybe Hurona wouldn't have come back for me after all. What if I hadn't seen the FOLROY drone? What if Hurona hadn't been out in the woods with me when Iva called? Would my sister have slipped through my fingers like smoke?

The woman across the aisle shakes her head.

"They don't care much about family," she says. "Been a long time since they cared about family. They care about work. They say they want 'skilled workers.' Of course, what they consider *skilled* usually has a snooty idea about what skill looks like. When they say *skilled*, they mean people with computers and engineering jobs. Not ag workers. But if you ask me, that's skill too. Somebody just decided that it's not the kind that makes you rich."

Hurona stares straight ahead at the orange lights. Our bus is so close to the checkpoint now that the colors flash on her face. I glance up and find the bus driver eyeing us through the big rear-view mirror, frowning. It's like she knows we're somewhere we're not supposed to be. I wish she had warned us. I want to yell at Hurona. I want to say, *Why didn't Iva tell us any of this?* But my sister's face looks like a broken window, and I keep everything inside.

The woman across the aisle clears her throat, leaning a little way across to close the gap between us. She looks over the top of her glasses, the gold chain glittering. Her eyebrows are at different angles. She looks the way Mr. Lunder's wife always looked before she died: *Are you hungry? Need a bandage for that blister?*

"Do you need papers?" the woman says quietly. "You two look awfully young to be heading to the city alone. You said you have family there?"

Hurona shoots a look at me.

"Kind of," she starts. "A friend meeting us. She told us to take this bus...."

"Can't be much of a friend if she didn't tell you you needed papers."

Maybe it's the woman's worried eyebrows, or maybe it's the fact that she's echoed my fears about Iva. It occurs to me that maybe Iva isn't to be trusted at all, and maybe this woman is.

"Do you need papers?" she repeats softly.

Hurona doesn't answer. So I whisper: "Yes."

"I can help," the woman says. She's digging into her purse, a big clunky thing on her lap with shiny buckles. Her rings shine. "I have something...."

The bus is creaking to a halt when she pulls her hand out. In her fist are clutched two documents, sheathed in plastic. They're small enough to fit in a wallet. They both have what looks like a

116

raised stamp at one corner. At the front of the bus, the driver is reaching to open the door to admit a white man in a blue uniform. As he climbs up the steep stairs, the driver glances at me in the rear-view mirror again, frowning.

There's no way she knows if we have them or not, I think to myself. My heartbeat feels too slow. *If she tells on us, she can't prove we didn't already have these.*

The man in the uniform is speaking to the driver. The woman across the aisle from us reaches over and plunks the papers in my lap, withdrawing her hand quickly.

"Are you sixteen?" she whispers to Hurona.

Hurona nods, silent, nervous.

"Today you're fifteen," she says, her eyes bright and reassuring. "They make you put a photo on the doc when you turn sixteen. So today, if they ask, you're fifteen."

"Okay," Hurona whispers.

Neither of us say thank you—the woman has turned back to face forward and hums a little under her breath. The uniformed man makes his way down the aisle, and up front one of his colleagues climbs the second staircase to the top level of the bus. I can hear his feet, heavy over our heads.

"Paperwork, everyone," the man on our level calls as he makes his way. "You know the drill. I need everyone's papers out. Children under three are exempt. But if you have children under three, I will ask why you're taking the night bus."

"Not part of the job," a Black woman behind us mutters. "They

117

just like judging folks for what they have to do. Some mothers have to take their babies to work. The governor doesn't know how much child care costs if everyone in the home is working!"

I don't know either, but I peer up at the driver's daughter sitting behind her mother. Her mom doesn't have to worry about where she is—she's right behind her while she works. My guilt stabs me in my stomach. Or maybe that's hunger. My stomach growls.

The white woman across the aisle hears it groaning and smiles kindly.

"We'll be to Petrichor soon," she says.

The man in the uniform smells like soap and metal. I can smell him as he moves down the aisle. His belt is shiny black, and he uses a tiny flashlight from one of its loops to illuminate each passenger's paperwork. I don't know what he's looking for, but I pay close attention to the other people's eyes and faces. None of them really look at him: They all just hold the paper up, then take it back when he's done. Most of them still seem half asleep. This is what Mx. Amur says I do best—watch.

"You look too stiff," I whisper to Hurona, who glances at me in surprise. I raise my eyebrows high. *"Relax."*

I almost add, *You lied to me and Mom no problem. This shouldn't be any different.* But I don't.

When it's our turn, the man's gloved hand extends for my pass first, since I'm sitting on the aisle. I hold it up and yawn like I nap on this bus every night. Hurona does the same. Maybe it's because I'm nervous, but the man takes forever with our papers. Way longer than with other people's. I don't even know what correct ones are

118

supposed to look like—what if the woman across the aisle is playing a trick on us? She could have given us a lottery ticket and I wouldn't know the difference.

"How old are you?" the man says. His eyes are sharp blue and fastened on Hurona.

She pauses for just an instant. But—my smart sister—she hides it with a yawn.

"Fifteen," she says.

He studies her. Maybe he's seeing the circles under her eyes, thinking she looks older. She does. So do I. But he doesn't look twice at me, even though it feels like my heartbeat should be an alarm giving us both away.

"Did you drop a dollar?" the woman across the aisle says, her sudden voice almost making me jump. She holds a bill out to me. "I think it fell out when you were getting your pass out."

"Th-thanks," I say, and take it, and the man's blue eyes have shifted to the woman across the aisle now. He hands our papers back to us without looking, asks the woman for hers. She offers it with a thin smile. In the rearview mirror, I can only see the bus driver's eyes, but there's a frown in them.

The man moves on, and the woman winks. The smell of soap and metal fades a little. Out the window, two women with dogs circle the bus. The orange lights flash on and on until the uniformed men get off the bus, shouting goodnight from the ground outside.

When the bus glides forward, Hurona and I don't talk for a long time. I didn't shake when I was showing the pass, but I do now.

"Thank you," I whisper to the woman across the aisle, and I try to give the pass back.

"Keep it until we get to Petrichor," she says, smiling. "Sometimes there's one more check at the off-ramp. Can't be too careful."

I nod silently. Hurona says nothing. She's probably thinking the same thing I'm thinking: that this woman we don't even know helped us out of trouble, and Iva only helped us into it.

21

I DON'T SLEEP again. I sit straight up in the seat with the borrowed papers clutched in my fist. Every time I blink too long, I think checkpoint lights flash through my eyelids. And eventually there is light—but it's not a checkpoint. The bus turns onto a new road, and suddenly ... there's the city.

"Do you see ... ?" I whisper. I can see my sister nodding from the corner of my eye.

"Petrichor," she says.

The city rears up through the windshield like a kingdom of gold stars. Buildings taller than the lockwood stretch their heads toward the sky. Everything is covered in dazzling light, and the light illuminates all the trees. Planted on rooftops and also on terraces that cling to the sides of skyscrapers like moss. In some places the gold light shows trees growing between the buildings themselves.

And above it all, the stars. I wish I could walk up to the windshield and press my face against the glass. I wonder if the people who live in Petrichor know what it's like to see the stars whenever they want. What it's like for the trees to be a neighbor and not a threat. If they even notice. It feels like ivy is growing through my stomach, but the city looks beautiful. Full of promises. Still, I can't help but think of what people like Mr. Ovitt have always said about the city: how no one cares about one another, they're just a million strangers stepping over and sometimes on each other. How nothing ever feels like home.

"You see the lockwood?" Hurona says. "At the edge?"

I do. I thought they were normal trees at first, since they're not trying to curl and twist over the head of Petrichor. But as the bus gets closer, the city brighter and brighter, I see she's right.

Around the perimeter of the city, there's a tree wall: all lockwood, knotted and knitted together like someone turned trees into thread and sewed them into a scarf that drapes comfortably around the city's neck. Not choking it. Just there, a fireproof barrier to keep the wildfires out. The bus drives through a tunnel a lot like the one that leads to Prine, and I can't help but feel that mad-at-everybody feeling again. Why can't we have this? Why is everybody in Prine like cavefish when we could have…this?

The bus hums through the glowing streets, and it's easy to forget it's nighttime. The lights are so bright and they're everywhere you look. There are even trees with lights strung through their branches. So much solar power that they don't have to fight the lockwood for.

The bus swings off to the side of the road, where ahead a tiny blue house glows. People stand all around it, in rumpled and untucked shirts, hats off. I know the look on their faces—they just got off work. Probably not the lockwood, but I know what

122

work-tired looks like. They all pile onto another bus ahead, and the driver of our bus uses an intercom to speak to us.

"Last stop, everybody. Petrichor. Everybody off. This is the end of the line for me too."

She's opening up the plastic box that protects the driver's seat and speaking a few words to her daughter. The girl stands and stretches. Across the aisle, the white woman who gave us the passes stretches too.

"Here," Hurona says. She collects the paperwork from my hand and leans across to give them back. The woman accepts them with a smile. "Thank you for your help. You didn't have to do that. We really appreciate it."

"The pleasure is all mine." The woman yawns, smiling. "I know what it's like to be off on an adventure. Don't want it to be over before it begins!"

People are filing off the bus slowly. I wait until Hurona hefts her bag on her shoulder before I do the same. I can taste the staleness of my mouth after napping on the bus, and I'm glad I brought my toothbrush.

But that's when it really settles in: Where are we going to sleep? Does Hurona know where Iva lives? Will we walk? I peer out the bus windows as we make our way to the front. With all the millions of lights, it could never be as dark as Prine. But somehow all the lights make the shadows between them darker. I'm suddenly a little nervous about getting off the bus. Hurona walks behind me in the aisle, and she must notice the way my feet slow. She leans in close.

"It's going to be fine," she says, but she doesn't say, *I'm going to call Iva.*

We step off the bus.

"It's so warm," I say, surprised. I'd been shivering a little at the bus stop thirty miles away, but the city seems to breathe warm air.

"The humidity from all the plants helps," the woman who had been sitting across the aisle says. She's clambering down after Hurona and me, yanking her big purse farther up her shoulder. "It'll be colder away from the bus stop. They have heat fans this time of year, though."

Hurona just nods. She's trying not to look at her phone, and I'm trying not to look at Hurona. I don't want to say it but I have to: "Are you going to call Iva?"

"No," Hurona says, her voice tight. "She would've called me by now if she actually wanted to help."

"Maybe she . . . ," I start, but Hurona slices me with her eyes and I go quiet.

Nearby, the woman from the bus lingers, frowning.

"Do you two know where you're going? Is someone picking you up?"

"Yes," Hurona says, but even someone who doesn't know her as well as I do could tell that she's not telling the truth.

"If you want to wait for your friend," the woman says, "you can come with me and sit. I can give you a meal."

In Prine, there's a plant called a touch-me-not, and Mom says it didn't use to grow around here until the world started getting warmer. But now it does, and it's a plant that moves when you touch

124

it. You can just brush your finger along its stem and it shrinks away, shriveling up. Then when you walk away, it blooms again. Me and Hurona must look like a touch-me-not when the woman makes this offer, because she laughs.

"Not to my *house*." She chuckles. "To my job. I'm a waitress. My boss won't mind if you sit and have a bite—we're slow this time of night. If people look in the windows and see people eating, it'll be good for business. Come on. Two young girls shouldn't be out on the street alone. You can come sit until you make a plan."

I can feel Hurona hesitating, standing closer to me than she was a moment before. I get the feeling she's deciding whether she needs to whisk me away. Little sister. Her responsibility. But I think about what might have happened if I hadn't demanded to come. I imagine Hurona out here on this street alone. My heart clenches at the same time my stomach growls.

"See?" the woman says, laughing. "Come on. It's Tuesday night. That means stew at the diner."

I think of my mother's soft bread. Part of me wants to turn and press the button on the bus stop that I now know will make it glow blue. If there was a bus to Petrichor, there is a bus *from* Petrichor. But Hurona is saying yes, and she's giving me a look that says *we'll see how this goes*, and we're wandering down the street after the woman.

Her name is Shelly, she tells us, and as it turns out, she does actually work at a diner. It doesn't have a name—just a glowing sign over the low roof that says HOT SANDWICHES AND SOUP. By the time Shelly directs us to a table in the corner, I don't even care about the *hot* part. I just need to eat something. There are plastic-wrapped packets of crackers sitting next to the salt and pepper shakers. I eye them.

"Do you think those are free?" I whisper.

"Look at all that plastic," Hurona says, shaking her head. "Just wait a second."

It's more than a second, but not much longer than a minute. Shelly comes from the kitchen with a tray for us and slides it onto the table between us. Two bowls of stew with a red basket brimming with brown rolls.

"Thank you," Hurona says. "How much is it?"

Shelly just waves her away.

"You can do the dishes," she says. "And I spoke to my boss, Dale. He doesn't mind if you rest here for a while."

She walks away before either of us can answer. Hurona gazes after her, but I don't waste any time before eating. The stew is potato and lentil and carrot. The bread isn't as soft as Mom's, but it's not stale. In Prine, I would take small bites, thinking about fitting through the lockwood. But this is one morning I won't be going to the trees.

"Aren't you going to eat?" I say.

Hurona picks up the spoon, nudging a potato in the bowl. She scoops up one bite, chewing, still looking past me, where Shelly is now taking the order of two skinny women wearing pink blazers.

"Why do you think she's being so nice to us?" she says without looking at me.

"I don't know," I say around my stew. "Maybe she has kids."

"Hmm," Hurona says. She eats more, but she keeps her eyes on the restaurant behind me. The bright light of this place reminds me of Mom's workshop. And in it, Hurona kind of looks like Mom. I tell her so.

"You think I look like Mom?" she says, and laughs low. "I don't usually think so."

"You do to me."

"I think I look more like him."

I stop chewing. Like Mom, Hurona never talks about our dad. I have no memories of him: not a voice, not a shadow. But Hurona was older when he died. In Prine, she follows our mom's example: Don't talk about him. Pretend it never happened. It's easy, kind of. There are no pictures of him anywhere. Even a ghost leaves a mark, but he doesn't. But we're not in Prine anymore, and if there were unspoken rules about what can be talked about, Hurona is breaking them.

"What about you looks like him?" I say, studying her.

"The shape of my face," she says. "The way I smile."

"No wonder I never notice," I say, making a sour face, and she laughs. I wonder if I'm laughing *his* laugh. She takes another bite and then squints at me.

"Are you nervous?" she asks. "Being away from home?"

"No," I say, but I can't look at her when I say it. My *no* is half true. If I was alone, I think my whole spine would be shaking. But I'm not alone—I'm with her. Here, in this bright restaurant eating warm food, the shake is just a shimmer.

I want to ask her if *she's* nervous, because I can never tell. Even when we were kids and she was guiding me through the trunks around Prine. She always had an eye on the forest around us. And she still does. She squints toward the kitchen before I can ask her anything.

"This must be her boss," she says.

I turn and glance over my shoulder, spoon in hand. A white man has appeared at the kitchen door, clean-shaven and wearing a white apron. His skin looks like a cut onion—pale and a little damp from working in a hot kitchen. He stands rigidly in the doorway talking to Shelly, who hasn't spoken to us since she dropped off the food. Neither of them look at us, but I can tell they're talking about us. There's music playing through the ceiling. I can't even understand what the singer is saying because the speakers sound garbled. I glance around for a clock, but then remember Hurona has a phone.

"What time is it?" I ask.

"Four forty-five," she says.

I almost say *I'm tired*, but I don't want to sound like the whiny little sister. But the short nap on the bus hadn't done much for letting me rest. I'd be useless in the lockwood today. Fifty miles away in Prine, Banneker is already at the top.

"Banneker is fine," she says.

I snap my eyes up to look at her. I can't read her face.

"I know," I say.

"I can tell you're worried," she says. "We're doing something we don't do. We're doing something Prine doesn't make space for us to do. We have to make our own space, Erie."

Shelly appears at the table's edge, plopping down more bread and some water. In the tall clear glasses, it looks cleaner and colder than what comes out of our filter in Prine. I drink it eagerly while she stands with her hands on her hips, glasses on her nose.

"If you two need a place to sleep," she says, "I have a friend stopping by in a bit. He has a youth hostel. You know what a hostel is?"

"Yes," says Hurona. "But we have a friend."

"Well, you know, just in case," Shelly says, and winks before she walks away.

Outside, the city is waking up. The lights seem to have all been turned up, every building glimmering a little brighter. The sun isn't up yet, but it's on its way. In Prine, it will be hours before the vines are cut back enough to let it in. Here, though, I can see all the solar panels outside, on almost every surface, ready to soak it all up.

The streets start to thicken with people. Not like the Spine, with clusters of skinny kids like me making their way to work. Here, adults carry lunch bags and wear uniforms. Some of them look at phones like Hurona's. Some of them have pods in their ears and bob heads to music no one else can hear. I feel a little out of breath seeing all these people. I see more people staring out this window for five minutes than I do all day in Prine.

"Banneker's brother could be out there right now," I say to Hurona, who's watching too. "Isn't that weird? He could be walking past *right now*."

"I hope so," she says. Her eyes pry at each face, like one of them really might be Carver. "That would mean he found work."

I think of all the other people who had left Prine for Petrichor.

129

Big sisters and big brothers and dads. The occasional mom. How many never came back. It feels like Petrichor is a huge syringe, sucking the blood out of a heart. This is what Mr. Ovitt warned about, and Mx. Amur too. But we're here.

We stare until the light stains the sky, and until a bell on the door tinkles over the garbled music. Hurona looks and so do I, eyeing the man who walks in. My mom is tall, so I measure everyone against her, and this man is tall. He has the same pale skin as Shelly's boss, the same strong frame. He doesn't move for a table right away: He stands just inside the doorway and looks around. When his eyes fall on us, he smiles. Only then does he sit at the counter.

"Are you done eating?" Hurona asks, but she doesn't look at me. Her head tilts. Looking at her, I realize I know this face. This is the face that had told me to walk very slowly, backward, down the path when I was five. Prine hadn't seen a mountain lion in years, Mr. Ovitt said later. But we did that day. Hungry and thin, driven in after a fire outside the lockwood.

"No," I say.

"Finish."

"Why?"

"Finish, Erie."

I wish I had a headlamp that shone a light inside her head. It's like the lockwood is inside my sister sometimes. Knots and vines that I have to squeeze through. I take a few quick bites of stew. I watch as Hurona takes the basket of rolls from the table and dumps them in her bag.

"Come on," she says, and stands. She has money in her hand.

I take one last quick bite and follow. Dawn is starting to tinge the streets pink. I want to get out and see the sunrise. But the number of people in the street makes me feel shrinky. In the restaurant, it's just us, Shelly, and the two men.

"Thank you," Hurona calls, as Shelly comes out of the kitchen wiping her hands. "We're going to head out. This should cover the food."

She places the money on the counter, and I look up at Shelly just in time to see her shoot a look at the taller-than-my-mom man who'd come in.

"This is my friend," Shelly says. "The one who runs the hostel. How about you talk to him and see about staying over there for a few days."

"We have a friend," Hurona says, but the man at the counter is turning to face us.

"I don't see a friend," he says. His smile is friendly, but when he talks, his top and bottom teeth are a little too close together. Like the smile only smiles so it doesn't become a bite. "Have you ever been to Petrichor? I don't think I'd be comfortable letting two girls wander the city alone when they're not familiar."

"It's not about whether you're comfortable," Hurona says. She sounds like Mom, which is a little embarrassing, but it still makes me step closer to her. "It's about whether *we're* comfortable. And we are. We're fine."

"You weren't too comfortable on the bus," Shelly says from across the counter. She hasn't taken Hurona's money. "You needed help then, and I think you need help now."

"We don't," Hurona says, and she walks backward toward the door. I hadn't even noticed her holding my wrist until now. I walk backward too. We're in the lockwood all over again, and I remember the sound the mountain lion had made. A low rumble that might have sounded like a purr if you didn't know better. I think Hurona knows better.

The man has swiveled the counter chair toward us and stands. Shelly's hands are pressed against the countertop, but his are out of his pockets and hang by his sides, the fingers a little bent. He looks ready.

Hurona snatches for the door and swings it open, jerking me outside. It hasn't even closed yet when the tall man lunges toward it.

"Run, Erie," Hurona says, and maybe I'm just scared and nothing makes sense, but she doesn't sound scared at all. We could be running through the lockwood. She doesn't let go of my wrist.

We wind in and out of the crowd, and I look back only once. The man is chasing us. He looks mad, and his legs are long. I'm not used to running—I'm used to climbing. But Hurona drags me on, and at the end of the street, we hear the sound of many voices. To our right, the next street opens up into what looks like a square, like the clearing in Prine where the FOLROY trucks circle. It's full of people, someone's voice booming out over a microphone.

Hurona heads right for it, still squeezing my wrist. I think I would run faster with my hand free but she won't let me go. She charges toward the crowd. People are shouting and waving banners. I feel dizzy again—overwhelmed by the people, by the sounds. But when we reach the edge, we pause, both of us looking back.

The man from the restaurant skids around the corner, stops, then sees us. His big hands still look ready.

"Follow me," Hurona shouts over the noise, and I don't tell her I don't have a choice, that her hand is still locked around my wrist. She plunges into the crowd, I plunge after her, and we're lost in the blur of noise.

22

HURONA PUSHES THROUGH the crowd, ducking her head left and right to dodge elbows. It's just past dawn. What are all these people doing here? Is this what people do in the city? I pant after my sister, and I refuse to look behind me to see if the man from the diner is still following. Hurona ducks around a larger cluster of people, all of them with work gloves poking out of their pockets. Once past them, we find ourselves near the front of the crowd. There's a raised platform, where a man in a jacket stands smiling at a podium.

"Good morning," he shouts, and an invisible microphone throws his voice high and wide. "I'm so glad to see you all here today, here to watch the sun rise with me!"

We pause here and catch our breath. I don't see the onion-faced man from the restaurant, but that doesn't mean he's not about to pop out of the crowd. It feels at least a little safer here, hidden by all the people.

I've never seen so many people in my life. Young and old, all colors and frames. Everyone looks a bit like their gloves—tired, and a little worn. All of them watch the man on stage, a white man whose skin is as tan as the people watching him, but even and smooth. I think he's the same kind of boring handsome as Arlo Kylak, but a little older.

"My job is to address the problems that I see in the city I represent," he says, throwing his arms wide. "And I see where we're lacking. I see that Petrichor has problems with its pass system—"

Around us, people grumble.

"—and I see that the competition for well-paying jobs is fierce," the man says.

"And decent housing," someone near us calls. "And medical care!"

"All of that will be solved with Dolosalvus," the man calls to the crowd. He never stops smiling. "You'll have everything you need! A new town, a new chance. Dolosalvus is the solution."

Then Hurona yanks my arm, pulling me sideways. I don't see the onion-faced man but she must have.

"Where are we going?" I pant.

Her head is swiveling and she doesn't answer.

"Maybe we can just stay here," I say. "He can't do anything in front of all these people!"

"We don't know that," she says, and pulls me after her.

All around the plaza there are big statues of vegetables. There's huge silver celery, a big shiny potato. But they're out in the open. Not a good hiding place.

"Oh no," she says. When I look where she's looking, I see a flash of the man through the crowd. He's pushing through, his head moving back and forth. My heart flips.

"There," Hurona says, pointing at something ahead of us, and keeps pulling me. I go along behind her, looking over my shoulder the whole time. Part of me just wants to stand still and scream, the way they say you should do if you see a coyote. But this isn't Prine. This is Petrichor, and I don't know what they do with coyotes here. For all I know they keep them as pets.

The next thing I know, I'm being dragged down to the ground. Hurona pulls me down, pressing my head lower. It's only then that I actually look away from the bald head of the onion-faced man and see where we're hiding.

It's a cart selling food.

I smell grilled bread and zucchini, and get a glimpse of bottles of sauces and ketchups before Hurona pulls me fully under the cart. There's a fringe of ribbons hanging down like a skirt, and we huddle under it like mice. I imagine the man like a hawk swooping down. What will he do if he finds us? What will he do if he doesn't? There are other kids walking around the plaza—I saw them. Will he chase them instead?

From here I can only see the knees and feet of all the people gathered to listen to the smiling man on the stage. And then, the face of the woman running the cart as she crouches down to squint at us.

"You can't be under there!" she scowls. "Get out of here!"

"Please," Hurona pleads. "Someone is chasing us! I'm sorry... we don't know what..."

But then the woman's eyes are angling upward, and when I look back at the crowd, I see a pair of feet break away, moving slowly in the direction of the cart. The woman stands up.

"It's him," I whisper, and Hurona elbows me hard. She presses a finger to her lips and I clamp mine shut.

The man's feet don't move. I wonder if he's looking down, if he sees our shoes too and is just deciding how to pounce. The woman who owns the food cart is standing now too. Hurona told her that someone was chasing us, but what if she doesn't care? What if she's one of the people who keeps coyotes as pets?

But then I see another pair of shoes.

Smaller, and bright pink, walking past the onion-faced man. The pink shoes move toward the crowd, then pause. Then they walk back, pause again. Pacing. Waiting for someone. I don't know, but when the onion-faced man's shoes move toward the pink shoes, my heart starts screaming.

"Hurona," I whisper, but I see her eyes narrowing already. Her head tilts. She has a feeling, and we're seeing the same thing. Thinking the same thing.

I tear some of the fringe when I struggle out from under the cart.

"Erie!" my sister shouts, and her voice makes one of the man's shoes turn back toward us a half step.

But I'm already standing up straight, and I see his pale face and his bald head.

And I see his hand reached out toward the kid in the pink shoes. She sees me the same time that I see her.

The bus driver's daughter.

The woman who owns the food cart yells when I grab the bottle of sauce from the metal top. The onion-faced man is stepping back toward me when Hurona crawls out too. But by then my hands have already decided what they're going to do.

I squirt the sauce directly in the man's face, right in his eyes. It's red and green and comes out faster than I thought it would. Behind me, the food cart woman shrieks. The girl in the pink shoes opens her mouth but I can't hear what she says—the man on the stage is shouting, and the crowd applauds right as the man chasing us yells, rubbing his eyes. He staggers sideways and bangs into the cart, and the woman screams again. Everything sounds quiet compared to the crowd, like it's happening through a wall.

Then Hurona grabs my arm and we're running again, this time away from the plaza and down a sidewalk. I still have the bottle of sauce in my hand but I can't let go—my hands feel robotic. My bag across my chest makes me feel slow, but we don't stop until we've run six blocks.

"Why did you"—Hurona pants—"why did you . . . do that?"

"I don't know," I wheeze. I'm still holding the bottle. It's splashed all over my arm and I just stare at it, heart pounding. "I just . . . I didn't want . . ."

"You thought he was going to grab her," she says.

"Didn't you?"

Hurona breathes deep, trying to catch her breath. She nods.

"We should go home," I say. I don't want to cry. I think I still want to scream. "This was a bad idea."

Hurona doesn't say anything. I want to hug her but I know she won't let me. I wish I was home, but could I even hug Mom if I was? With Banneker fifty miles away in Prine, I feel lonelier than I've ever felt. I want to reach into my bag and hold Aunt Josie's voice. It feels a little like she's the only one close enough to touch, even with Hurona right here.

"Who was that guy?" Hurona mutters. I don't think she's really talking to me, so I don't answer. But someone else does.

"A hamster, probably," says a voice, and me and Hurona both jump, whirling around.

It's the girl in the pink shoes. The bus driver's daughter. She stands staring with wide brown eyes, one hand on her chest as she catches her breath.

"What did you say?" Hurona says.

"I saw you run into the crowd when I first got to the plaza," the girl says. "Then I saw him run after you. You don't know him, then?"

"No!" I cry.

"He was acting like he wanted to help us, and I got a bad feeling," Hurona adds.

I expect the girl to question Hurona about this, but she just nods. I like this about her right away—some people like to act sarcastic about Hurona and her feelings. But I've known my sister long enough to know that she's rarely wrong. She'd saved us from a mountain lion, and now something else.

"Definitely a hamster," the girl says, making a face.

"What does that mean?" I ask.

"A hamster," the girl repeats. "It's what they call men in the city who make kids disappear."

It feels like my heart is walking on a wire. The girl's words make it wobble.

"Why do they call them hamsters?" I ask.

"Because hamsters eat the young."

"No one was going to eat us," Hurona snaps as I shiver. "I wouldn't let anyone make us disappear."

"I'm glad you got away," the girl says. She doesn't seem to notice my sister's tone. "And, uh, nice shot with the sauce."

I almost forget what she means until she reaches for the bottle in my hand. I finally make my fingers unclench and she pulls it from my grip. Then she pokes one finger in the spilled sauce and dabs it on her tongue. She winces, then smiles.

"Habanero," she says. "His eyes are going to burn for a week."

She throws her head back and laughs. It makes me laugh too, and even Hurona smiles. Now that we're away from the plaza and the onion-faced man is no longer a threat, it does seem kind of funny.

"And I'm glad you didn't run into the cops, either," the girl says when she stops laughing. "They're not as bad as hamsters, but they're all pretty crappy to kids from the townlands. They would have just taken you into custody and sent you home. Eventually."

"Did you follow us from the bus?" Hurona says. I glance at her, wondering if she's getting another one of her bad feelings. But she doesn't look on edge—just tired.

"Not exactly," the girl says. "I went to the plaza with my brother to watch the speech. He runs a channel documenting stuff in Petrichor. It's not every day the governor does a speech at dawn. Let's see if we can see my brother's drone from here."

She turns, shielding her eyes. As it turns out, we only ran four streets over. It's far enough, but still close enough to where we can hear the occasional applause from the crowds. The girl points, and even from here we can see a drone circling the plaza. It makes me think of the FOLROY drone over Prine. It reminds me why we're here, and my stomach sinks a little.

"He's taking footage now," the girl says. "He'll edit it and all that stuff later. He's really good. He has like eighty thousand subscribers."

"Wow," I say. I don't really understand a lot of what she's talking about, but Hurona seems impressed.

"You look tired," the girl says. "I'm guessing you haven't slept since you got off the bus? My mom was worried when that lady gave you fake passes. She didn't want to rat you out to the checkpoint cops, but she didn't like that lady's energy."

"I didn't either," Hurona mutters, mostly to herself.

"You're from Prine, huh?" the girl asks.

"How did you know?" I ask. I feel like I can talk now. The tall man is gone and this girl is nice. When I think back to how Shelly was nice, I realize it was a different kind. It was like the hard bread that they sell in the general store. This girl is the soft bread my mom makes.

"We see Prine girls sometimes," she says. "Boys too. But you can always tell. It's different than the other townlands. Prinians are all so ... skinny."

I want to tell her there are reasons for that, but I realize I don't really want to talk about Prine. And I don't want to talk about people being skinny in front of Hurona. My heart is still beating faster than it ever has in the lockwood.

"You can come to my house if you want," the girl says. "My mom will probably be glad to see that you're okay."

The girl turns to look down the sidewalk. Me and Hurona look at each other while her back is turned.

"Oh, here comes my brother!" the girl says.

I see the shape of him moving down the sidewalk from the plaza. When he gets closer, crossing the streets between us, I see he's cradling a red drone like a baby.

"You're done already?" the girl shouts when he's a block away.

"Security started kicking everyone with drones out," he shouts back. "But I think I got enough!"

He crosses the last street.

"Hi." Her brother smiles when he joins us. His eyes angle down at the outer corners, and it makes him look like he just woke up from a pleasant dream. Then his eyebrow raises when he sees the bottle of sauce.

"Why do you have habanero sauce?"

"This rad girl attacked a hamster with it." His sister chuckles; then we're all laughing again. "What's your name anyway?"

"Erie," I say, and when Hurona doesn't speak, I introduce her too.

"I'm Pinnia," the girl says. "This is my brother, Mento."

"A hamster," Mento says, suddenly serious. "Are you two okay?"

"We're fine," Hurona says. "Now."

"Good," he says. He turns to Pinnia. "I wanna get home so I can start working on this before I go to work later. Are you coming?"

"Yeah," Pinnia says. She eyes us. "Do you wanna come? You don't have to. But it's probably safer than being out here by yourself. Especially without passes. Plus, that guy isn't the only hamster."

"I know we don't have to," Hurona says, sounding sharp again. I think she's mad at herself for following the Shelly woman to the restaurant. But it hadn't been her fault. It had been my fault.

Pinnia kind of shrugs.

"Our address is Twenty-Seven Hauc if you change your mind," she says and waves. Then she and her brother are walking away. She reminds me of Banneker. They both walk like cats. Calm and sure-footed.

Hurona and I stand at the corner watching them go. I don't want to say we should follow them—half the reason we ended up with Shelly is because I accepted the passes on the bus. I don't want to be to blame for everything going wrong. But the woman driving the bus hadn't been like Shelly. She was soft bread too.

"What do you think?" I say after a minute. "Do you have any bad feelings?"

"I feel like my sensor is broken," she says softly, and I'm surprised, because she actually told me the truth for once. Without me having to pry at her like a screwdriver under a stuck lid. She sighs. "But no. No bad feelings."

"Her mom seemed nice," I say. Pinnia and Mento are turning the next corner, chatting and laughing. They'll be out of sight soon.

"Yeah."

Everything inside me feels shaken up, like baking soda and vinegar. So far the city is what Mr. Ovitt warned about. Hamsters, liars, people made to vanish. But it's also not. In the version of the city the older folks in Prine warned of, there was no Pinnia.

"We don't have to go inside," I say. "We could sit on their porch."

"They may not have a porch."

"Yeah, but..."

She raises her hands and rubs her eyes. Her phone is in her pocket for once. I wonder if she's thinking about Iva.

"If they don't have a porch, we're leaving," she says. "Okay? And we don't talk to them about what we saw in the lockwood. We can't trust anybody. Deal?"

At home, when Hurona would talk to me, sometimes it would feel like she was talking through a blanket. Never really looking at me. Always something between us. But right now, the only thing is air. We look at each other in the shadow of a tree with no vines and we nod.

"Deal," I say. And we go.

23

AS IT TURNS out, Pinnia's house does have a porch. A big one. It wraps all the way around their yellow house. And as it turns out, Pinnia's mom *is* relieved we're okay. When we turn into their yard, walking with Pinnia and Mento, their mom is stepping out onto the porch.

"You should all be sleeping," she calls. She's patting her hands dry on a blue towel. "You've all been up all night! And you two"— she points at me and Hurona with two fingers on the same hand— "look terrible."

"Mami, you're doing it again," Mento says. He closes the gate behind us just as two dogs rush down from the porch. They're red-brown and fluffy, with ears that perk up halfway and then flop at the tips. Hurona and I both jump back. There are no dogs in Prine. They never want to stay.

"I'm doing what again?"

"That thing where you talk to people like you already know them."

"I do know them! They rode my bus. What are you girls' names?"

"Erie."

"Hurona."

"Lakes!" she says, her eyes glittering. "Do you know why those lakes were named what they were?"

Hurona and I blink at each other.

"The Huron nation," she says, beaming. "The Wyandot people. And Erie. Iroquoian people both. Superior was the first to dry up, then Ontario, then Michigan. The lakes disappeared, but the people didn't. No matter what folks say. I wonder if your mother knows the history of the names she chose for you."

She studies us, still smiling. I wonder too.

"Mami is a self-taught historian," Mento says.

"As we all should be," his mom says. "Remembering is an important job."

"There was a man chasing them in Edible Square," Pinnia says. "Seemed like a hamster."

Pinnia's mom throws her hands skyward, the towel she carries flopping.

"Ay, dios mío santo!" she says. "I knew that woman was no good! I had a bad feeling."

"Me too," Hurona says. "But..."

"You had to get to the city," Pinnia's mom says. "I understand. I'm just glad you're okay. They didn't touch you? You're not hurt?"

I'm a little surprised she doesn't seem to care that we used fake passes. I wonder for the first time how we're supposed to get real ones in the first place. I know there's no place in Prine that gives them out. It's kind of like there's an invisible moat around Petrichor.

146

"No," I say. The two dogs are sniffing around my feet now, smelling my pants. "We're okay. Do your dogs bite?"

"Only if you're made of food and not flesh."

"Never sit on the floor while you're eating," Pinnia says, shaking her head. "They'll take everything."

"Can you blame them?" Her mother laughs. "Dogs gave up being wolves to be with us. Bless them! But every dog has limits. Deep down, they remember what it was like to be a wolf."

They don't look like wolves to me—they look kind of like four-legged mops. But with her assurance that they don't bite, I lean down and pet them. Their fur feels thick and squishy, like there's a layer of foam underneath it. I squish them, then let go.

"I do that too." Pinnia laughs. "They're like furry marshmallows."

"What kind of dogs are they?" Hurona asks.

Pinnia shrugs.

"No idea. They wandered into our yard one day when they were tiny."

"Someone busted a puppy mill, and the puppies went everywhere," Mento says. He's walked over to the porch and sits fiddling with his drone. The porch, like the yard, is extremely clean. The grass is patchy, but here and there are small scrubby trees whose names I don't know.

"What's a puppy mill?"

"A place where they raise special breeds of dogs that people pay a lot of money for," Mento says. "They don't care about the dogs and don't treat them well—all they care about is the money."

"If they actually cared about dogs," their mom says, making a sour face, "they'd adopt one. Paying all this money for these poor animals! Basura."

"Mento actually testified as a witness in court about it," Pinnia says, her eyes bright. "His drone got footage of them selling the dogs, and they used it to put the mill owners in jail. It's happened a couple times since then. This company, Goldigo, got shut down because of what Mento filmed. Workers' rights violations. All because of Mento's channel."

"Not *all* because of me," Mento protests. "The workers testified too."

"Still," Pinnia says, clearly proud. "My brother and his drone babies are kinda like heroes. At least to our pups."

"Wow," I say. I can't think of the word *drone* without thinking about what I saw over the lockwood in Prine. The two dogs have realized I like squishing them, and both press against my legs now. "That's really cool. It's like these two came to find you to say thanks."

"That's what I said!" Pinnia cries. "Like they came just to say thank you but then decided to stay. I always said they're brother and sister, like us."

"What are their names?" Hurona says. She's crouching down now too, and I like how her eyes seem soft.

"Head and Tail," Mento says, smiling.

"These names," his mother says, shaking her head. But she laughs too. "Mento said they were too hard to tell apart, but one of them had a crooked tail, so the other had to be Head."

"Head and Tail." I laugh, and Tail—I see the crooked wagger now—licks my cheek.

148

"You two come inside," Pinnia's mom says, turning back to the house. "It's going to rain. And you *all* need to sleep. Yes, you too, Pinnia! Don't make that face! You can't ride the bus all night half napping and then not sleep. You think I homeschool you so you can become a zombie? It's bad enough I let you ride with me last night. Did you do any of the homework I gave you?"

She disappears into the house, still scolding. I can hear music from inside, a woman's voice sailing and soaring in Spanish. Pinnia pats her leg for Head and Tail, who follow after her cheerfully. My hands feel smooth, like their squishy fur had left a powder on my fingers. I look at my sister.

"Any bad feelings?" I say, but I already know the answer.

"I think they're good," Hurona says, and good from her mouth sounds like more than *safe*. She means *good*.

Inside, the house is just like the yard: clean and bright. If the yard was a little dry and bare, the house makes up for it. It's like the yard is actually inside the house: planters mounted on walls, big pots on the floor. Plants over doorways, flowers at the windows, and vines snaking on bookshelves. It's like if the lockwood was smaller. And friendly.

There are just as many picture frames as plants. Faces crowd the walls and tables. Pinnia's mom and her wife, cheek to cheek at their wedding. The two of them holding one baby, Mento, then other photos of little-kid-Mento with baby Pinnia on his lap. He smiles nervously out of the photo, his moms with a hand on each shoulder.

"You can call me Ms. Mari," their mother calls from the

kitchen. The kitchen is straight back from the front door, and I can smell whatever she's cooking as soon as we step in. Head and Tail trot in eagerly, snouts raised. I'm not even hungry after the stew at the restaurant, but my stomach shifts anyway. I feel the same way I felt on the bus before the checkpoint disaster. Safe. Still. As excited as I was to leave Prine, the wideness of the world makes me feel fizzy inside. But Pinnia's house is like a bottle that keeps it all in.

"Are you girls hungry?"

"No, thank you," Hurona says. "We ate. Before... well, before things got weird."

Pinnia flops on a big puffy chair that seems to swallow her. She reaches behind her where a stack of crocheted blankets towers. She grabs one and tosses it at me. When I catch it, it feels almost like Head and Tail.

"Before the hamster," she says.

"Yeah."

"Well, you're here now," Ms. Mari says. "And what brought you girls to Petrichor? One of you looks a little young for city work. Are you runaways?"

"I mean, not exactly," Hurona says. I sink onto the couch that Pinnia is pointing at, a big green thing the size of a boat. Hurona sits next to me. When I spread the blanket Pinnia gave me out, Hurona lets me spread it over her too. "It was just kind of... last minute."

"Do your parents know you're here is the better question," Ms. Mari says, and turns to stare at us. Even if I didn't know Pinnia and Mento existed, I'd know she was a mom because of the face she makes. Guilt flutters in my stomach.

"She knows," Hurona says, and I'm glad she said it so I didn't have to lie. Mom *does* know we're here, but she didn't know until we were already gone. I think of how I'd stood in her workshop. I press my hand against my bag, where the sparrow I'd taken is nestled in my clothes with my toothbrush and Aunt Josie's voice.

"Mm-hmm," Ms. Mari says, and she doesn't look like she buys it either. I mean, *I* barely buy it. "Well, you're safe here. If your mother ever asks, let her know there was a mother in Petrichor who tried to look after you. That's more than I can say for Prine, from what I hear."

She disappears into the kitchen before I can ask what she means. I hear the sound of popping oil from the stove, and on the roof rain starts to patter. My eyes feel heavy. Pinnia leans her head against the arm of the chair she's bundled in.

"What did you do in Prine? Lockwood?" she asks.

"Yeah," I say, so Hurona doesn't have to answer for herself. I don't know if I've ever heard her actually say *I'm too big.*

"Do you ever get mad?" Mento says. He's sitting at a desk by the plant-lined bookshelves, fiddling with his drone.

"About what?" I ask.

"About the lockwood," he says. "It seems so unfair that they didn't figure out they could plant it in strips until after they made, like, a chokehold around Prine. Now you're stuck with a plant they can't burn or uproot."

"I guess they think it's better than the fires," Hurona says. "We're just one town. Nobody cares."

They don't know Hurona like me—but I know she's being sarcastic.

"If they had just listened to Indigenous people earlier," Mento says, frowning down at his gadget. "They could have made the fires better a long time ago. We wouldn't even have needed lockwood."

"What do you mean?" I say, interested. My whole life I've been told that even though the lockwood has turned us into part-time cavefish, it's a necessary evil.

"My other mom's people," Pinnia says. "The Mono people. Native folks lived in California before anyone else and had their own ways of handling wildfire. Then white people came and said our ways were wrong."

"What did the Mono people do?" Hurona asks. "For the wildfires, I mean."

"Controlled burns, for one thing," Mento says. "Our ancestors would burn the vegetation that would overgrow. It was like kindling out there in the plains and near the forests. They'd clear and burn the underbrush, but really carefully. Always with a plan and a prayer."

"That's really cool," I say. "I'd never think about burning something to keep things from burning."

"Neither did your ancestors." Pinnia laughs, her head still resting on the chair's arm. "They didn't start realizing we were right until it was too late."

"And by then we needed the lockwood," Hurona says. I can hear the bite in her voice.

"What's it like there?" Mento asks. "In Prine?"

"Dark," my sister says, and that's all.

"It's the same every day," I add. "Work and school, unless you skip and go sleep. Boring. Nothing happens."

Unless someone gets hurt, I think to myself silently. *Then there are funerals.*

"I don't know why people stay," Pinnia says, and then her mother's voice joins us again from the kitchen.

"People need money to move, mi amor!" she calls. "Not to mention someplace to go. Something to go *to*."

She's right, but I know it's not only that in Prine. I think of my mom, huddled inside the lockwood like it's a life vest. Like the world outside is still on fire.

"I would just go wherever there's sunshine at this point," Hurona says.

"Well, you'll find plenty of sunshine in Petrichor." Mento yawns. "But if you're here to find work, it's harder than you think. If you don't have a pass, they're only going to let you do a few things."

I listen to them talk, and I try to ignore the dropping feeling in my stomach, but I can't. Hurona said she was going to come and find a job, but what if she can't find one? Will she go back to Prine? Or will she go and live with Iva and forget about me and Mom?

"What do your parents do?" Hurona asks.

"Mami's been driving the bus for two years," Pinnia says. She has her blanket over her head like a hood. With the rain coming

153

down on the roof, it makes it feel like we're all sealed into a cave together. "Before that, she was doing the same thing as Mom. Ag work."

"What's ag work?" I ask.

"Agricultural labor. Farmwork. Cutting Brussels."

"Ag work is what the governor was talking about in the plaza," Mento says. "Did you hear? They're opening a new town called Dolosalvus and inviting ag workers to come live. Say they'll give health care and housing if you go live there and work for them."

"Doesn't sound too bad," Hurona says. I hear the gears turning in her head. I imagine her settling not in Petrichor but in a new town, one like Prine. Would it be even farther away?

They go on talking and I stay quiet, trying to find places in what they say where Hurona will fit. Ag work sounds a lot like lockwood work, and Hurona says so. Ms. Mari pops her head in, onion and knife in hand.

"It's very similar," she says. "Long work, short pay. Petrichor loves to call itself a green city"—she pauses and rolls her eyes dramatically—"but who keeps this city green? And where is *our* green?"

She rubs her thumb and fingertip together, then dodges back into the kitchen without answering the question she asked. I think the answer is supposed to be obvious but I'm still looking for it.

Ms. Mari hums in the kitchen. It sounds as unusual as the music that floats out, carrying her voice. At our house, all the doors feel closed, even when they're open. Mom in the kitchen with invisible walls around her. I peek at Hurona, wondering if she feels it

154

too. The way Pinnia's house makes my shoulders feel like shoulders and not like stone.

The smell of cooking onions and Mento and Hurona's talk lulls me. The rain is so peaceful—I hear it alone, not the distant sound of Prine's pulper. My eyelids are fluttering. I glance over at Pinnia, like I need to check whether it's actually safe to sleep here. But she's half asleep too, and when she sees me looking she smiles lazily.

"What do you think Petrichor would do if they didn't have pods anymore?" I hear Hurona say to Mento. She sounds far away even though she's sharing the blanket with me. She's warm and close and the rain is coming down harder now.

"More like, what would *you* do?" Mento says. "If you didn't have to pick them?"

I'm asleep before I can hear my sister's answer.

THERE'S A WINDOW seat at the back of Pinnia's kitchen, where I sit with *The Encyclopedia of Entomology* on my lap while everyone else is still sleeping. In the backyard I can see through the window, Ms. Mari is asleep in a hammock, protected from the rain by a little gazebo. She has a book open on her stomach.

But when I open the encyclopedia, the map of Petrichor is staring up at me, and now that we're here, I can't help but set the book aside and look at the map instead.

Some of its edges are a little tattered, and some of its ink is a little faded. But most of it I can read easily, and I sit studying all the different roads, thinking about Banneker's brother, Carver, and whether he lives on one of them. And then of course I think about Aunt Josie and wonder how much time she spent here, whether she had a pass. If she knew what a hamster was. If she ate from the food carts. If my mom did any of those things with her.

And that's when I see it.

Right there on the map near my right thumb.

Eccles-Tillery Conservancy.

It takes me a minute to connect the words on the paper with the sound of them in Mom's voice. Eccles-Tillery.

That was where Aunt Josie worked.

I stare at the big green square, trying to imagine her there. Trying to imagine her at all. I don't even know what she looked like. But I know what she sounded like, and I reach into my bag. A second later I have the old phone pressed against my face.

> *Nadine, it's your sister. Remember me? Just kidding. Look, are you still mad about what I said? Please don't take it personally. I said I don't trust him—I didn't say I don't trust you. You can be as smart as you are and a genius inventor and still get fooled. Anyway. I'll let it go if you let it go. Let's talk. I got to hold a golden eagle today. Barely older than a chick. Can't wait to tell you about it. Later.*

This message makes me stare at the phone for a while after listening. It seems different than the other ones, like she and Mom reached a forked road. Who did Aunt Josie not trust?

"Is that a *phone*?"

I look up to find Pinnia standing in the kitchen doorway, her hair fuzzy from sleep.

"Not anymore," I say. "I mean, I'm pretty sure it's older than me."

She pads in and settles in the window seat next to me.

"That's what I mean." She laughs. "It looks ancient. Why do you have it?"

157

"It has voice messages from my aunt on it. It's kind of like... like a time capsule."

"What do you mean?"

"She died. I never got to meet her."

Pinnia's brow wrinkles. "Oh. I'm sorry. That's sad."

I shrug, feeling awkward. I'm not used to talking about Aunt Josie out loud. Or my family at all, really. Not even with my sister.

But Pinnia seems to know I feel weird, because she lets her eyes drop to her lap. She has what looks like a glass jar in her hand, a small tool in the other. She fiddles with both.

"What's that?" I ask.

"I'm trying to build a flower pot that can plug into an outlet," she says. "Then you could put a grow light in it and grow flowers in dark places. Like Prine, maybe."

"Cool," I say, and she grins.

"I like making stuff for plants," she says, then waves her arm around at her house. "My mom has so many. For her birthday I made her a necklace of succulents. You know, the little rubbery plants? They don't need much water, so she wore it around for six weeks until it started growing roots. Now it's in the backyard."

"My mom's an inventor too," I say. I don't add that she hasn't really invented anything major. A jar to grow flowers in dark rooms is one of the coolest things I've ever heard of. But maybe that's because I'm from Prine. "I think it's really cool that you make stuff with plants."

"Eventually people will see that this is the only way." She shrugs. "There are still people who call that kind of thinking activism, but

158

how is wanting to live in harmony with the Earth activism? That's just...life."

"I think so too." I nod. "I've just never heard anybody say it like that."

She grins at that. "My mom says everything anyone thinks they know about justice, a Native woman told them."

Then Pinnia sets the jar aside and crosses her arms over her knees. She rests her chin in the middle and stares at me. There used to be a cat that would show up in Prine sometimes, orange and brown and white calico. She would appear through the lockwood, and people would see her winding around front-porch steps and on windowsills. She never came close enough to touch, but she would sit and watch us as we went through our days. Pinnia kind of feels like that. Her eyes aren't green like the calico's, but they're intense the way cats' are.

"What?" I say, after I try to pretend to read for a few more minutes.

"Nothing. Just wondering."

"Wondering what?"

"What it's like in Prine."

"Dark, remember?"

"Whenever we see townland kids come into Petrichor, they're always a little different. But people always say Prine is different because of the lockwood. Like living underground."

I've never really sat and talked like this with anyone but Banneker and my sister. But unlike other people my age in Prine, Pinnia doesn't know the way my mom marches to the circle every Tuesday, the way she tinkers all day and never talks to anyone. All the mean things people say about my mom, calling her crazy and weird, usually feel like pinches. But talking about home with Pinnia is like being pinched through a raincoat. I don't really feel it.

"It *is* kind of like being underground," I say. "But only until we clear the lockwood. Once it's cut back, the sun comes in and the solar panels can charge and then you can do stuff like normal."

"So you go to school and stuff? Me and Mento are home-schooled. My mom pulled us out of public school after two of our teachers said the Dakota Access Pipeline wasn't that bad."

"Whoa," I say. "Were they like a hundred years old?"

"Not even!" She shakes her head. "Do you have teachers like that?"

"We only have one teacher," I say. "We go to school in shifts. They don't really care if we skip, though, because they know we're tired from being in the trees."

"Wait, what do you mean?" she says, looking confused. "Who's we?"

"Huh? The lockwood kids. Us. Me."

"Wait, *you* cut the lockwood back?"

I'm so surprised I laugh.

"Yeah, who do you think does it? Adults can't fit through. I mean, some kids can't either. Once you get too big..." I stop, thinking of my sister just through the kitchen door. I lean sideways to see her. She's still curled in sleep, her head squished into the couch cushion. "Once you get too big, you have to find something else to do. Groundwork, gathering pods. But that can really only last for so long. A lot of people just...leave."

"I can't believe they have kids up there," Pinnia says, her cat eyes wide. "Isn't it, like, really dangerous?"

"Yeah, kinda," I say. I think of Helia. I can still hear her mom crying. It wells up in me, like water pressing at a dam. "Sometimes people get hurt. My best friend, Banneker, is the best climber and even they slip sometimes. I worry about them all the time. I worry about..."

I trail off. Saying *me* out loud at the end of that sentence feels embarrassing somehow. Pinnia looks outraged either way.

"It makes no sense that no one can figure out how to make it stop growing," she says. "They'd rather let kids die than figure it out?"

I frown and look again out at my sister. I know she had said not to talk to Pinnia about it. Hurona doesn't trust anyone. Maybe she wants to talk to Iva about it first, since she works for FOLROY. But it ended up that we couldn't really trust Iva either when it came down to it. Pinnia helped us stay safe, and gave us a place to sleep. Her mom is asleep in a hammock with a book—that doesn't exactly say *evil kidnapper* to me. And something about our conversation before we went to sleep makes me think she would understand.

But Hurona said not to tell. I feel like a pod half picked, dangling from the vine.

Luckily Pinnia is leaning forward and looking at the map still open on my lap.

"Is that Petrichor?" she says, eyebrow raised.

"Yeah," I say, and turn it so she can see. "I was...I was thinking about my aunt. She worked here for a while before she died."

"Where?"

"Right there," I say, and point to the green square: *Eccles-Tillery Conservancy*. It still feels weird to see those words right there on the page. All the questions I want to ask my mom swell higher in my throat. Now that I'm out of Prine, maybe she's not the only one to turn to. With my finger on the conservancy, I hold the map higher for Pinnia to see. "Have you ever heard of this place?"

She peers at the faded paper, frowning. Then her eyes brighten.

"Oh, I know that place," Pinnia says. "That's only a few blocks away."

I don't really know how big a block is, or what that even really means, but she looks so hopeful. It makes my heart grow feathers.

"Really?" I squeak.

She points, her finger following the line of a street.

"See? Warren. Then Hauc. That's us. It's super close. I used to pass it on my way to school, before homeschool." She pauses and frowns. "It looks a lot bigger on the map."

"Wow," I say. "She was right there."

I can feel Pinnia looking at me, and my cheeks feel hot. Somehow, the empty space that is Aunt Josie at home feels less empty here.

"Do you think...do you think you could take me?" I ask. "I...really need to see it."

She puts down her plant invention and sits up, eyes shining.

"Sure! Everybody is still asleep—we can walk over there really quick before anyone even wakes up. It looks like the rain is stopping."

The green square on the map is only two blocks away. Sometimes it feels like Aunt Josie exists only to me. And barely. She's a voice in a box. Maybe walking where she walked will fill the space a little more.

I close the map inside the book and smile at Pinnia.

"Let's do it."

25

THE GATE OF the Eccles-Tillery Conservancy is the biggest part about it.

"Wow," Pinnia says, standing next to me on the sidewalk. "It, uh...looked a *lot* larger on the map."

On the map, the conservancy took up blocks and blocks of Petrichor. Maybe even miles. But instead, me and Pinnia stand outside of one single square block of trees, with a few buildings beyond the fence. The gate is huge and copper and arches over the entryway, with all the words carved in. It's dull and mossy and looks like it's been there for a hundred years.

I'm definitely going inside.

"That map looked kinda old," Pinnia says as we step under the archway. "I guess things changed."

Inside the grounds, everything is cooler and shadier. Not like Prine—the light filters down through the layers of leaves and makes everything a little green. I hear what I think are birds calling. Not the usual kind, the twitterers and the cheepers. Big birds. Birds with voices that rise and fall and echo so that I can barely tell where they're coming from.

"This place is amazing," Pinnia says, craning her neck to look up.

This is the only part that reminds me of home—vines and strings of moss connecting some of the trees. We take it all in as we walk across what feels like carpet but is actually a thick bed of leaves and pine needles, so soft they don't even crackle. The trees block out some of the city noise. Everything is muffled.

"There's a visitor center," I say, pointing. I can't help the feeling that bubbles up in me. Being here, a place that I've heard come from my mother's lips, feels like stepping into the past itself. I've thought so much about ghosts, but this is the first time it feels like I'm actually close to meeting one.

The visitor center looks as old as the rusty gates. The wood is dark with age and half covered in moss. There used to be a story Hurona would tell me when I was little, about two kids who went into the forest and found a witch's hut. This looks like that. Like in wandering through this shady little jungle I might stumble across magic. But when we walk through the door to the visitor center, it's not a witch.

Maybe a wizard instead.

At first I think he's old because he has white hair, but his face says different. Behind the round glasses are bright eyes, and below them a nose like a beak. He fits right in, because the room is absolutely filled with birds.

They're everywhere. Some of them are in roomy cages, but most of them are free, fluttering up into the rafters, landing on window-sills. Inside, the building is kind of like a cabin. It's weird to see a building made of wood. I know wildfires don't happen as much anymore, but it still makes me shiver. I've never actually seen one, but it's like my mom's memories are my own. The pieces of them she shares, anyway.

"Oh," the man says when he sees us, looking up from his book. He looks surprised. "Can I help you?"

I can barely hear him because the birds are so loud. They squawk and warble and trill. One swoops down from the rafters and barely misses Pinnia's head. We both leap back.

"Albert," the man scolds the bird. It's already back up in the rafters. He looks at us, lowering his eyebrows apologetically. "Don't mind him. He's a bit of a brat."

"The bird is a brat?" I ask. Then repeat it, almost shouting, when the man holds a hand to his ear.

"What is this place?" Pinnia calls. "What are all these birds?"

"It's all that's left of the conservancy!" the man calls.

"All that's left?"

"Petrichor seized more and more of the land," he answers. "Needed more farmland as the city grew. They relocated most of the animals to the Bastida-LaDuke Reserve in the south! So now it's just me and the kids!"

It's almost like "the kids" don't like sharing the man's attention—they seem to get louder and louder the more he talks. And he seems to notice. He scowls around at them and throws his hands up. Then he stands up and closes his book, shaking his head, and walks around the long desk where he's been sitting.

"Let's go outside so I can actually hear you," he shouts. He strides toward us—definitely not an old man. His silver hair is long and wavy, but he looks strong and quick. He opens the door and waves us out. It's not until *he* moves to walk through the door that the birds all try to follow. A big flightless bird darts over with the speed of a snake.

"Now, Achebe, you stop it! Siguete haciendo el chistosito y te encierro!"

He struggles out of the door, me and Pinnia watching with our mouths open. He wrestles with the big white bird at his feet, using his book as a shield, while also using his head to keep a bright red parrot from slipping out at the top. When he finally gets the door closed, he's breathing hard.

"Dios," he mutters.

Pinnia giggles.

"You talk to them like my mom talks to me," she says.

He takes off his glasses and wipes them on his shirt. His white hair is ruffled but he doesn't seem to notice.

"Well, some of them I hatched from eggs," he says. "So in some ways I'm the only mother they've known."

"You've worked here a long time?" I ask.

"Long, long time," he says. "Now. I'm Arturo. What can I do for you?"

"We just wanted to check this place out," Pinnia says. "I used to pass it on the way to school but never came in."

Arturo nods.

"This conservancy is a lot like that for many people. You know, the shirt in your closet that's been there for so long you stop seeing it when you're choosing your clothes for the day. This place was here before the city, but the city grew up around us. And eventually closed in on us."

Arturo has the same hunch in his shoulders that some people in Prine have. It's a different kind of shrinking, a different kind of crushing.

"They tell me I should be grateful for this little patch," he goes on. "But there used to be so many animals here, and so many people who took care of them. Now it's just the kids. And me."

"Her aunt used to work here," Pinnia says, nudging me. The ghost feeling creeps back over me. I'm glad Pinnia is here. My lips feel sandpapery.

Arturo pops his glasses back on his face and turns to me now, focused. With his eyes and his beaky nose pointed at me and his head tilted a little, he looks even more like one of his birds.

"What was her name?" he asks.

Such a simple question. But saying it out loud feels sticky. I don't even talk to Banneker about Aunt Josie. But my sandpapery lips open and I hear her name come out of my mouth:

"Josephine Neaux."

Arturo's eyes get big and round like an owl, and his mouth falls open just a little.

"Josie?" he says. "You're Josie's niece?"

"I . . . yes," I whisper.

Someone else outside the Neaux household knows she existed. I hadn't realized it until the light sparked in his eye...that I wondered if she was even real. No photos. No memories. Just a name and a word or two until I found Mom's old phone.

"Which one?" he says quickly. "Are you Erie or Hurona?"

"E-Erie," I say.

"No puedo creerlo," he breathes. "I can't believe it. You! A Neaux! After all these years."

"So you knew her," Pinnia says, grinning. She looks delighted. I want to smile too. I want to laugh and shout. But I also feel too frozen. Part of me wants to cry.

"Knew her?" Arturo cries. "We worked together for many years. Drove buses of animals back and forth between the conservancies. Your tía was one of the funniest people I ever met! She would talk the whole time and I would laugh the whole time. Even the animals would laugh."

"You knew her," I repeat, but he doesn't seem to notice.

"Oh, I was so sad when she passed," he says. His eyes glitter behind his glasses. It makes my eyes sting too. It feels weird that he knew her better than me. That he met her at all when I didn't. "A true friend. To me, and to the Earth. Oh. Oh. Oh, I think about her all the time."

He's silent for a moment, and I feel Pinnia looking at me, seeing the tears in my eyes. She looks like she wants to hug both me and Arturo but isn't sure.

"I looked and looked for next of kin," he goes on, poking a pinky under his glasses to dab at his tears, his book tucked under his arm. "She didn't leave much but I held on to it. Couldn't bear to just throw it away."

My tongue comes unstuck in my mouth.

"You have something of hers?" I rasp. "That she left?"

"It's been a long time," he says. "But it's still here. Her niece. I can't believe it. Dios mio."

I watch him walk away. Do I follow? What if he has a picture? Do I even want to see it? It's not until now that I realize I've had an image of Aunt Josie in my mind. She smiles more than Mom. She laughs. She tells the truth. Part of me wants to run out toward the street and not look back. Maybe this is how Mom feels when she thinks about her secrets.

But then Pinnia is touching my arm. "Are you okay?"

I nod. Because I am. But I also think about how sometimes in Prine I think I can feel myself growing, getting too big for the lockwood. This feels like a different kind of growing. What else can I outgrow, even if I stay the same size?

But my curiosity is stronger than my nervousness. I take a deep breath, and I follow Arturo.

26

BEHIND THE VISITOR'S center is a metal shed, its roof just as mossy as everything else. Arturo already has it open and disappears into the shadow. Then farther back behind the shed, nestled in the trees, is another cabin like the one we'd just walked out of.

"Do you live here?" I ask.

"Sometimes," he calls from the shed, where I can hear him banging around. "The employee cabin is set up for emergencies. Used to stay there with your aunt sometimes, when the fires were bad. They would have us here around the clock, waiting to receive injured animals. It's just me now."

He pops out of the shed and extends the book he'd been carrying to Pinnia, who's closest. She takes it, and he disappears back into the shed.

"It would be lonely if it wasn't for mis hijos," he says. "They're loud, but they're good company. Birds and their personalities."

He continues digging around, and I look over at the book he gave Pinnia. She tilts it so I can see: *Raptors of the World*.

"I know raptors aren't just dinosaurs," Pinnia says. "But it's still weird to see *raptors* on a bird book."

She plucks at a piece of paper poking out of the top of the book, and it slips out. When I bend to pick it up, I see a familiar word: *Dolosalvus*.

Pinnia sees it too, and points.

"That's what the governor was talking about at the plaza," she says. "The town they're building."

I say it out loud: "Dolosalvus."

Arturo pops out, his hair a little dusty. He's carrying a small box.

"Oh that," he says, when he sees what we're looking at. "They've been passing them out in this area. All the markets and changarros and tamale carts. I've never done ag work, but I might start now if it means I can get a medical card."

"What about the birds?" I say.

He looks sad.

"I don't know," he admits. "But I don't have any help here. You two are just niñitas so you don't know yet, but eventually the body gets old and tired."

"You're not old," I say quickly.

He smiles, a little weakly.

"Not yet," he says. "But I will be."

Then he retrieves the book and the Dolosalvus pamphlet from Pinnia's hand, and uses them to gesture for us to follow him. He chats as he walks.

"I wonder if the governor gets old as quickly as the rest of us." He chuckles. "Dolosalvus. I just know this will show up in his campaign videos. What won't show up will be whether he takes anything off the top."

"What do you mean?" I ask, curious.

"My abuela always said that citizens march and politicians slither," he says with a wink. "If the governor is saying Dolosalvus will help people, it might. But I don't watch his mouth when he talks...I watch his bank account. I'm pretty sure your Aunt Josie told me that." He chuckles. "If someone calls something the best solution, but they're getting rich off that best solution, the word *best* should raise all our eyebrows."

We end up on the front steps of the visitor's center. Behind us, the birds start their chorus when they can see Arturo again. He turns and raises a fist, shaking it at them. He's smiling, though.

"Now," he says, turning back. "Jo's things."

He starts to open the box, then pauses, and hands it to me instead. Beside me, Pinnia scoots a little closer.

The box is dusty but I don't blow it off before I remove the lid.

"There's not much," Arturo says softly.

There's not. It's just two things.

A jacket folded up small and a single envelope.

"I could never find any family to send it to," Arturo says. "I think she meant to put it in the mail but she...never came back from her last rescue trip. I'm glad you're here now."

"Me too," I whisper. I stare at the things in the box, almost afraid to touch them. This had been Aunt Josie's stuff. She wore this jacket. She sealed this envelope. I don't have to lift it out to see the word written in small tight lines on the front: *Nadine*. A letter for my mom. I hoped that by coming here, everything about the past would feel a little more real. And it does. It also stings a little bit more. I hadn't expected that.

"Your aunt was good at so many things," he says, smiling. "She had a little camera that she rigged up to fit on some of the birds' tracking bands. There was a golden eagle named Samantha...un cuata de tu tía. Buddies. Jo would let Samantha fly above the reserve and take footage on her camera."

"Like a drone." Pinnia grins.

She's thinking of her brother. But I can't help but think of FOLROY and Prine.

"Like a drone." Arturo nods. "La antigua. I think your tía wished she was a bird. Of all the animals we kept here at Eccles-Tillery, she always loved the birds the best. Me too."

And now I'm thinking of Hurona. Is it possible to be like someone you never met? I pick up the letter and hand it to Pinnia. She accepts it so gently that I think she might be my best friend, even if we barely know each other. I slide the jacket out of the box too. Is it wrong to put it on? It's dusty and smells kind of stale. But I don't care. I slip my arms through. It's light green and it's not until I'm fully wearing it that I notice the patch on the left lapel.

"*Neaux says no*," Arturo reads, grinning. His eyes brim and he pokes at them with his pinky tips again. "That was her. Never did nothing she didn't want to do."

"Thank you for keeping this," I whisper.

"Thank you for coming," he answers, and behind us his birds start singing so loud, I think they're happy to see the jacket again too.

Pinnia and I walk back to her house in silence. She'd given me back the letter and it's stowed in the big pockets of my aunt's jacket.

"Are you going to open it?" she asks.

"No," I say. "It's for my mom."

"You're not curious?" Her voice dances. "It's been waiting for...how many years?"

I think.

"Ten at least," I say.

"It's been waiting for *ten years*," she repeats. "And if you hadn't gone, it would've stayed there forever. What if Arturo left for Dolosalvus, and the person who replaced him just threw it all out?"

"Or what if you had never taken me?" I say. Her excitement is contagious. "Like what if you hadn't said anything about the map, or what if I didn't bring it with me at all?"

"I love what-ifs." She sighs as we walk. "A what-if can reimagine the whole world. Like what if my mami had never cut her finger chopping okra? What if my mom's headphones hadn't died the day she met my mami? She wouldn't have heard Mami ask for a bandage. They never would've met."

"What if I didn't come on this trip?" I say, going along with her. "What if I stayed in Prine?"

Then I'm thinking of bigger what-ifs—what if my father never died, what if Aunt Josie didn't either—and I go silent. But Pinnia goes on.

"And what if Prine didn't have the lockwood? Or like, had

normal lockwood? What if it grew like normal and you didn't have to cut it? Your whole life would be different."

My breath catches, because I'm toe to toe with the thing Hurona told me not to say.

Pinnia keeps walking, kicking a pebble. She can't see in my head, so she doesn't see the seesaw inside me, going back and forth. Hurona had said we can't trust anyone, but I think we can trust Pinnia. I never would have gone to the conservatory if it wasn't for her. Would never have found these pieces of Aunt Josie.

"I'm going to tell you a secret," I say, and she looks at me then, her eyes bright.

"What kind?"

"The big kind. You can't tell anybody, okay?"

"Deal. Promise."

And I believe her.

"What you said about Prine," I say slowly. "That's . . . kinda why me and Hurona are here. Because we . . . well, I . . . figured it out. Why the lockwood won't stop growing."

Pinnia stops walking and peers at me, and it makes her look even more like a cat.

"What did you figure out?"

"They're watering it," I whisper, even though we're on an empty sidewalk. "FOLROY. They send a drone at night, and it sprays something over the lockwood to make it grow back while we're sleeping."

Her eyes widen again, her eyebrows arched over them like black crescent moons.

"You saw it?"

"Yes. That's why we came. We're going to go talk to Lunata Elemnieri and tell her to make them stop."

"Lunata Elemnieri?"

"Yeah. She's the person who invented the lockwood. She's—"

Pinnia waves her hands, shaking her head.

"No, no, I know who she is. *Everybody* knows who she is. You think she'll care?"

"She *has* to care," I cry. "She's a scientist. She needs to know what they're doing with her invention. No one will listen to us," I say, repeating my sister's words, "but they'll listen to her. I've been seeing her on TV for as long as I can remember: *the scientist who saved us all*. Well, she didn't really save us all if some of us are . . . you know."

"Screwed," Pinnia says, and I laugh quietly.

"Yes, screwed," I say. "So I just have to figure out how I'm going to find her and talk to her, and I think it will be simple if she hears it from someone who actually lives in Prine."

"Well, I think you got on the right bus," Pinnia says, smiling.

"Huh?"

"So many what-ifs!" she cries. She sounds like one of Arturo's birds. "What if you had gotten on another bus? Not my mom's? Then you wouldn't have met me. And it's a good thing you met me, because *I* know how you can meet Lunata Elemnieri."

27

WHEN WE GET back to Pinnia's house, everybody is mad.

Hurona is waiting on the front porch and springs up when we open the gate.

"Erie!" she yells. "Where have you *been?*"

On the way back, me and Pinnia had gotten so excited about our plan that we'd run the last block. But now we both grind to a stop at the gate. Behind my sister, Ms. Mari appears in the doorway, with another woman close behind.

"We just went down the street...," I start.

"Why didn't you wake me up?" Hurona snaps. She leaps over the last two steps up to the porch and strides up to me. "I woke up and you were gone!"

"Sorry," I say. Beside me, Pinnia stays silent. Her mom glares at her from the porch. "We weren't gone that long. We just had to..."

"To do *what?*" Hurona snaps. "What did you have to do *alone*, in a city you've never been in? What did you—"

But then her eyes take in the jacket I'm wearing, and she stops. Her eyes fix on the patch, then dart up to my face.

"Where did you get that jacket?" she whispers.

"The Eccles-Tillery Conservancy," I answer. "Aunt Josie used to work there."

"It's two blocks away," Pinnia answers. I think she thinks because Hurona's not yelling anymore it's okay to talk. Then she looks up at where Ms. Mari stands. "The conservancy!"

"You still should have told someone," Ms. Mari scolds. Beside her, I realize from the wedding picture, is her wife. Her skin is a darker brown and she wears a dusty-yellow scarf tied around her hair. "I don't mind you being off by yourself, but these girls don't know the city and her sister was worried! Usa la cabeza!"

"I could have been asleep," Pinnia's other mom says, crossing her arms. "You know I need a nap after work!"

"I'm fine," I say to Hurona while Pinnia talks to her parents. "We weren't even gone that long."

"You can't just do that," Hurona says. She's still mad, and it starts to make me mad too. "You have to—"

"Maybe I should have left you a note," I snap. "Would that have been better?"

She gets my meaning and narrows her eyes.

"Actually, yes," she says, and my anger falters. I know she's right. But I'm still not sorry. I keep thinking about Pinnia's *what-ifs*. What if I hadn't gone? I had to. It almost feels like I was meant to.

This would be the time to tell my sister, to share it all—tell her about the letter addressed to our mother. We could open it together, maybe. But Aunt Josie has been my private obsession. Hurona has her secrets—bigger ones than this. Having my own feels important all of a sudden. The decision to keep the envelope in my pocket makes it feel heavier.

"You won't be so mad when I tell you some news," I say to Hurona as we walk toward the house. She doesn't answer, just raises her eyebrow. "Pinnia knows how we can meet Lunata Elemnieri."

"Wait, really?"

I nod, grinning. I feel a little lighter.

"Erie, Hurona," Pinnia says from the porch. "This is my mom."

"I'll tell you in a minute," I whisper to Hurona.

Pinnia's mom's voice is scratchy and her eyes are tired. But they're gentle too. She shakes our hand.

"You can call me Eya," she says. "Everything okay between you two?"

"I'll make it up to her," I say, shooting Hurona a look. "Sorry if we worried you."

"I wasn't worried." Ms. Mari shrugs and leads the way back inside. "Pinnia knows not to go more than six blocks. But you're new here. If your sister is fine, I'm fine."

Inside the house, all the blankets are folded and a wonderful smell is coming from the kitchen. My stomach immediately wakes up. Hurona's must too, because she stops trying to catch my eye to tell her about Lunata Elemnieri and looks toward the kitchen.

We can hear Mento singing:

"Pero, ah-ah-ay, ¡cómo me duele!"

"What are you making?" Pinnia shouts, but he doesn't hear. The music and the popping oil are too loud.

"Tacos de papa," Eya answers, peeking into the kitchen.

"Yesss." Pinnia grins.

"You girls must be hungry," Ms. Mari says.

"How can we help?" Hurona says in answer.

"You were raised right," Ms. Mari says, and I flush with pleasure, even though Hurona said it. I don't know if she's right or wrong. This house feels so full: of people, of singing, of talking. Prine and our house feel so empty. But I push up my sleeves to help, and try not to think about it.

We eat in the backyard, half in and half out of the gazebo. At first Hurona and I both paused to watch how we were supposed to eat what was on our plates—golden semicircles, bright radishes and tomatoes on top, a pale orange sauce. White cabbage. Pinnia and her parents laughed when we drank lots of water for the spice, and Mento looked proud.

"Sometimes I think I miss meat," Eya says, "and then I eat your tacos, Mento, and I forget all about it."

Mento looks even prouder.

"It can be hard to unlearn," Ms. Mari says. "Harder if you don't want to. You've come a long way."

"There are people in Prine who still complain about not eating meat," Hurona says.

"Who?" I ask, shocked.

"Thatcher," she says. "Gaetz."

I frown. Two kids her age. I didn't know that. Sometimes when I looked down at the ground from the lockwood, I would imagine being on a spaceship, looking down on another planet. When Hurona says stuff like this, it makes me feel like my imagination pulled from a textbook instead.

"When I was growing up," Ms. Mari continues, "we learned about the future from what la chancla warned us about." She laughs, then takes on an older woman's voice: *"Don't leave the fridge open. Don't waste your food! Don't touch the dial—put a wet towel on your neck instead! Share with the neighbors! Check on los ancianos!"*

They laugh and talk while me and Hurona listen. I wonder if she's hearing the same thing I'm hearing. Not the talk of Pinnia's family, but the silence of ours. And then I think of the letter in my pocket, and my stomach, full of taco de papa, twists. Is this why Mom doesn't tell us about the past? About anything? Because she wants to keep some things for herself?

"Wait, where did you get this?" Pinnia says, and I start paying attention again. Pinnia is slipping something off her mom's lap. A pamphlet.

"They were passing them out when I stepped off the bus," Eya says.

I recognize it too—the same red floral design as the one Arturo had at the conservancy.

"Is that a Dolosalvus brochure?" Mento asks. "We saw the governor talking about it in the plaza this morning."

Ms. Mari frowns.

"I don't know if I trust anything the governor is advertising," she says.

"I know, I know," Eya says. "But they're offering so many benefits. All the things they keep from ag workers in Petrichor they'd be giving us in Dolosalvus. Medical cards! I could have my surgery. No more waiting."

Ms. Mari bites her lip.

"I just have to wonder why they can't give us those things here," she says. "Why make a whole new town?"

"You're going to be late for work," Eya says to Mento.

I may have only one parent at home, but I see what Eya is saying plain as day: This is a mom conversation they need to have alone.

"I'll clean up," Ms. Mari says. "Thank you for cooking, Mento, mi conejito."

When Mento moves to stand up, Pinnia shoots me a look and a nod. I tap Hurona, and the three of us trail him to the front yard.

"Mento," Pinnia says. She uses the kind of little sister voice that I wouldn't dare use on Hurona. Maybe it's different when your big sibling is a brother.

"Whaaaaat?" he singsongs, still walking toward the gate.

"Can we come to the Buzz Yard," Pinnia says, "and you scan us in?"

"I've already scanned you in twice in the last month," he says, not stopping. "And last time you talked until everyone's ears were smoking. No way. I need to focus."

"What's the Buzz Yard?" Hurona says to me as Pinnia and Mento talk. Her head tilts. She's getting a whiff of our plan. "And why do you want to go there?"

I ignore her at first—how mad will she be that I told Pinnia about the FOLROY drone? Maybe she'll be less mad once she realizes that I figured out a plan for us to talk to Lunata Elemnieri.

"Mento...," Pinnia whines.

"No way, manita."

"But we need to talk to Zizi!"

Only then does Mento pause, midstride.

"Zizi, you say?" He turns, smiling. "Why didn't you say so?"

Pinnia rolls her eyes toward me.

"I knew that would do it," she says. "He has a crush on Zizania."

"It's not a crush," he corrects. "It's adoration."

"Who is Zizi?" my sister says. She's looking at me for the answer. Hurona and her hunches. She knows I'm up to something.

"Zizi is their friend," I say, repeating what I learned from Pinnia on the walk back from the conservancy. "And apparently she works at Lunata Elemnieri's house."

"Erie," she says quietly, slowly.

I look over at her even more slowly. She knows I told Pinnia.

"She can help," I say quickly. "Pinnia thinks Zizi can take us to Lunata's house and maybe introduce us. Isn't that great?"

Hurona raises her eyebrow but doesn't say anything right away. I can see the wheels turning, a whole factory of thoughts.

Then I hear a tiny beep. Her phone. I almost forgot she had it—it's still so weird to see her with one. She glances at it, and I know it must be Iva, the way that factory of thoughts whirs faster. She shuts the phone off.

"What did she say?" I ask.

"And what's the Buzz Yard?" Hurona says, ignoring me. She moves her eyes from the phone to Pinnia.

"Do you not have one in Prine?" Pinnia says. She's trotting after Mento toward the gate, and we follow. "They're all over the city. They're kind of like farms, but they have all different kinds of bugs. Like bees, of course. Did you know bees can be trained to smell diseases? Mento taught me that."

"You hear that, Erie?" Hurona says. She even smiles a little. Maybe she won't be mad at all. "Bugs."

"I saw your encyclopedia," Pinnia says with interest. "So you're like really, *really* into bugs?"

"Bugs love Erie," Hurona says. "A bee has never stung her. A mosquito has never bit her. They have...mutual respect."

I smile at that. It's kind of true.

"Mento *loves* bees," Pinnia says. "He does part of his home-schooling at the Buzz Yard. He takes the bees on pollination tours."

"The bee tours are my favorite part," Mento adds. "Because even now, with climate change all around us, people still don't know how important bees are. And *all* bugs! People have gotten so used to thinking that our comfort matters more than nature—they don't even know how bad it messes up the planet when we get rid of bugs. So on the bee tours we can educate people a little bit more."

I nod. I remember Banneker telling me that their brother, Carver, worked on the bee tours for a while when he first got to Petrichor. With help from humans, the bees were able to travel around greater distances and pollinate more flowers and gardens. I've heard that FOLROY has their own bees, but I didn't know it was called a Buzz Yard.

"And your friend Zizi works there?" Hurona asks. She's following along now, which makes me feel hopeful. Maybe she won't be mad at all.

"Yeah," Pinnia says. "She works with the flies."

"Do you need to tell your parents where you're going?" Hurona says. Big sister.

"I'll text them," Pinnia says. "They need to talk anyway."

Mento glances up at the sky while we walk. It's raining again, but only a little. A light mist settles on his long black hair, making it sparkle. This is the kind of rain that never makes it onto the street in Prine. Too light and fine. At home it's licked up by the lockwood high above. So it feels nice, walking to the Buzz Yard with Pinnia and her brother.

We've slept, and we're walking around in the daylight, and I'm wearing Aunt Josie's jacket with secrets inside. The world and the sky feel huge and wide. Back home, the lockwood makes Prine feel like a cave. Here, the city streets are broad and everything feels *open*.

Pinnia tells us about everything we see—I feel like one of the bees that Mento takes on tours. Everything looks like a flower. She points at restaurants and bicycle shops and bakeries that sell loaves of bread that seem to shine as bright as the signs. Everything has signs! Even if the air isn't noisy, the signs are loud in their own way. Everything glitters and shimmers and glows.

But there are still trees. Planted between and on top of every building, sprouting from awnings. Some of them are willows, spidery

186

vines like a curtain people have to push past to get through a door. Some are thick as columns and join with brick and stone. They seem to fit into every crack, every gap of the city—trees and trees and trees.

None of them are lockwood. It makes me feel like I can breathe.

28

WE HEAR THE Buzz Yard before we see it. It's not an actual buzzing—it's a hum that grows and grows. Gentler on the ear than a machine, but it rises and falls the same way. The gates outside are arching wood beams that must have been from a redwood. BUZZ YARD is carved into it. All around the words are intricate designs of bees and beetles. I've never seen anything like it. I remember lying on my stomach in the lockwood when I was little, using twigs and leaves to make tiny houses for ants. The Buzz Yard is almost like the same thing, but a grown-up version.

Mento leads us under the arch of redwood, pulling a slim wallet from his back pocket. It's attached to his belt loop with a brightly beaded chain. There's a shiny gate ahead. He slaps the wallet down against a pad by the gate, and a light above the door glows green.

"Come on," he says, waving us after him.

"We won't get in trouble?" Hurona says, reluctant.

"No, no," he says. "People bring people inside all the time. They mostly have the gate up to keep the cops out."

He rolls his eyes, and we follow him through the door and into the Buzz Yard.

"Whoa," Hurona says. I watch the closed envelope of her face crack open. The misty rain is only barely coming down now, and it's like we're walking through a cloud. But on all sides, instead of sky, are huge clear tanks filled with...bugs.

"What do you think?" Pinnia says, grinning. "You said you like bugs, but do you like bugs...this much?"

Nearby, one of the tanks flickers like lightning, purple and white.

"What was that?" I gasp.

"Illumabeetles," Mento says. "Come see."

We approach the tank, which is about the size of our kitchen at home. It's clear like all the others, the ceiling lined with bulbs, all of them dark. Through the glass, we can see the swarms of bugs. There are so many that the floor looks like it's solid black, moving and roiling. Hurona shudders.

"Gross!" she cries, and Mento laughs. I just stare, in awe.

"Watch this," Pinnia says, pointing.

Two people, one an older woman and the other around Hurona's age, stand near a control box. They study the tank, then the older woman says something to the younger person. They flip a switch.

Something inside the tank hums, and then all of a sudden the clots of bugs rise up. They fly up to the ceiling, swarming over the unlit bulbs. There's another humming sound and then a purple pulse of light fills the tank.

"It's coming from the bugs," I whisper.

The purple light flickers through the swarm, like a chain reaction. Then there's another humming sound, and all the insects fly low again. Returning to the floor. At the ceiling, the light bulbs are all illuminated.

"Illumabeetles," Pinnia repeats. "They raise them to help with blackouts. When communities lose power, they can send the illumabeetles to charge certain kinds of bulbs and devices."

"There's a frequency that calls them back," Mento says. "Pretty cool, right?"

"Amazing," I breathe. Even Hurona nods.

"This is the kind of stuff Buzz Yards work on," Mento goes on, waving for us to follow him. "Right now Petrichor is still putting solar panels all over the city and selling them to people, but charging tons of money. We're trying to make alternatives."

"They help people get light and other stuff from the bugs they take care of here," Pinnia adds. "Also, did you know they use lockwood to make the tanks?"

"What, really?"

"Yeah. They make it from the pulp. It's stronger than glass and everybody knows plastic sucks."

I feel like I don't know anything, like Pinnia and Mento are plugged into some huge fountain of information. I think of what Mom always says: *The opposite of ignorance is humility. You have two ears and one mouth, so sometimes shut the one and listen with the two.* So I listen, and learn, and I marvel at the tanks, wondering if the hatchet I use in the lockwood would cut right through this container.

It's cool to think about how something can completely change form, but still hold on to what it is. I wonder what Hurona would be like if she moved to Petrichor—or Dolosalvus—and left me in Prine. Whether she would be different, but still my sister at the core.

Mento leads us across the yard. The humming is all around us like an orchestra. It's so soothing I could sleep. But that's when I realize it: I'm not tired. I still didn't have a full night of sleep, but this morning was the first morning since I was ten that I hadn't gone into the lockwood. My muscles don't ache. My head doesn't hurt at the temples from my headlamp. I follow Pinnia and Mento and wonder if this is what normal must feel like.

"But this," Mento is saying, "is the most popular bug."

This tank is even bigger, closer to the size of my house in Prine. The insects in this tank don't swarm the floor: They fly in clouds around the tank, coating the walls and clogging the air. Hurona steps back, like the swirling black billows might come right through the tank wall. But I step closer.

"What do they do?" I ask, staring. I've always thought that you could learn a lot from insects, and I'm curious about what I can learn from these.

"They save our butts," someone says, and a Black girl with her hair in thick twists bounds down from the control panel platform nearby. She's my sister's age, and her confidence glows out of her like her own private star. She beams, and behind me I actually hear Mento sigh, dreamy. I realize this must be Zizania.

"What are you doing over here?" Zizi says to him over my head. "I thought you were assigned to the skeeters today?"

"The kiddo needed me to bring her and her friend to talk to you," Mento says, patting Pinnia's head. She shoves him off.

"What do you mean they save our butts?" I say quickly, before the conversation can derail.

"I'll show you," Zizi says. She has heavy-lidded eyes, painted gold, and a round face. Her smile is like a solar panel. She looks like an angel. I see why Mento has a crush.

Zizi climbs back up onto the platform. She taps out some instructions, and a moment later my nose fills with the rank smell of rot.

"What smells like trash?" Hurona says, wrinkling her nose. Like Mento, she can't take her eyes off Zizi either. I smile to myself, wondering if she might forget Iva after all.

"Surprise, it's...*trash*!" Zizi laughs.

Sure enough, a heaping mountain of trash has appeared. I'd been so focused on the bugs I hadn't noticed the big metal box behind their tank. It's actually more like a house—even bigger than the bug tank. A metal door has slid open, and a mechanical arm the size of a crane moves smoothly out. It heaps with garbage. Under Zizi's direction, the arm travels up to the top of the bugs' tank. It lowers down into a chamber, and I can hear the hushed metallic movement of it being closed in.

"Now I open the secondary roof so my babies can chow down," Zizi says. "Watch this."

The secondary roof must open, because all of a sudden the trash-heaped arm moves down into the fly tank. The black flies swarm to it, swaths of them crawling and buzzing over the arm and its contents. I can't see the trash at all, just clouds of teeming black.

And just like that, in maybe two minutes, the trash disappears. The arm is empty and Zizi directs it outside again. She smiles down at us.

"How...?" Hurona says in wonder.

"Savior flies," Zizi says. "Bred from black soldier flies. A couple of decades ago people realized that trash was going to flood this planet if we didn't find a way to do something besides dump it. Enter these little babies."

"They just...eat the trash?" I say. I'm standing so close to the tank my nose is almost touching.

"Yep. Everything but plastic. They breed fast, and when they die, they're chicken feed. A lot less taxing on the land than corn. We raise them naturally, but I hear a lot of the higher-tech places like FOLROY use frequencies to train them to clear land and stuff like that."

"That makes sense," I say. "Some grasshoppers and locusts can hear frequencies up to one hundred thousand hertz. And some moths can even detect ultrasound."

Zizi looks impressed, and shifts her eyes to Hurona for explanation.

"She loves bugs." My sister shrugs. "She has a whole encyclopedia. I dunno."

Zizi laughs and goes on, telling us all about the larvae and how the Buzz Yard takes care of them before they grow into the flies. The smell of the trash has faded a little, but I don't notice anyway. I'm listening to every word Zizi says about the Buzz Yard and drinking it in.

Bugs with jobs. Prine doesn't make a lot of waste because we compost and don't use plastic, but I look at the big metal building next to the bug tank, imagining how much garbage must be inside. I look in at the insects swarming—slower now that they've eaten— and have the urge to thank them one by one, a billion individual gratitudes.

"I'm taking classes," Zizi says. "Environmental entomology. I want to study this forever. They keep saying college will be free one day, but for now...I pay for one class at a time. Maybe you can do that too," she says to me, "and maybe by the time you're old enough it will be free."

"Yeah, maybe," I say. There's a feeling of yearning inside me. It chews at my heart the way the dustnose beetle had chewed on my lockwood pencil in Prine.

"So why did you want to come see me?" Zizi says, smiling kindly at Pinnia. She and her brother have been waiting patiently while me and Hurona learned about the savior flies.

"Well, really, it's them," Pinnia says, pointing at us. "They need to see Lunata Elemnieri."

"Oh," Zizi says, squinting, but still smiling. "Superfans, huh?"

"Um...kind of," Hurona says.

"You work at her house?" I say, turning away from the bugs. "What do you do?"

"I cart the babies," Zizi says, jerking a thumb at the fly tank. "Big houses tend to have their own food- and house-waste collector, and I bring the buggies to eat it up."

"Just how big is her house?" Hurona says.

"Massive." Zizi laughs. But then she gets serious. "I can't take you there, though."

Pinnia looks even more disappointed than we are.

"Why not, Zi?" she cries.

"I'm not gonna get in trouble for bringing some random girls to her house," Zizi says. She glances at us. "No offense. But I represent the Buzz Yard when I go, and it wouldn't look good to essentially sneak two people inside. She has a fence and full security. I'd probably be breaking some kind of law if I took y'all inside."

"I understand," I say, even if I'm actually frustrated. The idea of being so close to finding a way to talk to Lunata Elemnieri and then realizing we're still not close at all stings. And I can't help but look at the sun and realize the day is just ticking by. I picture my mom back in Prine, alone. Part of me wonders if she even notices, but part of me imagines her alone, waiting. Worried. It makes me want to get on a bus and go home right now.

But while our mom would be waiting for us, so would the lockwood. We can't go back until we talk to Dr. Elemnieri.

"What if we paid you?" I hear my sister say, and I glance at her, surprised. Usually when someone tells Hurona no, she grits her teeth and figures it out on her own. *Independence run amok*, my mom always says.

Zizi laughs.

"Nice try," she says. "But if you paid me, it would be like trading my whole paycheck for ten bucks. Because I'd get fired, get me? I can't get fired. Who would look after the babies?"

She laughs again, and pats the savior fly tank. I stare in at them, and I realize how much I want to do this job. I could do this job. I could find ways to make bugs our allies. I could...

"What if I didn't give you money," Hurona says. Her tone pulls my eyes away from the tank. "What if I gave you this instead?"

My sister reaches into her bag, and when she pulls her hand out, she reveals a round brown nut, pointy at one end, coated in a slight fuzz.

"What is that?" Zizi squints. "Is that a lockwood pod?"

I stare at Hurona. My confusion hatches into concern. Why would she think anyone wants a lockwood pod? I know Hurona feels me looking at her because she refuses to look at me.

"Yes," Hurona says. "And to the right buyer, you could pay for ten classes with this."

Zizi looks skeptical, but when I look at Mento, his expression of adoration has shifted into thoughtfulness.

"I've heard rumors about this," he says. "That they secretly make chips and computers and stuff with a mineral inside the pod. I know a couple of droners who have been trying to get footage at a FOLROY factory, but those places are so tight with security, you know? You can't even blow your nose without security watching."

"They use the minerals in the pods in everything," Hurona agrees. "Computers. Memory chips. Even rocket engines."

Zizi considers this, gripping the pod between her fingers and holding it up in the sunshine to study it. The rain has passed and the clouds have started to part. The pod glows brown-gold. I realize I've never actually seen one up close outside of Prine's gloom. In real sunshine, the pod is actually pretty. The same rich color as Mx. Amur's old violin.

"Okayyy, so I'm interested," Zizi says, tilting her head. "Where did you get this?"

"Hurona and Erie are from Prine," Pinnia says eagerly.

Zizi's eyes widen.

"Oh, that makes total sense," she says, studying us with new eyes. As pretty as she is, and as nice as she is, I can't help but feel a little annoyed. I'm tired of everyone acting like we're creatures from outer space. Even if Petrichor does sort of feel like another planet— the way I once thought of Prine from the treetops.

"That's why we need to talk to Dr. Elemnieri," I say quickly. "We need to talk to her about the lockwood."

"What about it?"

"It's crushing us," Hurona says, and I'm surprised. She hadn't wanted me to tell Pinnia, but now it's like she can't keep her mouth shut anymore. "Kids are getting killed and..."

She pauses, and looking at her feels like staring directly at the sun. Her pain is bright and hot. But I do it. I look at her. And it hurts as much as I thought it would. My sister is tall and strong, but in her eyes I can see how small Prine has made her.

"It's bad," she says. Her face closes. She looks at Mento. "What's happening there is exactly the kind of stuff you make videos about for your channel. FOLROY is secretly making the lockwood grow back every night because they want us to keep harvesting the pods that make them rich."

"But why do they want the pods so badly?" I burst out. "FOL-ROY doesn't give us hardly any money for them."

"Because no one in Prine"—my sister starts, then stops and scowls—"because *hardly anyone* in Prine knows how valuable the pods are. FOLROY has kept it a huge secret. I didn't even know until Iva told me."

And you're just now telling me, I think. But I don't say it. Like Pinnia's parents, I know there are some things we should talk about in private. But I ask one more thing:

"Why did you bring them if no one else knows how valuable they are?"

"I don't know." Hurona shrugs. "I thought they might come in handy. Either as proof or trade or both. I figured some people *have* to know the pods are valuable. That must be why FOLROY does the checkpoints on the way into the city. Not just to check for people coming in without passes, but so they can make sure no one is messing with the trucks."

"They don't give y'all good money?" Zizi says, looking surprised. "Lockwood harvest is hard ag from what I hear."

Hurona opens her mouth to answer, but I jump in. She may be the big sister, but I know things too.

"They give us some money," I say. "But we have to use all of it to buy the blades that cut the lockwood anyway. Nothing else works, and they're the only ones who make the hatchets. And now they said they're going to start paying people in tokens. Tokens that we can only use to buy stuff from FOLROY."

"What?" Hurona says, snapping her head to look at me.

"Yeah," I say, and I try to keep my face smooth when I say it. "You didn't know? You were talking to Iva that day in Prine, so..."

Her eyes flash, then cloud. I'm never nasty. Not out loud. I guess we both see each other in a new light.

"It sounds like they own everything in your town," Mento says, frowning. He doesn't notice that things have shifted between me and my sister. All the stars in his eyes from staring at Zizi have faded. He looks as angry as Hurona. As me. "This makes me think about Dolosalvus. Remember? What the governor was talking about in the plaza. The new town."

"Maybe they're trying to fix everything for the new towns?" Pinnia offers.

Mento makes a face that says *don't hold your breath*. He nods back at Hurona and the pod.

"Do you think Dr. Elemnieri knows?" he asks.

I blink. Dr. Lunata Elemnieri has been on TV as the scientist who "saved us all" for as long as I can remember. Her smile is one I know well. I can't imagine that a smile like that knows that the thing she had invented to protect people was being used to hurt them instead.

"I guess we'll see," Hurona says. But I can tell by her voice that her mind is made up, and I wonder how long she's looked at Dr. Elemnieri's face and seen a monster instead of a hero.

Zizi stares at the pod in her hand, still held up to the sun.

"So will you take us?" Hurona says quietly.

Zizi turns her eyes from the pod to us.

"I'll take you to her neighborhood tomorrow morning," she

says. "She doesn't want people to know where she lives, obviously, because she's famous. So me showing you will be bad enough. I'll drop you at the closest corner. I can't take you in, but I'll get you close. Okay?"

Hurona nods, and there's something in her eyes I don't quite recognize. It glints like a silver cap over a tooth with a cavity.

"That's fine," she says. "Close is all I need."

29

PINNIA'S HOUSE HAS a spare room filled with plants, which she turns into a guest bedroom for me and Hurona. It almost feels like being in Prine again, the plants blocking the streetlight from the window. Everything smells green. But instead of being on the other side of a wall, Hurona is next to me on a couch that Eya pulled out and popped up into a bed.

The whole house is asleep, including Hurona. We'd all had dinner together, and Hurona had surprised me when she pitched in and made dinner rolls. I thought bread took hours, but she made them quickly, and when I asked how she knew, she said, *Mom showed me.* And I don't know when she would have, but maybe it was when I was still a baby.

It seems like so many things happened when I was still a baby. The Arborklept. Our dad dying. Aunt Josie dying. It feels weird and unfair that things happened while I was alive but that I'm still not part of them. I think about the lockwood pods, and how they're not just big seeds going to a compost pile somewhere. Buried inside is a mineral that has made everyone who knows about it rich. I imagine my brain the same way—somewhere buried deep are all the memories. But no way to extract them.

Beside me, Hurona's breath sounds like a hum. I should be sleeping, but it's almost too quiet and my head is too busy. I think about the pods Banneker picks in Prine—how if they knew what was in them, they could pick for one day and never have to climb again. And what about me? All my futures, having to stay small to fit in the lockwood. Futures that never actually feel within reach—being a teacher, working with bugs somehow. The imaginary sound of the lockwood seems to rustle in my head. In the end, I turn over as slowly as I can and reach for my bag, inch it closer and closer until I can get my hand inside.

I keep my back turned when I press Mom's old phone against my face and listen to Aunt Josie's next voice message.

> *Nadine, I know you're still mad. I know we don't live the same lives. But you have to trust me on this: There's just something there, okay? Something not right. If it means you stop talking to me, then that's your choice. But I wouldn't be a good sister if I only told you the things you want to hear. I know you want me to meet the girls. I do too. I promise I will soon. Later.*

"What are you doing?" Hurona says, her voice groggy.

I place the phone flat against my chest to hide the glow. "Nothing."

"Why aren't you sleeping?"

"I just...can't."

"Tomorrow is going to be busy. You should really sleep."

"I said I *can't.*"

She's silent, and I can tell she's surprised that I snapped. I'm surprised too. A second later, she shifts, rolling toward me.

"What's going on with you, Erie?"

"Nothing."

"You've been different."

Even though it's mostly dark, I shrug.

"Everything is different," I eventually say.

"And a lot is still the same," she says. She sounds tired. And not just because it's late.

"No, it's *not,*" I insist. "We're away from home. Mom is alone. It turns out FOLROY has been lying to us: about the trees growing, about the pods. The only thing that's the same is that you and Mom are both keeping secrets like you always do!"

By the end, I was raising my voice over a whisper, and I swallow. The last thing I want is to wake up Ms. Mari or Eya or anybody else and have them wondering why the two girls they let sleep in their house are yelling in the middle of the night. But all the anger that's been bubbling since the Buzz Yard feels like it's spilling over now. I remember when I thought of Hurona and everyone else as brimming cups. I didn't realize how hot the water was.

"Anything else?" Hurona says. She's fully awake now, and her voice is clear. And mad.

"You still act like I'm a little kid," I say. "And you keep

everything to yourself. And it's stupid. When telling me could actually help."

"Help what?" she snaps.

"I don't know! Anything. Everything."

"I don't know why you want to know some things, Erie." She sighs. She's turning back over to face the wall. "Trust me, some things, once you know them, you wish you didn't."

I don't know what to say to that, and I'm too mad anyway. I can feel a tear spilling out of the corner of my eye, and I feel more like a full cup than ever. There's no point in saying anything else anyway—Hurona is like Mom. I can tell when the door of her is closed.

I don't know how she can say that things are still the same when everything has changed. On the other side of the room is the jacket that used to belong to Aunt Josie, and now the envelope inside is my secret, one I've chosen to keep for no reason other than to have something of my own. What happens when you keep a secret? The one Hurona kept eventually leaked out and spread onto me. Will mine? It feels like balancing in the dark, the path ahead in shadow.

I lie there in the dimness, feeling unsure about everything. And for once, I miss the lockwood. At least up there I know where to put my feet.

30

THE STREET THAT Lunata Elemnieri lives on is deep green, the trees like leafy hands clasped around it. It almost reminds me of the tunnel out of Prine, if any sunlight passed through. When we'd left our town, we'd been huddled in the back of a FOLROY truck. As we make our way, Zizi humming as she steers the Buzz Yard truck, I think about what it would be like to drive out of Prine like this—on our own terms. We'd need a car first. Maybe one day Mx. Amur will fix her busted-up teal van.

When the Buzz Yard truck pulls over to the curb, Hurona flings the door open, and I hear what sounds like millions of birds calling. It's different than Pinnia's neighborhood, where all the houses are close together. Here, I can't see any houses at all from the street. Just trees and trees and trees. But Zizi said she'd drop us off close, so we have to be nearby.

Me and Hurona climb out of the truck silently. We haven't spoken much since last night. I'm so used to Hurona being mad at everyone and everything, it feels weird to be mad *at* Hurona. At home, there's a wall between us. Now it feels like something thicker. I thought coming with her to Petrichor would bring us closer together. Maybe I was wrong.

The huge tank attached to the back of the truck seems to spin with the movement of the savior flies inside. I almost get dizzy staring at them until Zizi leans to talk to us from the truck window.

"You'll see me turn in up ahead," she says. Her dark eyes look even darker with worry. "That'll be her house. Be careful, okay? Don't get in trouble. And don't get *me* in trouble."

"We won't," Hurona says.

"Do you know how to get back?"

Hurona glances at me.

"Twenty-Seven Hauc," I say.

Zizi tips an imaginary hat and the truck purrs to life again. It hums down the emerald street and we stand watching.

"Do you like her?" I ask. "She's really pretty."

"Yes, she is," Hurona says, but doesn't answer the first part. I can feel Iva there with us on the curb. It's like the birds on the street are singing her name.

"Do you still love Iva?" I ask.

"Who said I loved her to begin with?" she says.

I shrug. I don't know anything about love. The only person I love besides my mom and sister is Banneker. Sometimes when we laugh together or when they put their arm around me on the way to school, I feel like maybe something grows in my heart, even faster than lockwood. But most of the time we're just friends. And watching them disappear behind me in Prine had felt like the opposite of love.

206

I glance at Hurona and find her checking her phone.

"Has she called you?" I ask.

"Yes," she says.

"And?"

"I don't trust her anymore."

She puts the phone away. She has that small look in her eyes. I remind myself that I'm here on Lunata Elemnieri's street for myself, but for Hurona too. And Banneker. They want to be a scientist like my mom. They *could* be if the lockwood didn't put a shadow over their whole life.

"Zizi's turning," Hurona says, pointing down the street.

Sure enough, the truck is pulling left, disappearing into a shaded drive.

"Guess that's where she lives," I say. "So what do we do?"

But Hurona doesn't answer. She's already walking down the sidewalk toward where Zizi and her truck had pulled in. If my sister is nervous, she doesn't seem like it. I trot next to her, thinking of what Zizi said about there being security outside the house.

"I mean, we could just walk up and be honest," I say. "Or if we lie, maybe say we're big fans and just want to say hi?"

She snorts.

"What?" I demand.

"This woman is a superrich inventor," she says, still marching along. "If we're going to get in, we're going to have to sneak."

"Sneak?" I whisper, even though nobody's around to hear us. The only sound on the street is birdsong.

"When we pass the entrance Zizi took," Hurona says, "just

glance in. Don't stare. Erie, stop making your eyes all big! Just look normal and glance. You notice everything. Tell me what you see."

"What are we going to do after that?" I press.

"We're going to see what we're dealing with," she says. "Just pay attention."

We're approaching the entrance where the Buzz Yard truck disappeared. I try to notice if my eyes feel big, but they just feel normal to me. I sigh, getting ready. I tug at the bra strap under my shirt.

"Are you wearing a bra?" she says.

Of course she noticed. And of course she's going to know I took it from her room.

"No," I say.

"Liar," she says, but she's smirking.

"Whatever," I mutter. We're almost to Dr. Elemnieri's entryway.

"Okay, check," she whispers as we cross.

I look to my left. The trees that arch over the quiet street also arch over the entryway. The light that makes it to the ground is green-gold. It's so different from the lockwood: The branches here knit together gently, like a leafy blanket woven loose for summertime. But in a way, I think, scanning the entry, they're similar: They've been planted close and tight. Not to keep out the sun, but to keep out people. And the gap left for entry is barred by a heavy black gate. Two signs: SERVICE IN FRONT and DELIVERY IN BACK. There's a booth with two people in gray uniforms. The woman glances up as we pass by. I give her a half smile and look away, trying to seem casual.

Hurona doesn't speak until we reach the next corner. If we didn't already know Dr. Elemnieri lives here, we'd have no clue standing here. The trees completely shield everything from the street. I think of Pinnia's square, clean yard, the way the scrubby trees barely provide shade. I think of what Ms. Mari said: *Petrichor loves to call itself a green city.* But even this green city is greener in this part of town.

"What did you see?" Hurona says once we reach the corner.

"Not much," I say. "The trees block everything. Couldn't see the house at all. But there are guards like Zizi said. I guess she already knew to come to the front."

"What do you mean?"

"There was a sign that said SERVICE IN FRONT. The other one said DELIVERY IN BACK. But I guess she's not really *delivering* the savior flies."

Hurona's eyes light up, and that shiny look is back in them— the same look they had when she took the pod out of her bag to pay Zizi. I squint at her.

"Why do you keep making that face?"

"I'm not making a face," she says. "Come on."

She tugs on my arm, turning the corner now and marching down the next street.

"What? Where are we going?"

"Deliveries in back," she says. It dawns on me slowly.

"Deliveries in back," I repeat, and quicken my step to keep up with her.

"We're not exactly delivering anything either," she says.

"Yes, we are," I say. "Information."

She laughs quietly and I breathe just a little freer. It's the first time she's smiled since yesterday.

"Special delivery," she says under her breath.

We almost pass the alley at first. It's not narrow, but it's unpaved and almost looks like a dead end. But something catches my eye, a silver truck with a wide bed, people hopping up and then down, carrying sacks. I snatch at Hurona's arm—she's still moving down the sidewalk.

"Hurona," I whisper. "Look!"

She doubles back, then peers. Her smile spreads like melting butter.

"Deliveries," she says, almost singing like one of the unseen birds above us.

"Let's go," I say, but I'm already walking down the alley. A plan is hatching in my head. As we get closer, I can make out the clothes of the people on the truck. Shades of gray and brown, smudged with dirt and dust. The clothes aren't the same things we wear in Prine, but close. These are people who work with the land, and we might just blend in. We work the land too, after all. Just a little higher up.

Hurona nods as I tell her this, the factory in her head spinning again.

"You should hide your bag," I suggest. I'd left mine at Pinnia's, but Hurona had insisted on bringing hers. She looks up at the truck then back down again, deciding. Eventually she bends down, pulls what looks like a slip of paper from her wallet, and stuffs it in her back pocket.

"What's that?" I say, curious.

"Just something I don't want to get lost," she says, but she's turning away, stowing her bag in the green crush of leaves that border the alleyway. "Ready?"

"Ready."

We lope up to the truck, me a step behind. My heart feels like a scurrying mouse in my chest. Hurona still doesn't seem nervous at all, and I can't help but think it's because she's used to sneaking around. She, after all, climbed the lockwood by herself once too. Hurona and her secret girlfriend and secret plans. Her closed-envelope face.

But this was my idea, I remind myself, and when she climbs up onto the back of the truck, I jump up too. It's full of sacks of I don't know what, loose straw, and dirt. A few vests. A stack of brochures catches my eye: *Dolosalvus.* I almost point it out to Hurona, but I don't. For all I know, Dolosalvus is a hundred miles away. At least Petrichor is only fifty.

Hurona grabs for a sack of whatever is in the truck, strong from groundwork. I'm not as strong, but I grab the smallest of the bags I can see and struggle down off the truck, hoping I don't stand out too much. I don't dare look around to see if anyone notices. The other workers are young but not quite as young as we are, and they seem busy going in and out through the back gates, which, unlike the front gates, are open. Hurona doesn't speak, but she catches my eye, and together we move through the ivy archway into the backyard of Dr. Lunata Elemnieri's house.

This is why they planted the trees so thickly around the

211

property. I see very quickly that Lunata and her husband, Arlo, want to feel like they're in their own world. And in here, that's what it's like.

The sunlight pours down in golden pools. A sapphire pond ripples with a gentle waterfall. The grounds of the house stretch the entire block: There's a walking path and rose gardens and a greenhouse. Far across the yard, I spy the yellow Buzz Yard truck, the back open. I catch a glimpse of a figure that must be Zizi forking garbage in for the savior flies to crunch through. But I don't watch long, because that's when I actually see the house.

I'm pretty sure it could fit the entire town of Prine inside. The windows look like frozen lakes. The walls are pale pinkish-gold, like each brick was dipped in sunset. My eyes travel upward...and upward...and upward. It's massive. There are pointy turrets and then arching sections of roof that I can imagine over big empty rooms. They have to be empty. What would you fill a house so big with?

"Come on," Hurona mutters, and we trail the line of workers. They're making their way toward the greenhouse, which is also bigger than the house I share with Mom and Hurona. It's like a work of art: thick panes of glass bordered by curling ironwork. Inside, humidity clouds the glass and rolls down like slow rain.

The other workers drop the sacks by the greenhouse door, and we move to do the same. I feel like one of the ants I've spent so much time watching in Prine. All of us working together in a line, carrying and dropping, carrying and dropping. Does that make Dr. Elemnieri the queen? I learned when I was younger that an ant

212

only becomes a queen by accident. It's all about diet. One ant happens to get more protein in its diet, and suddenly she's the queen. But could a house like this ever be an accident?

I drop my sack, rubbing my aching arms as I straighten up. My eyes are still on the greenhouse, and I barely have to pry for my eyes to find the shape of a person inside.

"It's her," I whisper, grabbing for Hurona. "She's right there!"

It is.

Dr. Lunata Elemnieri, the woman who had saved so many lives with her invention of the lockwood. She's just beyond the glass, standing at her long worktable that's covered with plants and tools and scatterings of dirt. A workshop like my mother's, but instead of a soldering iron there's water and soil and sunlight.

Dr. Elemnieri is like a version of sunlight: Her dark skin seems to soak in the warmth of the greenhouse, the humidity almost making her glow. Gold glasses are perched on the end of her nose as she studies something in her palm. Her hair is pulled up into a puffy bun. She looks older than on TV, and more beautiful.

"We could just go in," I whisper, taking a half step forward. "Right now."

Hurona's staring through the greenhouse glass intensely, but not at Dr. Elemnieri. Her eyes dart past her, seeking something more. Whatever is in her eyes seems to glow brighter now that we're here.

"What?" I demand. "What is it, Hurona?"

But before she can answer, someone else is saying her name. We spin around, and I trip on one of the sacks we'd dropped off at the greenhouse door. I stumble backward, bang my elbow on the glass. It doesn't break, but it sounds like it. I'm expecting security, and my heart is already hammering, but when I look up I don't find a gray uniform. Instead it's someone wearing a worn brown shirt, and a thin brown face above it, with eyes I know both well and not well. A patchy beard I don't recognize.

"Oh my god," Hurona cries, and jumps to hug him. My sister never hugs anyone, so it takes me a minute to see why. She's beaming his name:

"Carver!"

31

"**WHAT ARE YOU** two doing here?" Carver says. He looks so much like Banneker in small, quiet ways that it makes me want to cry.

He used to be skinny like Banneker, and parts of him still are. His wrists are fine; the work gloves he wears are loose around them. But he has new muscles, and his shoulders are broad. Other things are different too: He doesn't have the circles under his eyes that we all do in Prine, from too little light and too little sleep. In Petrichor, Carver has bloomed. I wonder if he knows how much Banneker misses him. How the envelopes of money he sends are enough to pay bills, but not enough to fill the Carver-shaped hole in Banneker's heart.

"I came to find work," Hurona says. "Do you work here? For Elemnieri?"

"Not exactly." He shakes his head, then raises his eyebrow. "I do what you two were just *pretending* to do. We take care of the land. Bring mulch and supplies. Mulch right now. Dr. Elemnieri likes to do the stuff in the greenhouse herself, though. So we just leave it here." He lowers his voice. "I saw you two grabbing bags and sneaking in. What are you *doing?*"

"A question I, too, would like the answer to."

The greenhouse door has just swung open, and Dr. Lunata Elemnieri steps out into the sun, peeling off her gloves. Hurona jumps back and Carver goes very still.

"Anyone?" she says. "Anyone?"

"We...we need to talk to you," I say, and feel Carver's eyes on me. Nearby, a few of his fellow landscapers slow their steps and watch.

"There are phones, you know," Dr. Elemnieri says. She's half smiling, but her eyes are like scorpions. "I don't typically have interviewers show up at my house." She lets her gaze wander from the sacks we had dropped to the walkway leading to the back gate. She puts it together in her head. "Many shades on the spectrum between *calling first* and *sneaking in the back door.*"

"It's important," I say. Hurona had said the truth wouldn't get us inside, but we're already here. And Dr. Elemnieri's eyes are like two searchlights sweeping over our faces. I don't think I could lie if I wanted to. But how do I even start to say the truth?

Two security guards wearing gray uniforms have paused where they're walking near the house. I see Dr. Elemnieri's eyes take them in, and they notice, then, that it's her, that she's out of the greenhouse and talking to us. They immediately make their way over, and Dr. Elemnieri doesn't wave them away. I think of how I would feel if two people snuck in my house while I was trying to read a book or take a nap. I feel squirmy with guilt.

"Is everything all right, Dr. Elemnieri?" one of the guards says as they approach. Their frown is like the crease in their uniform pants. "Is there a problem?"

"Well, there definitely is," Dr. Elemnieri says, and her eyes are still like scorpions. But I had learned at some point that scorpions aren't always trying to sting you. Most of them are just trying to live, like everything else. "But I'm not sure how big that problem is at this point."

"You two," the guard says, settling their eyes on me and Hurona. Carver's work gloves must make it more obvious that he's where he's supposed to be. "Come with me. We're going to have a chat with your boss."

They curl a finger at us, stepping away. I look at Dr. Elemnieri, who watches with an almost amused look on her face. She had already put together that we aren't landscapers at all, and I think for her it's like an experiment. Waiting to see what will happen, what we'll do.

Hurona doesn't move right away, and I don't either. Carver's big brown eyes glance between the two of us, the same worried face as Banneker's. The security guard notices, and snaps, "Move along, sir."

Carver hesitates, then slips his phone out of his pocket and bumps it against the square shape poking through Hurona's back pocket.

"Transferred you my number," he says. "Call me. If you need me."

"Is this your boyfriend?" Dr. Elemnieri asks Hurona, not

teasing. Actually curious. She has the same kind of mind as my mom, I think. Probing. Always looking for answers.

"No," Hurona says, flustered. "An old friend."

But the security guard is tugging at her sleeve now, their eyebrows like caterpillars.

"Young lady," they say. "Come with me."

The other guard has a device that they're speaking into, telling someone on the other end to prepare an "incident report." That's when I start to feel a little wild. Because paperwork is what Miss Jinnah pulls out when the FOLROY trucks are about to purr to life and leave Prine. Paperwork is what happens when things are finished. And I'm not finished here.

"We're from Prine," I say quickly. I only look at Dr. Elemnieri. Not the guards. Not even Hurona, whose face has lost that closed envelope look and is something else entirely now. She looks lost. She looks like the younger sister. "We came all the way to Petrichor to talk to you. We need your help."

The guards stop, surprised. The puzzle in their heads adjusts, like a maze cube being twisted and turned. They realize what Dr. Elemnieri had known all along: We are not gardeners. We are here for another reason. The tall one's face flushes red.

"Both of you are coming with me," they say, and now rather than Hurona's sleeve, they're holding her arm.

She doesn't pull away. She doesn't say anything until the other one grasps my elbow, and then she snaps. "Get off my sister!"

"Everyone, please relax," Dr. Elemnieri says, sighing. "It's barely ten o'clock."

"Ma'am," the guard says, and I'm not sure if it means *okay* or *what now?*

Dr. Elemnieri doesn't even reply. She studies us a moment longer, and I can almost hear the sound of scorpion claws clicking together as she thinks.

"All right," she says, as if deciding. She turns and opens the door to the greenhouse, leaning in to toss her gloves on a bench inside. She points at me and Hurona. "You two, follow me, please. At ease, folks."

The guards exchange a confused glance, but Dr. Elemnieri is already marching off toward her massive sunset-colored house. She doesn't even look back to make sure we're following. I guess she doesn't need to—it's either go after the thing we say we came for, or go with the guards and their incident report. Hurona touches my shoulder. Not a push but a question: *Ready?* I don't know. So I just shrug, and we both follow.

Dr. Elemnieri enters the house through a side door, and as we step inside behind her, we're hugged by the smell of lavender. There are bundles of it hung everywhere. But they're the only plants I see. Pinnia's house had been covered in plants, but Dr. Elemnieri has only the lavender and a couple of ferns that I see hanging in windows as we're led down a long bright hallway.

"Here we are," Dr. Elemnieri says, and makes a turn into a wide doorway. We follow her, and I almost gasp when we step inside.

If the rest of the house is like a desert, with no greenery at all, this room is like a jungle.

There are plants on every surface. The gold-rimmed windows

are filled with leaves and blossoms. Hanging from the ceiling are planters like small boats, with vines overflowing. The wide desk that Dr. Elemnieri sits at is made of rich dark wood, but its surface is almost invisible under a combination of plants and papers. Dr. Elemnieri is sitting behind the desk and staring at us, her two pointer fingers propping up her chin, but I'm too busy taking in what must be her office. There is a gold chandelier at the center of the ceiling, and even it has plants weaving between its crystals. She looks up and laughs a little.

"Not many people come in here," she says. "I forget that it might seem a little shocking at first. I have to keep most of my plants here in the office, you see. My husband, Arlo, has a lot of allergies. He never sets foot in the greenhouse."

"Probably a good thing that he can't be around your work," Hurona says, and I glance at her, confused. She shakes her head. "So you can focus, I mean."

"I've never had an issue with focus," Dr. Elemnieri says. "I've realized that when you find the thing you're called to do, you have trouble focusing on everything else. But never that."

"Is that why you made the lockwood?" Hurona says. "You were called to do it?"

Dr. Elemnieri frowns a little, not angry, but serious.

"That was a different kind of call," she says. "I had already been working on a substance that made plants grow faster without compromising their safety. Fast-growing plants. There have been a lot of advances in science and society to tackle food insecurity. I was very successful at that. But then I was called—an actual call

220

on the phone." She pauses, smiling. "They wanted me to apply that research to a hardy plant they had already bred. They needed fast, and they needed fireproof. The fireproof part was easy, actually. There were already plants I could learn from that existed naturally: California fuchsia, French lavender, sage. Yellow ice plant. Ornamental strawberry. Then trees like hardwood and cherry. They're not quick to burn like pine or cedar."

I listen, fascinated. I've heard her talk about the lockwood on TV, but the interviews always seem so shallow. They ask her more about how her dress was designed than how the lockwood was designed.

"How long did it take?" I ask.

"A year," she says. "You would've just been babies when the lockwood first was planted. You probably don't remember how bad the wildfires were at that time. Do your parents talk about the Arborklept?"

I glance at Hurona, whose face is hard. She doesn't answer, so I don't either.

There's no more scorpion in Dr. Elemnieri's eyes now. She looks sad, like everything she's feeling drips blue paint. I know that look. That's my mother's face on the rare occasion she talks about the past.

"A lot of people were lost," Dr. Elemnieri says. "And a lot of trees. Forests older than us all, older than almost anything else."

"And you made something better," Hurona says. I find myself glancing at her again, shocked by how sharp her words sound. It brings the scorpion back to Dr. Elemnieri's eyes.

"Not better," she replies, just as sharply. "But something that will help us survive. Not just humans, but the remaining forests. We didn't just plant the lockwood around towns and cities. We planted it around *forests* too."

Hurona stares at her, and I can barely believe it, but her eyes are shimmering. Hurona is about to cry, and it makes me feel short of breath. She had cried out on the highway waiting for the bus, but her girlfriend had just abandoned her. That made sense. But this doesn't. And a Neaux crying twice in one week seems like a violation of nature.

"Hurona," I whisper, but she refuses to look at me. She's staring at Dr. Elemnieri like she hates her. And even though the lockwood has taken a lot from us, has made us shrink, I can't understand blaming Dr. Elemnieri. Unless she knew. Did she?

"Why are you here?" Dr. Elemnieri says, and Hurona opens her mouth to speak, but I'm afraid of what will come out, so I talk quickly instead.

"FOLROY has been secretly making the lockwood grow back overnight in Prine," I blurt. "And no one in Prine knows except us. My sister and I saw the drone. But everyone else thinks the lockwood grows back overnight by itself. And we can't get solar power if we don't cut it back. And I have to wake up at four every day to cut it back, because if I don't we can't live. And nobody can afford to move. We give FOLROY all our money to buy tools. And now they want to pay us in tokens. But they're the ones making it grow. And it turns out that the pods are actually super valuable? But no one in Prine knows that. And . . . and we never see the sun."

I pause, out of breath, and my eyes are stinging now too. Beside me, Hurona's jaw is steel. We both look at Dr. Elemnieri, waiting for her to speak, but she just stares at us. Then I realize that all my words had been as twisted and confusing as the vines of the lockwood. I take a deep breath, but it's Hurona who talks now.

"FOLROY is exploiting the town of Prine," she says softly. "FOLROY needs the pods, and they keep the lockwood growing so that they never run out. But we're running out of life. And we... we wanted to know if you knew about this."

There's a sound behind us, and me and Hurona turn to look at the same time Dr. Elemnieri's eyebrows arch up. There's a woman in the sloping doorway, as slender as one of the clippings of lavender. Her hair is straight and short and the color of bone, stopping at her chin. Her eyes shine green in the jungle of Dr. Elemnieri's office.

"Doctor Lunata," she says. Her voice is sharp and quick like hail on a window. "Your husband is back from the junket. He wants to know where you'd like him to put the letters."

Beside me, Hurona shifts.

"The letters?" Dr. Elemnieri says.

"Fan mail." The woman smiles. "There was a high school bused in to hear Mr. Arlo talk, and, as usual, they had words they wanted to pass along to you."

"Oh," Dr. Elemnieri says, then laughs a little. "He can bring them here. If they go out to the greenhouse the paper will get dirty, and I want to read them. Poor Arlo. I hope his feelings weren't hurt."

"I think he's used to being the . . . less cool scientist at this point," the woman says. She seems to look through us before she nods at Dr. Elemnieri and then disappears.

"My assistant," Dr. Elemnieri says. "A townland girl, like you. If you had told me twenty years ago that I would even have an assistant . . ."

She trails off, then her eyes fall back to us.

"Prine," she says slowly. "It was one of the first towns to get the lockwood, if I remember. Yes?"

"Yes," Hurona says. "The very first."

"They changed the approach after the first," Dr. Elemnieri goes on. "Instead of planting it in a ring, they planted strips. Firebreaks. We had never planted so much of it: We didn't understand how it liked to knot in on itself once it got out into the air. The governor begged us to move fast, so we did. But mistakes were made."

"Mistakes," Hurona says, and her voice sounds small. She sounds like she could fit through the lockwood again.

"It can't be uprooted," I say to Dr. Elemnieri. "You know that, right?"

"Of course."

"And they spray it every night. We can't leave. And they make it impossible to stay. So what are we supposed to do?"

"What do you mean they spray it every night? FOLROY?"

"Shouldn't *you* know?" Hurona says. "Don't you work for them?"

"I do not work for FOLROY," Dr. Elemnieri says evenly, seeming to ignore my sister's tone. "I am an independent researcher and always have been. The partnership with FOLROY was to quickly produce the lockwood, and since the completion of that partnership, I have continued working as I work best—alone. My husband is on the board of FOLROY and those are his affairs."

"FOLROY sends a drone," I say. "From Petrichor. I watched it water the lockwood. I watched it all start to grow. Everything we'd cut that morning, growing back like...like...magic. Like a monster."

"Who else knows about this?"

But before we can answer, there are heavy footsteps out in the hall, the booming voice I know from TV echoing against the windows.

"Where is my wife?" Arlo Kylak calls. "Where is my beloved and her green thumb? I come bearing adoration from your many devotees. Why are you in your office so early? Did you discover something in your greenhouse? Did you—"

He swings into the doorway of her office, his smile as bright and natural as it is on TV. His hair is a perfect shade of brown, combed up and back in a chestnut wave. He wears a suit with no tie, his shoulders broad underneath the jacket. His voice trails off when he sees us, all the boom trickling away. Me, Hurona, and Dr. Elemnieri are all turned to stare at him, and I wonder if she'll ask him to stay or if she'll want to finish talking to us alone. If he'll be as confused as she is.

But Arlo Kylak doesn't look confused. He looks pale. The healthy tan that Petrichor provides is like ink leaking out of his face. He's suddenly as pale as a Prinian. I glance around, alarmed, wondering if he's having an allergic reaction to one of Dr. Elemnieri's

225

plants. His eyes are locked, but not on Dr. Elemnieri. He's staring at Hurona.

"What—" he begins, but whatever is happening inside him grabs his tongue and holds it tight.

Hurona talks just fine.

"Hi, Dad," she says. "Nice to see you too."

32

WHEN I LOOK at Arlo Kylak again, I see my sister's nose and eyebrows. When his mouth opens, then closes, I see my lips. I'm too busy staring at him to see what Dr. Elemnieri's face looks like. I only hear the sound she makes, which is nothing. Which is to say I hear how silent she is.

We're all silent. Hurona seems to be the only one breathing. She had been tense and glinting before this, but now, with Arlo Kylak staring at her white-faced, it's like she's a rubber band that had been stretched between two fingers and finally shot across the room. Now she's relaxed and loose, staring at the man who she says is our dad. The man who I thought was dead.

When he finally speaks, his voice has lost the boom I heard from the hallway. Instead it sounds like dry leaves:

"What is happening here?"

"I came to find you," Hurona says. I don't even look at her. Just because I'm hearing something for the first time doesn't mean it's a lie. This is another thing that Hurona has kept behind the sealed secret of her face. "And Erie came too. You probably don't even recognize Erie. She was just a baby when you left."

"Arlo...," Dr. Elemnieri says slowly, quietly. If Arlo's voice was a dry leaf, hers is the wind blowing it.

"Lunata, I don't know what's going on," he says, looking past Hurona and me toward Dr. Elemnieri, who is no longer sitting behind her desk, but standing, fingertips planted on its surface.

"I was going to tell you too," Hurona says, turning to address Dr. Elemnieri. "But then Erie saw the drones. And that seemed a little more important. But honestly it's better this way. Telling you when he's here."

"Telling me what?" Dr. Elemnieri says. Her eyes don't shine and her lips don't tremble. A bit of that scorpion is back.

"We're his daughters," Hurona says. "He was with our mom, Nadine Neaux, for eight years. He left when I was little. We mostly just pretend he's dead, but ever since he married you, he's been on TV a lot, and it's kind of gotten a little hard to ignore. Here, I have this photo. You also left your toolbox when you went to Petrichor, Dad. But I didn't bring that."

Hurona reaches into her back pocket—it's the folded paper she slipped out of her bag before we snuck in. I only see it for a moment before Hurona passes it—my mother, young and smiling, and Hurona beside her, already tall. Arlo Kylak is in the photo holding a baby with serious eyes. Me.

"You left one more thing," Hurona says. "The map that used to hang in the classroom. Your classroom. Your map. Erie left it in her bag where we're staying or I'd show you. Just as a refresher."

"What do you mean *his* classroom?" I say quickly.

"He taught at the school before Mr. Ovitt." She doesn't even look at me when she says it.

My lungs feel like they're too small for my body. I think back to when Hurona came to get me from school early—a "family situation," Mr. Ovitt said. I remember Mr. Ovitt's face when Arlo Kylak was onscreen. *He knew.* The screen at home was smashed when we got there, and Hurona had asked if Mom watched the Newscast. The one with Dr. Elemnieri and Arlo Kylak. And Mom had said yes. The smashed screen, the screwdriver thrown across the room. How many of Mom's storms were from seeing his face?

"Erie," Hurona says. She turns to me. "I'm sorry I didn't tell you sooner. I was supposed to be coming alone. Then when you saw what you saw in the lockwood, I knew I had to change my plan. Originally I was going to come and show up at the press junket he did today." She glances at him and I do too—his eyes are wide, but the color is coming back to his face. "But I figured we needed to tell Dr. Elemnieri what we saw first."

I want to say something. I want to yell at her. I want to yell at everyone. But as usual, everything important feels stuck inside.

"Why?" Arlo says. "Why are you here?"

"Does that mean it's true?" Dr. Elemnieri says quickly. The photo tells her the truth, but I can tell she wants to hear it.

"No," he says. Then squeezes his eyes shut. When he opens them again, they're on his wife. "Yes. But it's more complicated than it seems."

"It's pretty simple actually," Hurona says. "You left us and you took what my mother..."

"Stop," he says. The boom is back in his voice. "You're a child and you only know what one person has told you. Your mother is..."

"What?" Hurona snaps. "Crazy? My mother is a genius. And you—"

"Hurona," he says. The sound of my sister's name in his mouth makes my knees tremble. I can tell by the way he says it that even if the photo wasn't proof enough, what Hurona is saying is true. He knows her name. Not just her name. But he says it like a name he's always known. "I know for you it must seem simple. Your mother has been telling you for years that I left, and now that feels like the truth...."

"Don't do that," Hurona says quickly. "You're lying. Erie may not remember because she was a baby. But I was not a baby. I remember."

"You were very young," he says softly. "Your mother asked me to leave. This was what she told me I had to do."

"You mean steal from her?" Hurona says, raising her voice. "And lie about it? For years?"

The woman with the bone-blond hair and green eyes is back in the room. I don't actually know when she got here—her feet are as soft as a cat's. She stands watching, listening. Dr. Elemnieri sees her too and says, "What is it, Urtica?"

"The landscapers need you to approve the placement of the samples before they plant them," she says.

"Don't they know what they're doing?" Dr. Elemnieri snaps.

"Ah, yes, I think so, but they say they always get your final confirmation before they put anything in the ground."

Dr. Elemnieri stares at her assistant, the room silent except for the air-conditioning blowing the leaves of a nearby fern.

"I'll be right back," my father's wife says, her scorpion eyes flashing. At us, at Arlo, at everyone in the room. "Maybe you three can decide what you're going to tell me by the time I get back."

Hurona and I stand aside to let her pass, watching as she pauses by Arlo's shoulder. She stares at him, a long stare, and I think if she actually was a scorpion, that barbed tail would be trembling. Instead she brushes past him, following Urtica down the hall. When we can't hear their feet anymore, Arlo begins to speak.

"I never wanted this," he says, his big hands held out in front of him. "I never wanted to be gone while you grew up. Honestly, I'm so glad this day has come. Now you're old enough to come and find me on your own, without your mother telling you what to think."

"If you're so glad we came to find you," Hurona says, "why didn't you send something so we knew *where* to find you?"

"I send money every month—" he starts.

"From FOLROY," Hurona snaps. "White envelopes. Not your name. Not your address."

"So how did you find me then?" he says sharply, and then closes his mouth fast.

Hurona doesn't even answer. She just smirks. When I was still little, this was the only thing we really fought about. How she could lead you into saying what she wanted you to say, even if you didn't mean to. Arlo Kylak didn't mean to say what he just said.

"For the record," I say. This is what Banneker always says when they're about to make a great point. "For the record, *I* wasn't even looking for you. I was looking for Dr. Elemnieri. And I found her. And I don't really want to talk to you. I want to talk to her."

"And tell her what?" he says. He looks kind of desperate now, and the paleness is back.

"That the lockwood is ruining things in Prine," I cry. "That I can't even go to school or finish a book. That all my friends' big brothers and sisters have to leave and move to the city if they want to find work. The lockwood is *her* invention. She should do something about it."

"Surprised you haven't found a way to steal that too," Hurona says, and Arlo looks at her with more of the whites of his eyes showing than he has so far. He reminds me of the mountain lion we'd seen in the lockwood all those years ago, fleeing the fire.

"Hurona," he says, "I don't know what your mother told you. . . ."

"I figured it out myself," Hurona says. "Mom just confirmed it."

"Confirmed what?" me and Arlo both say.

"That you stole Mom's discovery," my sister says, her eyes shiny. "That she was the one who first sliced open the pods from the lockwood and started running experiments. *She* was the one who discovered the mineral that has made FOLROY all that money. And *you* stole it."

The world seems slippery. Everything I thought I knew feels

232

like it's sliding out of my hands and out from under my feet. It feels like falling, and I can't help but think of Helia, the way I hadn't even seen her fall. Just heard her. Heard the slapping of her palms as she tried and failed to find a hold in the trees my not-dead father's wife grew. I can't find a hold either. When I do find a branch in my mind, it has Aunt Josie's voice: *I said I don't trust him. You can be as smart as you are and a genius inventor and still get fooled.* I know I don't know everything, but this feels solid: *This* is the man who Aunt Josie didn't trust. And my sister says she was right not to.

"You haven't invented anything else. Have you?" Hurona says. "Haven't discovered anything? That's because you never *have*. You attached yourself to Dr. Elemnieri the same way you attached yourself to my mom. You're like a . . . like a parasite."

"You don't know anything about me," Arlo says. He takes a step forward, finger outstretched. "I have taken care of your mother. I never stopped taking care—"

"Of *us*?" Hurona laughs. It's ugly and snarly and it makes me cringe. "How? Sending envelopes? Allowing your youngest daughter to think you're dead? Leaving us to rot in the townlands with no future? While you live . . . here?"

She gestures all around us, at the massive building that he calls home, and the grounds beyond it, like its own private park.

"Lunata does a lot of good," he says. "She donates a third of her income, did you know that? On top of paying taxes! She does a lot of good—"

"And what do *you* do?" Hurona interrupts. "What good do *you* do?"

The room returns to silence. I can't stop staring at the man who is—was—my father. He held me when I was a baby. How do you hold a baby and then leave? How do you decide her future isn't your problem?

"I can make this right," he says, sighing deeply. "I can move you to the city, I can find work for you."

"And leave my mother in Prine?" Hurona snorts.

"We can't leave Mom in Prine," I cry.

"No, no," he says quickly. "No, her too. Okay? How would that be? I'll pay for everything. I'll find you an apartment, I can help you find...what? A job? An internship?"

"What about everybody else?" I say. "What about Banneker?"

"Who's Banneker?" he says, bewildered.

"My best friend," I say. "What about them? What about everybody else? If we just leave, that doesn't help anyone left behind. The lockwood will just keep growing, and FOLROY will just keep using them. We can't just *leave*."

"I'll talk to Lunata tonight. How does that sound?" he says. His eyes are brighter, his eyebrows higher. "We can all fix this together. I can make this right, but I need tonight. Tonight I can discuss everything with Lunata, and then I can come pick you up tomorrow. Where are you staying? I can have Urtica drop you off and then tomorrow we'll go find an apartment. Okay?"

"What about Mom?" I ask.

"I'll send a car for her tomorrow if that's what you want," he says. He sounds like he does on TV again. Cheerful and in command. He talks like he's the captain of a ship steering across a wide blue ocean.

"And then what?" Hurona says. She sounds different. Hopeful. "You find us an apartment and jobs and then what? You go back to pretending we don't exist?"

"We can talk about that too," he says, and he looks hurt, but something about it feels like TV too. An advertisement. "I'll be whoever you want me to be."

I hear footsteps down the hall, two sets of steps.

"Tomorrow?" he says quickly. "Tomorrow. We'll get this all figured out. Together."

Dr. Elemnieri appears first, her eyebrows stormier than when she left. Urtica pops in behind.

"So?" Dr. Elemnieri says, eyebrows arching, but Arlo is turning to her with a hand held out.

"Urtica is going to give the girls a lift home," he says. "We're going to all meet tomorrow and discuss some things. I'll send a car tomorrow at noon. Girls, is that all right?"

"We know where to find you if you don't," Hurona says, and I try to keep my face flat, but I can't help but stare at her, at this person who is my sister. Hurona has never been sweet or friendly. It's just not who she is. But she's never been mean. I think again of brimming cups and jars. It turns out Hurona was brimming with years of anger, and now it's spilling over the sides onto Dr. Elemnieri's marble floor.

"You can follow me if you're ready," Urtica says. She's moved

235

out into the hallway to give us room to pass. Her eyes are less green away from the plants. I glance at Dr. Elemnieri. She stands stroking the leaves of one of the ferns, her gaze traveling between us and Arlo.

"I'll see you tomorrow," she says. It almost sounds like a question, like she's reluctant to let us leave. But I can't tell. She probably wants us gone so she can ask Arlo the questions that I can see stacked up in her eyes like a tower of books. I wonder if she's mad or sad. I think of my mom, the screwdriver she'd smashed our screen with. She doesn't choose between mad and sad—it always seems like she's both at almost every moment. Maybe Dr. Elemnieri is the same, and I guess I am too. Because when I look at her face, I see a woman who has spent the majority of my life with the man who was supposed to be my dad. But how can I blame anyone but him?

"Come on," Hurona says, and she follows Urtica into the hallway, taking us back the way we came. I walk alongside my sister, our hands almost touching. If we were alone, I'd already be talking to her, demanding answers and details. But the museum of Dr. Elemnieri's house doesn't allow it, and even after we retrieve Hurona's bag from the alley and get into the car—a small, zippy red thing with a solar engine—there's no space for conversation. I don't even know what to say. The farther away we get, the madder I feel. I'm glad when Hurona sits up front so I don't have to see anything but the back of her head.

Urtica is so skinny she might as well be from Prine, but her presence is like a giant balloon that squeezes against me in the back seat. None of us speak until we make our way down the front drive,

236

toward the gate me and Hurona had passed while walking. I peek out the window before we disappear down the lane. I don't see Zizi or the Buzz Yard truck anywhere, and I sigh in relief. Zizi technically did nothing wrong, but I don't want anyone looking at her for how me and Hurona came to be here. The same for Carver.

"Do you have an address?" Urtica says. Her voice is exactly what I would think of an assistant's sounding like. Chirpy like one of the birds on the green street we make our way down. A little like a robot.

I tell her, and she taps it into the screen on her steering column.

"I know you haven't been here long," she says. "Only a few days, I imagine?"

"How'd you know?" I say.

"You can always tell when people first get to Petrichor from Prine," she says. "Once you're here a bit longer, you'll blend in a little more."

"How long have you worked for Dr. Elemnieri?" Hurona asks.

"Four years."

She guides the car onto the speedway. None of us say anything for a while.

"You've come looking for work?" Urtica says eventually.

"Yep," Hurona answers.

I wonder if Urtica knows that the pods are worth a lot of money. I still can't make it make sense in my head—how basically everyone but the people of Prine know. The lockwood keeps out more than fire.

"What about your mother?" Urtica says.

237

"What about her?" Hurona says sharply.

"I may have overheard a bit of your conversation with Dr. Elemnieri," Urtica answers. "Does she know why you're here?"

"How many sources of pods are there?" Hurona asks instead of answering. I would say she's reading my mind, but she's not—our heads are both just filled with the same thing.

"What do you mean?" Urtica says.

"Prine isn't the only place with lockwood," Hurona says coolly. "So I'm assuming we're not the only town that harvests pods. Do you know how many other towns there are like us?"

Urtica pauses. I can tell Hurona notices it too, but in her way—her head tilts ever so slightly sideways, like a puppy listening. I realize more and more that me and Hurona really are like the lakes we're named for: two different bodies filled with versions of the same stuff. She has a feeling about Urtica. And even though I don't get a feeling, I notice things. I notice that Urtica is gripping the steering wheel very hard.

"Prine is the only town that harvests pods," Urtica says.

"Why?" Hurona says. But Urtica ignores her.

"If you're looking for work," Urtica says, steering the conversation the same way she steers the car, "there may be an opportunity you might be interested in."

"Working for Dr. Elemnieri?" I ask. I'm remembering what Hurona said, about coming to Petrichor and working for her.

"No," Urtica says, and clears her throat. "No, there's a new endeavor the governor is offering very soon. Good work with benefits—"

"You're talking about Dolosalvus," Hurona interrupts.

"Oh, you've heard of it!" Urtica says cheerfully.

"Seems like a lot of people have," Hurona says. I can hear the frown in her voice.

"The governor has everyone's best interest at heart," Urtica says. "It's an excellent opportunity if you're someone who likes to work hard."

She guides the car onto Hauc, then pulls up outside Pinnia's blue house. Urtica turns slightly in her seat to address both me and Hurona.

"Here we are," she says in her clipped voice. "I urge you to consider Dolosalvus. Your mother might prefer it to life in Petrichor. It can be difficult to adjust to city life after the townlands."

"You seemed to do just fine," Hurona says.

Urtica pauses again, and when she finally speaks all she says is "Yes."

A moment later, Hurona and I are on the sidewalk watching Urtica's red car murmur down the street.

"She seems like she knows more than what she's saying," Hurona says, but now that we're alone again, everything that has happened feels like it floods back over me. Sisters are supposed to be on the same side. But are we?

"Sounds like someone else I know," I snap, and turn toward Pinnia's house.

"Erie," she says, and I know I'm supposed to be mad, but I still look back. "I'm sorry I didn't tell you."

"So why didn't you?"

"Because I'm the big sister," she says. "I wanted to protect you!"

"Well, you didn't!" I cry. I have too many things I want to say. Everything feels upside down. "You knew about our dad. You knew about the pods. You knew about...everything!"

"What would knowing have changed?" she demands. "Other than making you sad?"

"I don't know! I always feel like there's so much I don't know and...and you're part of the reason why!"

I turn and stomp toward the blue house, hugging Aunt Josie's jacket around me. The farther away I get from my sister, the more everything hurts. But maybe that's just the way some things are.

33

FROM THE OUTSIDE of Pinnia's house, the roof is flat except for one place in the middle where there's a lone window sticking up like a periscope. This, I found out, is Pinnia's room. It's tiny and kind of hot and basically an attic, and it's the coolest place I've ever seen. When I stand up and explore her space, she lets me, not asking any questions about Lunata or Arlo.

"What's your room like in Prine?" Pinnia asks from her bed.

"Not like this," I say, admiring everything. "My room is like a cupboard. Like somewhere where you store crackers."

"Do you decorate it?"

"Not like this," I say again.

Pinnia's room reminds me of my mom's work shed, but more cheerful. She has these tiny strings of what look like beads strung back and forth over our heads, attached to the walls. They glitter with light from the window.

"What are these?" I ask, touching them lightly. "Crystals?"

"Nope." She grins. "Guess again."

"Glass?"

She opens a drawer in the small dresser next to her bed. She pulls something out and holds it up.

"Is that a mushroom?" I ask.

"Yep," she says. And then she points at the strings of light. "And so are those."

"No way!"

"Uh-huh. They're fungus filaments. I was messing around with them one day in the backyard and realized when you dry them out, they get really sparkly. So I started experimenting with them, rolling them out to see how thin I could get them."

"They look like thread!" I cry. I get my eye really close to them now, examining them.

"Cool, right? Now if only I could get the polybeetles to stop eating them in the backyard. I might try selling shroomstrings at the market if I can get a good supply of them. That's what I call them—shroomstrings."

"Good name," I say. "Have you tried sprinkling garlic around the garden bed? Polybeetles are like vampires. They won't go anywhere near garlic."

"Wait, seriously? How do you know?"

I shrug. "Learned it from *The Encyclopedia of Entomology*. Then I did it on my own to see if it worked."

"That is so cool." She grins. "You should work at the Buzz Yard!"

I keep studying her shroomstrings. I feel like all the things I want to say are too big to fit in my mouth, or even in this room. I *want* to work in the Buzz Yard. I imagine everything happening the way Arlo Kylak—my father—said today at the mansion where he lives with Dr. Lunata Elemnieri. Moving to Petrichor. My mom leaving not just our house, but Prine. And Banneker. Could we really make it so that Banneker can come too? But what about everyone else?

"You thinking about your dad?" Pinnia says quietly.

"Kind of," I say. "But he's not really my dad."

"You still thinking about *that guy*," she says, and smiles.

I smile too. "Yeah, I guess so."

Pinnia had noticed right away that I didn't want to talk to Hurona when we got back. So we came up here and everything came flooding out of me. I have no idea what my sister is doing. I don't care.

"I just don't know why nobody told me," I say. "Like I'm a baby."

Pinnia makes a face and leans again the wall behind her bed. "I don't get why parents decide you can know some stuff and not other stuff. They think they know what we can handle and what we can't, but I'm kind of the only person who knows that. Nobody knows me better than me."

"Exactly!" I cry. She scoots over on her bed, and I take it as permission to flop next to her.

"Did you tell your sister what we found at the conservancy? The letter?"

"No," I say, frowning. "And I'm not going to."

"Petty," she says. "But I get it. I had an aunt that died too."

"Really? In the fires?"

"No. It was actually a doctor's fault."

"Oh…"

243

"She was having stomach pain and kept telling her doctor, and he didn't believe her. Kept telling her to lose weight like that would solve everything. It turned out she needed surgery, but by the time they figured it out it was too late."

I look down at my fingers. They're knotted together.

"I'm really sorry," I say.

"Thanks. Mom was sad for a long time. She still gets sad. Her sister, you know."

"Is the surgery your mom needs the same kind of surgery your aunt needed?"

She shakes her head.

"No, Mom is going to have surgery to finish her transition. But it's really expensive without a medical pass." She pauses, frowning. "I really hope we don't move to Dolosalvus, though."

"The lady who brought us here from Dr. Elemnieri's was talking about it too," I say. "So at least if you go, maybe we'll be there together."

"Well, that would be cool, at least," she says. "But if it's anything like Prine..."

She looks at me sideways and we both laugh.

"I think my mom was mad that my aunt never visited Prine," I say. "But...it's *Prine*."

We laugh some more. It feels weird to laugh about the things that hurt. But it does make them hurt a little less. I don't think anyone could ever laugh about the Arborklept, but maybe if Mom would at least talk about it the pain would begin to fade.

"Can I listen to one of your aunt's messages?" she asks. She seems a little hesitant, like she's asking me something personal. I guess she is. But I kind of get it. She has a dead aunt too. She probably thinks about ghosts as much as I do.

"Sure."

I reach into my bag and find the phone, and we both lean close to hear Aunt Josie's voice.

> You can't ignore me forever, Nadine. I need to talk to you. Not everything is always as it seems. You don't have to believe me. But what if I had proof? Remember icebergs? I know there aren't many anymore, but I like the way they remain in our language. Just like that, when something dies, we shouldn't forget it—we should discuss it and love it even if we can't bring it back. Otherwise how do we really know what we've lost? I hope the elephants never leave us, but if they do, I will go on saying the elephant in the room. Like the one between us. Please, Nadine. This is an iceberg, I know. A little above the surface, but so much more below the water. What is it that's under the water for you? So cold and so deep you can't talk to your sister? I'm still here. Later.

It feels like we're quiet for a long time after the message ends.

"They're not usually that long," I say.

"It sounds like your mom—Nadine?—hadn't been answering her calls. So I guess your aunt had some stuff stored up."

"I wish I knew what made them stop talking," I say. "It must have been really bad."

"Maybe. But maybe something small. I mean, you're not talking to Hurona right now."

My heart feels stretchy, like one of the shroomstrings strung from wall to wall.

"It has to have something to do with Arlo," I say. "I wonder what the proof is she was talking about. Proof of what? Proof that he was going to leave us?"

I hear someone shouting downstairs, and I jump, startled, until I realize it's just Ms. Mari. She's yelling something in Spanish, and then singing.

"Time to clean." Pinnia grins, standing up. "We're having a cookout!"

I'm not exactly sure what a cookout is, but I stand up eagerly, because she seems excited. And it sounds like food.

"Is your mom mad?" I ask, listening.

Pinnia listens too, then shakes her head, rolling her eyes.

"No, she's still talking about some cleaning product they stopped making a long time ago. Fabuloso. Every time we clean she goes on and on about how nothing else is as good. We still call all the cleaning stuff Fabuloso, though."

"Like icebergs and elephants," I say, and she laughs, and we go downstairs and sweep all the dust from the house out into the sunshine. By the time people start to arrive, everything sparkles, and it makes it easier to forget everything in my life that doesn't.

34

I'VE NEVER SEEN so many people laughing in my life. Maybe once when I was still a little kid, when a bunch of us played hide-and-seek in the lockwood before we knew what the lockwood really meant.

But it was different than this: here, out in the last hours of the sunshine, everyone crowded together and showing off different dances. I watch from the gazebo, where I sit by myself in the hammock where Ms. Mari takes naps. Zizi is at the cookout too, and Mento makes his way over to her. He cruises through the party little by little, winding an indirect path. It makes me want to smile. But I can't quite make myself.

The envelope from Aunt Josie's box sits on my lap. In the light from the lanterns in Pinnia's backyard, I can easily read my mom's name on the front. I said I wasn't going to open it. It's for my mom. But now I know for sure that if I gave it to her unopened, what's inside it would disappear into a hole along with everything else: the truth about the pods, the truth about my father. Hurona and Mom keeping all the secrets, and me like a hound dog always trying to sniff them out.

So I open it.

It was written a long time ago, and even though the envelope is made of thick paper, it barely resists my thumb under the flap. Inside is a tiny memory chip housed in a plastic case, and a single piece of paper. The words written on it only take up half the page. A feeling of disappointment gnaws at me. I had wanted pages and pages. A whole book even. Everything that Mom and Hurona ever kept from me spelled out letter by letter. But Aunt Josie wouldn't have known that—she never even met me. And that fact makes me feel even worse.

Dear Nadine,

Maybe by the time you're ready to talk to me, I can give you this in person. You haven't been answering my calls, so I figured I'd do things the old-fashioned way. Did you know Mama used to write letters? I've always been a chatterbox just like her. You're more of a steel trap, like Dad. Anyway, they're sending me down to rescue birds. You've probably heard by now—there's a big fire that they say is getting bigger. Might be the biggest. I'm glad you're safe in Prine—I know they're working hard to plant more of that tree everywhere else. But remember, Dina: You can't stay there forever. We can't hide from the world and still make it better. I believe that you will make the kind of choices that will create the changes we've already dreamed about. Sometimes we just have to get out of our own way first.

I won't repeat what I told you during our last phone call. You're like Dad in another way too—you only really hear something when you're ready. But when you're ready, watch what's on the chip. It will prove what I told you. Footage from Samantha. I know you don't see it, Nadine, but I'm your sister. I have to tell you the truth, even when it hurts.

Love,
Jojo

All the letters swim together when I finish reading. I hold the paper close to my face, but I don't smell anything. It smells like nothing, the way there's so much nothing around Aunt Josie. I don't understand how Mom can just walk around and pretend she never had a sister. Especially one who told her the truth.

I take out the chip that has been in that envelope at the conservancy all these years. It fits in the center of my palm. I imagine what's on it: a bird's-eye view of the treetops, Petrichor like an ant city far below.

"What is that?"

I jump, almost dropping everything onto the floor of the gazebo. Hurona stands in the entryway. Behind her, everyone is still dancing and laughing and eating. But I don't answer her. I fold up the letter and tuck it away inside my bag with the chip.

"Nothing."

It makes me feel a little queasy. I know she doesn't believe me—I don't have as much practice with lying as she does. I wonder if this is how she felt when she lied to me about our dad, about the pods, about Iva. I guess she wasn't even outright lying. She just wasn't telling me. Is a blank space still a lie? I suddenly think about the lakes that dried up—empty craters where water used to be. Even if we fixed everything on Earth that needs to be fixed, would they ever fill up again? Or are some things—and people—just gone when they're gone?

Hurona crosses the floor and plops into the hammock next to me. We swing back hard and I gasp, steadying myself.

"You're missing the party," she says.

When we first got back from Dr. Elemnieri's, we had to promise Ms. Mari that we were okay and everything was fine. Then we jumped into helping get ready for the barbecue, slicing jicama and jackfruit and pushing sweet potato fries around in the ovens. Ms. Mari had been impressed that I knew how to make black bean burgers. By the time the guests had started arriving, the whole house smelled like a party. But the party hadn't made its way into Hurona's eyes, or mine.

We both stay quiet for a long minute.

"Mom wanted to pretend he was dead," she says suddenly. "That was easier for her. You know, after what he did."

This time I stay quiet because I'm surprised. Hurona talking first is like a dog opening its mouth and meowing. Down in Pinnia's yard, her dogs Head and Tail move through the party like fluffy tumbleweeds, looking for scraps. Hurona keeps talking.

"It wasn't my secret to tell," she says quietly. "And eventually, as you got older, I realized why she didn't want you to know. She wants you to be strong. And with everything that happened, Mom doesn't think she's strong. I think it's less that she didn't want you to know about...*him*. It's more that she didn't want you to know about her."

I'm confused, so I finally speak.

"About Mom? Know *what* about Mom?"

"That she's not a fighter," Hurona says. "As the years went on and they started sending kids into the lockwood, she knew that we would need to be fighters. To...to make it. And she isn't. I think she's ashamed."

"But Mom *is* a fighter," I say. "Every Tuesday she goes to the square and tries to sell an invention, even though they always tell her no!"

Hurona sighs.

"She could have left Prine, Erie," she says. "But she didn't. She's known about the pods all this time—they were *her* discovery. She could have spoken up. And she didn't."

On top of my bag, I can feel the shape of the sparrow I had taken from Mom's workbench the day we left Prine. I reach inside and pull it out. It seems like we left a long time ago. I stroke its tiny, smooth body, knowing it was built by my mother.

"Does anyone else know?"

"About the pods?" She shakes her head. "Maybe a few. Like Mr. Ovitt. But he never liked Mom. So I think he lets himself believe that Dad...Arlo...was the one who discovered the pods and Mom is just jealous."

I think back to school, the day Helia died. Mr. Ovitt had behaved so strangely when Arlo Kylak was on the screen. I thought it was because he had a crush on Dr. Elemnieri, but he had looked right at me. Then I remember what I told Banneker in the trees when they asked about what my mom was working on: *She hasn't invented anything but the headlamps.* It's like I had swallowed everything that Prine says about her, and made it my truth. But it's not the truth.

"So everybody knows Arlo is our dad," I say quietly.

"All the adults. And most of the older kids. Banneker doesn't know, I don't think. Unless Carver told them. But everyone sort of agreed not to talk about it."

"Why?"

"Because it's ugly," she says, shrugging. "And they have bigger things to worry about, I guess. It's hard to care about two kids when you have your own and FOLROY is taking every penny you earn. Plus Mom has always been ... you know, the way she is. Antisocial. She never left Prine, and after Aunt Josie died, she never left the house. Then Dad was gone pretty soon after that."

"Are you two going to come dance?" Pinnia says, hopping up onto the gazebo. Her bangs are stuck to her forehead with sweat. She looks down at the sparrow in my lap. "What's that?"

I hold it up. I suddenly want to brag about my mom. I want to tell the whole world how brilliant she is, what she has done. What she's lost.

"One of my mom's inventions," I say. "It's called a sparrow. She's still working on it—this is a prototype. But it's supposed to be a robot that can fly up into tight spaces and run tests and emit frequencies."

"Can I see?"

I place the sparrow in her palm, and I watch her face as she admires it. I want everybody to look at what my mom has done this same way.

"This is beautiful," she says. "Your mom is really good. How does it turn on?"

"I actually don't know," I admit. "It has those tiny solar panels, but they're not activated."

"Let me see," she says. She pulls a bobby pin from her hair. "Do you mind?"

"I mean, okay," I say. "But please please please don't break it."

"I've never broken anything in my life," she says with a smile. But I believe her.

Her eyebrows bunch down and she holds the sparrow as carefully as if it's an egg. She uses the bobby pin like a tool, finding a tiny little latch I hadn't even noticed. It lifts a solar panel and exposes a little patch of circuits, the inside of the sparrow.

"I think I see . . . ," she says to herself. Then her eyes rise to my face. "Be right back."

She darts from the gazebo to her back porch and inside, leaving me and Hurona looking at each other in surprise. But she's back a moment later with a little jar of what looks like white dough.

"What's that?"

"It's this stuff I made," she says. "I call it Puttia. Get it? Putty, but my name, Pinnia?" She laughs to herself. "It's kind of like a glue you can use to stick wires and stuff together. But it's semiperma-nent, and it lets currents pass between it."

"You just…made it?" Hurona says, impressed.

Pinnia grins. "I make a lot of things."

She places the sparrow gently on the gazebo rail and then unscrews the Puttia. Using her bobby pin, she dips out a tiny bit and quickly transfers it to the inside of the sparrow. She blows on it gently, then uses the other end of her bobby pin to replace the solar panel. I hear a soft click as it latches. When she places it on the rail again, the solar panel glows green.

"You did it!" I cry. "What did you do?"

"Just two circuits not quite connecting that needed to be bonded. No biggie."

"My mom would think Puttia is so cool."

"Thanks," she smiles. "Being an inventor is hard, though. Sometimes I make something and then it turns out that somebody already did it first."

"Our mom says the best inventions aren't always the ones that make something entirely new," Hurona says. "But making some-thing that improves what already exists."

"That's true," Pinnia says thoughtfully. After a minute she tilts her head at us. "So are you two talking about what happened at Dr. Elemnieri's house? I still can't believe you actually spoke to her. What was her house like? Did you get a tour?"

I shake my head. "We weren't there for very long—and just her office. Maybe I'll see more tomorrow. They're going to send a car to pick us up. I guess to have like an official meeting."

"About the lockwood in Prine?" she says, raising her eyebrows. "That's a good sign!"

"Yeah, I guess so."

She comes and sits next to us on the hammock, and we scoot to make room, the three of us swinging. I wish Banneker was here, squished between us, all of us in the sunlight. *Soon*, I think. *Soon*.

"I won't be mad if FOLROY flops," she says. "They're like the worst company ever. They treat their workers like mud, and it's going to end up biting them in the butt."

"What do you mean?" Hurona says.

"Mami has a saying too." She smiles. Ms. Mari is standing at her solar grill, flipping black bean burgers and doing a little dance, heel-toeing her feet and swaying her shoulders. She's laughing. I wish my mom would laugh like that. "She says that you can only treat people like mud for so long before the mud starts to thicken into clay, and clay will always become something else. Even if it only becomes a bowl, you can't step on a bowl like you step on mud without cutting your feet."

I think about this for a minute, and then Zizi and Mento are leaning over the rails of the gazebo, grinning. Their shoulders touch. It makes me blush for some reason. I think about Banneker, how often their shoulder has brushed mine. I wonder if we'll always be friends.

"Y'all talking about your little adventure today?" Zizi says. "Can't believe you did it. And without getting me fired. So, thanks for that."

She's wearing a flower crown and a bee appears out of nowhere, buzzing around her ear. She doesn't bat it away.

"We got lucky," Hurona says. "And Erie was smart."

I blush for a whole new reason now.

"We got lucky," I repeat.

"We're talking about how FOLROY sucks," Pinnia says.

"Don't say *sucks*!" Ms. Mari calls from the solar grill. Somehow her voice carries over the music.

"How did she hear that?" I whisper, and we all laugh.

"It definitely does, though," Zizi says, glancing over her shoulder at Ms. Mari and grinning. "Not too many corporations like them left. I guess it's easier to hide how bad they are when they pretend they're helping people."

"Dr. Elemnieri doesn't work for FOLROY," I say, still thinking about where she fits in. "So maybe she's not like them?"

"She works *with* them, though," Hurona says, and I can tell she's mad at Dr. Elemnieri. Even if it doesn't make sense to blame her for what our father did, sometimes pain doesn't make sense. Like accidentally stepping on a dog's tail, and the dog biting you. Dr. Elemnieri didn't mean to step on our tail. She didn't even know our tail existed.

"Sometimes when people do stuff like what Dr. Elemnieri's doing," Zizi says, "it's not out of a lack of goodness, but"—she pauses, thinking—"a lack of imagination."

"This conversation is really boring," Mento says, yawning loudly. But he bumps Zizi with his shoulder and grins and I know he doesn't mean it. He looks at me and Hurona. "You two haven't eaten yet. Stop moping and come get a plate. Your strategy session can wait."

Hurona glances at her phone—I wonder if she's still waiting for Iva to call. Or maybe she's thinking of calling Carver. I wonder if we can see him before we go back to Prine. I want to tell him about how much Banneker misses him. I wonder if when we have our meeting with Arlo tomorrow we can try to convince him to bring Banneker to Petrichor too. Let them see everything I have seen. Let them see the stars that the lockwood blots out.

"Come on, come on," Pinnia says, tugging on me. She waves at the sparrow. "Leave that and let it charge. I wanna see what else it can do when it's powered up. Come on, let's eat."

35

WE EAT. WE dance. I've danced before, of course. But not for a long time. The old speaker in our house hasn't even been turned on for two years, since I was old enough to go into the trees. But the speaker in Pinnia's backyard isn't a fossil, and Eya rigged it so it seems like the music comes from everywhere.

I don't know who the other party guests are, but Pinnia and her family seem to love all of them, and everyone eats and laughs, and when it starts to get dark, Mento programs one of his drones to circle above the backyard with lights flashing like a disco ball. I don't even know what we're celebrating, but it doesn't matter. I feel like I've known Pinnia and her family my whole life.

I'm out of breath, but Hurona is still dancing and I stand at the edge of the party watching her. She's smiling bigger than I've ever seen, and the drone's lights flicker orange and pink across her face.

And that's when I realize: She definitely can't go back to Prine.

She looks bigger and stronger right now, twirling around with Ms. Mari, than I've ever seen her. Well, not ever. Before she went into the lockwood, she could climb a tree faster than anyone else. I remember her standing in the branches and crowing down at me. She always wanted to be a bird.

But after the lockwood, she started to shrink. There's no space for my sister in Prine. And I think that even if we stop the lockwood and the people making it grow, Prine will always be a place that hurts. I want my sister to be somewhere she can dance. Arlo *has* to bring her to Petrichor. He has to. I want her to be where she lets this smile out of the envelope of her face.

So when Mento threads through the dancing crowd toward my sister, and her smile falls, I feel something like a tarantula grip my heart. It feels like a bite. I wonder what he's saying, but then her eyes wander the crowd and find me catching my breath. She says something to Mento and then comes over.

"Where's your bag?" she says.

"On the gazebo."

"Grab it. Dad is here. I mean, Arlo."

"What?" I say. "I thought they were coming tomorrow."

"There's a car waiting for us out front." She shrugs. "I guess he decided he wanted to talk sooner."

Pinnia meets me at the gazebo. I grab Mom's sparrow, which, with the help of the Puttia, is fully charged and glowing a ghostly white.

"Are you sure you don't want to tell them to come back tomorrow?" Pinnia says. "We haven't even brought out the cake yet! Mami makes really good cake."

"I bet she makes really good everything," I say. Hurona's already inside getting her bag, and I head that way too.

"It's kind of late," Pinnia says. I hear worry scratching in her voice.

When I pick up my bag, I slip the sparrow inside. It's nestled in there with Arlo's map of Petrichor and Aunt Josie's jacket, the envelope tucked back in its pocket. Everything and everyone together. I'd brought the sparrow so I could keep Mom with me on our trip to Petrichor, but now it also feels like I'm carrying a piece of Pinnia too. She's the one who made it glow, after all.

"Are you sure about this?" Pinnia asks.

"It'll be fine," I say. "I kind of think this is better. The sooner we can start talking about what's happening in Prine, the sooner we can fix it. And...I know it's weird but...I'm kind of homesick."

"I get that," Pinnia says. But she's still frowning, and she's frowning the whole way out across the front yard and to the sidewalk, where Urtica stands waiting by the car. It's not the red one from before, it's a longer black vehicle with dark windows. Hurona is waiting next to Urtica.

Pinnia's hand catches at the strap of my bag.

"Did you tell my mom you were going?"

"I couldn't find her," I say, hesitating. "Should I go back in? You can tell her we'll be back later. Or maybe tomorrow. Dr. Elemnieri's house is huge. We might just stay there. I promise we'll come and see you before they take us back to my mom."

"Okay," Pinnia says, still frowning. "I'll tell her. Be careful, okay?"

"I will," I say. "Don't worry."

"One more thing," she says, and catches my arm. She hands me a tiny tin, like something you'd put breath mints in.

"What's this?" I say, confused.

"Puttia." She grins. "Just a little bit. So you remember me. If, you know, you get too busy to come back and say bye."

I tuck the tin into my bag with everything else and look her right in the eye.

"I'm going to come back," I say. "We're friends."

Then I turn to the car. Urtica opens the door. Hurona is sliding in, and I move to follow.

"Thanks for everything," I say to Pinnia, who nods. But her eyes are on Urtica.

The inside of the car is warm after the chilly night air. The seats are smooth and it smells like cedar. I'm surprised when Urtica slips in on the other side of Hurona instead of riding in front. I press over a little bit against my door to give my sister more room.

"Nice to see you again so soon," Urtica says.

"Yeah," Hurona says.

"I thought Arlo was here?" I say.

I'm a little confused when the car starts to roll forward, because I assumed Urtica would be driving again. But there's a man in the front seat instead, not Arlo, who steers the car down Pinnia's dark street. I can see the stars out the window, and the skyline of downtown Petrichor. Something else glows in the corner of my eye, and when I look, I see that it's the driver's uniform.

It's bright white and glows softly. When the driver leans forward to check traffic on the street ahead, I see that the back of the uniform reads FOLROY.

36

JUST LIKE THAT, it feels like we're back in the lockwood around Prine.

My whole body is tense, like it's clinging to itself instead of a branch. Next to me, Hurona is motionless, but she's tilting her head the way she always does when she gets a feeling. There's a mountain lion in the car with us.

I slowly turn my head to look at Urtica, who is already staring at me. Maybe *two* mountain lions. But Hurona looks frozen. I remember the look on her face when she said she should have known better about Shelly, the woman on the bus. She has that same look on her face now.

"Dolosalvus?" the driver says. I don't understand, but Urtica ignores him.

"You gathered all your things from your host's house?" Urtica says to us.

"Yes," Hurona answers.

"What does Dolosalvus have to do with anything?" I ask, but

Urtica is typing something on her phone and ignores me. The driver might as well be a robot.

The car is cruising over a glittering bridge. We had driven to Dr. Elemnieri's house from the Buzz Yard this morning, but I can tell we're already on a different route. I suddenly remember Banneker mentioning the compass Carver used to carry in the lockwood—I wish I had a compass right now. But without one, something inside me says that the car is going the wrong way. *We* are going the wrong way. Hurona still sits frozen.

"Why are you picking us up tonight instead of tomorrow?" I ask. I can't let Hurona always be the one who has to speak up. "Did he change his mind?"

"There are some things that were said at Dr. Elemnieri's house today that are pressing," Urtica says. "Some things that can't wait until tomorrow."

"How do you know?" I say. "Did Arlo tell you?"

"It's my job to know," she says. Her green eyes are hidden in shadow now, but I'm watching close. I can see her eyes flick up toward the driver. He's looking back in the rearview mirror at her.

"Do you work for Dr. Elemnieri or FOLROY?" I ask her.

Her eyes zap back to my face just as the car exits the bridge. The highway is up ahead. A different highway than the one that had taken us to Dr. Elemnieri's.

"I work for the governor," she says.

And just like that, whatever was frozen in Hurona thaws. She turns to me, and I almost jump at the laugh that comes out of her mouth.

"Erie," she says brightly, chuckling. "What are you *wearing*?"

"Wh-what?" I stammer.

"Is that a *bra*?" She laughs. It sounds too loud in the car. It makes me feel scared. "Did you take that from my room? You have the strap all twisted, I can tell. Let me fix it."

She's stuffing her hand inside the neck of my sweatshirt. I stiffen. Her voice is weird and high, but her hands are steady. Determined. I can feel her fingers find the bra strap that I'm so unused to wearing. Then there's something cold against my skin and I almost jump again.

"Little sisters," she says to Urtica and the driver, who are both frowning. "Can't live with them, can't live without them!"

She's shoving something under the strap of my bra, square and thin. I realize very quickly it's her phone. With her body in front of me, blocking me from Urtica, she reaches with one hand and quickly unlocks my seat belt.

"Now," she says, leaning across. "The other side. Let me get that fixed for you."

Everything happens so fast.

Hurona yanks the seat belt off my body, untangling my arm. Urtica is quick too—she heard the click and saw the nylon belt whip off. She snatches Hurona by the shoulder, both of them still bound by their own seat belts. Hurona is the only one she can reach. But my sister has already grabbed the car door's handle. It swings open as the black car arrows toward the speedway. We're not going very fast—the ramp up to the quick-moving lanes is lined with other cars. Hurona shoves me hard, screaming, "Go, Erie! Just like I taught you to fall! Roll and then run! *Run run run!*"

I curl my body like she's shown me since I was little. I'm hurtling toward black pavement. The stars are a blur above me and my sister's screams are a blur behind me.

I land on my shoulder, rolling onto my back, then rolling again, three more times. I keep my neck curled, my face protected. Just like Hurona taught me. I can still hear her screaming for me to run, so even though my body aches and my head is spinning, I stagger to my feet. The squealing tires of the car are both a sound and a smell.

I turn and I run, away from the highway. Away from the bright lights. I see trees somewhere ahead of me, can hear the call of night birds. I think I'll be safe where they are. I just have to get there first.

I hear another car, close, someone shouting. Footsteps. I run and run. I know it's adrenaline that makes me move faster, even with my bag across my chest slamming against my hip. I've never been this fast. It feels like a gift from my sister. I run until I'm surrounded by the dark shadows of trees and don't stop until I'm surrounded by black. It's not as black as Prine, but it's close, and it's comfortable. I stumble, then slow.

My breath is wheezing out of me. I collapse against the roots of a tree, and only when I can feel its bark against my back do I start to cry. The Neaux household doesn't cry, but the Neaux household is in Prine. And this is Petrichor.

37

I CRY FOR a long time. Or what feels like a long time. I freeze every time the wind blows, wondering if Urtica and her driver have tracked me down. And every time I realize it's just the wind, I'm both relieved and crushed. Because if they haven't found me, that means Hurona hasn't either. It means Hurona is locked in the back seat of a car with two people who are worse than mountain lions. And I am here. Alone.

I sit curled with my arms wrapped around my knees until my chest starts to ache. It takes me a minute to realize the ache is from Hurona's phone pressing into me. I yank it out, my hands shaking. I hate that I'm holding this phone, because it means Hurona's not here. She had known what she was going to do. She had secrets, a plan to protect me. Hurona was doing her duty as a big sister.

Little sisters have a duty too, I tell myself, and that's when I stop crying.

Hurona gave me the phone so I could call for help. That's obvious. But who do I call? Pinnia had said that kids like us are never treated seriously. If I call Petrichor's police unit they'll just say we're runaways, and maybe even try to take me into custody because I'm a kid. With no papers. And Hurona will disappear with Urtica in the black FOLROY car. Would the police believe FOLROY had been involved? Would they even look for her? Probably not. I tap around on the phone's screen, figuring out the menu. There are only two names in the contacts: Carver and Iva. I call the one I trust most.

Carver answers quickly.

"Hurona," he says. I can hear the smile in his voice, the one that looks like Banneker's. "I'm so glad you called!"

"Carver, it's me," I choke out. "Erie."

"Erie? Are you okay? What's wrong?"

He's somewhere loud, but the noise behind him softens. I hear a door shut.

"Carver, they took Hurona," I cry. "They said they were taking us to see our father but they lied. They took Hurona."

"Your father?" Carver says. "Hurona told you? About Arlo Kylak?"

"Yes, but now they took her," I say. My voice is getting louder and louder. It doesn't matter out here in the trees.

"*Who?*" he says. "Who, Erie? Who took Hurona?"

"FOLROY," I sob. "They came in a black car and they took her. She made sure I got away but she's...she's..."

"Take a deep breath," he says. "Where are you? I can come and get you. I can help. We can figure this out."

"I don't know where I am," I cry. "I'm in the woods. Hurona pushed me out of the car and I ran."

"That's okay," he says. His voice is soothing. He's always been like this. The gentle big brother to Banneker. Now to me. "It's okay. Walk until you see a road—go a different direction than the way you came—and then when you get there, find the setting on the phone that says SEND LOCATION. It will send me your coordinates and I'll find you."

"Okay," I say shakily. "Okay."

"You can do that?"

"I can do that."

"Okay. Go. Don't stop. And if you see anything suspicious, run. Okay? Run. We're gonna figure this out."

I hang up, and with the phone screen dark, I'm soaked in the black of the woods again. Maybe I would be more scared if it wasn't for the moon. The moon, and the chirp of crickets. I know crickets, and crickets know me. I listen to their song the whole way out of the woods, and when I find myself on a quiet side street, I do what Carver told me to do.

There's one more number in the phone, and I dial it while I wait.

Iva's phone rings and rings but she never answers. I think of how I had climbed into the back of her van on Tuesday, and how she had smiled. Now I think of her smile and want to punch her in the teeth. I pull up the messages she and Hurona had sent back and forth. It feels wrong to read them, so I don't. But I do send one more:

FOLROY TOOK HURONA AND IT'S ALL YOUR FAULT.

Five minutes later, Carver is pulling up. He runs to me and pulls me into a hug.

"Did they hurt you?" he says. He looks like he's going to cry. "Are you okay?

"I'm fine," I say. I don't tell him that under the sleeve of my sweater, it feels like my skin is on fire from rolling on the road. I don't even want to look at it. Tears well up again. "But they have Hurona."

"We're going to figure this out," he says. But the look on his face tells me that he doesn't even know where to start. "Do you have any idea where they took her?"

"I can't think," I say. "The car was just...going. I don't know!"

"And it was a FOLROY car?"

"Yes. I mean, I guess. The driver had a FOLROY uniform."

"They must have somewhere they're going to keep her," he says. "They're probably going to be out looking for you in the meantime."

"But where would they take her?"

"I don't know," he says. "I still don't know Petrichor very well. I only go to and from job sites. I can maybe ask my friends."

"No, no," I interrupt. "I need to get back to my friends and ..."

Then another thought occurs to me—a piece of what Urtica had said that had gotten shadowed in all my fear.

Dolosalvus.

"And I think...I think I need to warn them, Carver. About Dolosalvus."

"The governor's new project? The ag work town? What's that got to do with anything?"

"I don't know," I say, shaking my head. "But the driver said something about it, and Urtica told me she worked for the governor.

Something is not right. Can you take me to my friends' house? I have to talk to them."

"You have friends?" he says, raising his eyebrows. "Already?"

I haven't seen Carver in two years. I realize how much older I must seem to him. I step into the feeling like new shoes.

"Yes," I say. "Now let's go."

But then I turn to what he drove.

"What ... is that?"

It's clunky and green and only has two tires.

"It's a solarbike," he says, smiling. "There's a sidecar on the other side, see? Get in."

I scrunch into the sidecar. With the helmet on, I feel like I'm about to blast off to outer space. Carver puts his on too.

"How's my sib?" he asks as the whole solarbike starts to vibrate.

"Banneker is good," I say. But then I realize that's not true. Not entirely. "They really miss you. Things in Prine are ... bad."

I fill him in while we drive, shouting over the sound of traffic. Carver zips us between cars, and by the time we pull up outside Pinnia's house, he knows everything. When I tell him I'll be right back, he doesn't speak. I've only seen Banneker angry a few times—once when I'd pretended I'd accidentally cut my finger off in the lockwood. They didn't speak to me for six hours. Carver has the same quiet storm in his eyes. Like everything I've told him about what FOLROY is doing to Prine is a smog that rolls over his face. I'm almost to Pinnia's door when he calls after me.

"So you're telling me I left Prine for no reason? That I could be with my sibling and my mom? If FOLROY hadn't been making the lockwood grow? Prine could have been—could *be*—something else?"

I nod, and the look in his eyes hurts. He shakes his head, silent, and I turn to knock on Pinnia's door.

It takes some knocking. Only a few windows are lit, and it's quiet. No music coming from the backyard. When the door eventually opens, it's Mento. He looks sleepy but not like he's been asleep.

"Erie," he says, surprised. "Sorry, I was in the basement working on footage now that everybody's gone. What's up? Where's Hurona?" He sticks his head out, looking around. When he sees Carver on the solarbike, he frowns. "What's going on?"

I take a deep breath.

"FOLROY kidnapped Hurona. I need your help."

If Mento looked sleepy a minute ago, now he's wide awake. He doesn't speak for a half second, and then he turns and shouts into the house.

"Pinnia!" Silence. "Pinnia, quick!"

She stumbles to the door, a book in her hand, and like her brother, when she sees me, her eyes clear.

"They took Hurona," Mento says before she can ask. "FOLROY."

Pinnia's eyes widen.

"Where? Where?" she says. Then she says it three more times, like she's short-circuiting.

"I don't know," I say. I ball up my fists. I feel like crying again, but now's not the time. I tell myself I left my tears in the woods. "I don't know what to do. Are your parents here?"

"They're both at work," Pinnia says, her voice trembling.

"Mami is driving the bus and Mom caught the line out to ag work. It would take them hours to get back."

"Eya didn't go to Dolosalvus, did she?" I demand.

Mento and Pinnia both look confused.

"No," Pinnia says. "She applied but she won't know until next week. The town doesn't actually open until..."

"She shouldn't do it," I interrupt. "I have a bad feeling."

I tell them what I told Carver, that Dolosalvus will just be another Prine that will leave its workers penniless and its owners rich. A storm cloud appears on Mento's face.

"This is why I went to the plaza that day," he says. "I don't trust the governor. He's never cared about ag workers before—he's part of the reason Mom hasn't been able to get a medical pass. They want us to keep their city green, but they want to keep us invisible. I knew if there was a reason he was suddenly acting friendly, it had to be a trick."

"But what kind of trick?" Pinnia says.

"I don't know," Mento says. "But I'm going to find out."

He turns back to me.

"I know where FOLROY headquarters is," he says. "In the financial district. I've filmed them tons of times with my drones. Should we go and see if they have your sister there?"

"They wouldn't take her there, would they?" Pinnia says. "It's in the middle of the city. People would see!"

Carver joins us, walking up from the solarbike. I introduce him and they all mutter hellos. Everyone is grim, scared. But I think more than scared, I'm angry.

"Or I could go to Dr. Elemnieri's house," I say. "She and Arlo have to know where they took her, right?"

"How would you get in, though?" Carver says. "It's almost the middle of the night. With her security, you wouldn't even get close."

I ball my fists up even tighter. I feel helpless. I feel like I'm dangling from a lockwood vine, about to fall. In my mind Hurona is already falling. I have to catch her.

Suddenly I hear music. Soft and low, just a few bars of a tune. Then it repeats again.

"Erie, is that your phone going off?"

"I don't have a..." I start, confused at first. Then I remember. Hurona's phone in the pocket of Aunt Josie's jacket. No one has ever called it before, not while I was around. I pull it out and we all stare at the message on its screen.

Iva: *She's here.*

And then her location turns on.

"Oh crap..." I breathe.

"What is it?" Pinnia cries. "Is it Hurona?"

"No," I say, and I want to cry again. I shove all the feelings down. "It's my sister's girlfriend. She...she knows where Hurona is."

"She does?" Carver cries. "How?!"

"Because her girlfriend works for FOLROY. She just sent me the location. It can't be Dolosalvus—it's too close."

"If it's close, then let's go," Carver demands. "Now!"

"We're coming too," Mento says quickly, and Pinnia nods.

273

"You can't," I cry. "I have no idea what's going to happen! And your parents are going to freak out...."

"I like to think my parents would freak out if they knew I stood by and did nothing," Mento says seriously.

"And this is about us too," Pinnia adds. This is one of the first times I've seen her not smiling. "If Dolosalvus is some type of trick or a trap, then we need to stop it."

They both look so determined I know there's no sense in arguing with them.

"Okay, but *how*?" I say. "We can't all fit on your solarbike, Carver!"

We all look back toward the road. We would look ridiculous, the four of us smashed and piled into the bike and its sidecar.

"True," Carver mutters.

"Then we have to make a call," Mento says, and even though everything is terrible, he smiles. "And there's only one person I can think of."

Pinnia groans, and even I can't help but laugh. Even as my eyes feel burny with tears.

38

TWENTY MINUTES LATER, Zizania pulls up in the yellow Buzz Yard van. She leans out of the window, smiling.

"I just left the party two hours ago! You already miss me?" But when she sees our faces, her smile drops. "Oh no. What happened?"

"We'll explain on the way," Mento says. He climbs into the tiny seat behind the driver's seat, the drone he had insisted on bringing in his lap. Pinnia and Carver follow. "Erie, you ride shotgun so she can see directions."

I climb in next to Zizi, and as soon as my seat belt is on, we're moving. It's hard to believe that at the start of this day, I got in this truck to go to Dr. Elemnieri's house, thinking my biggest problem was the lockwood. How can so much change in a few hours?

"Do you think your dad—" Zizi begins.

"He's not my dad," I snap. "He's just some guy who used to be my dad."

"Okay, fair. Do you think…*he* did this?" she asks, following the map my phone gives. "Like, would he order the kidnapping of his own daughter?"

"He didn't *seem* evil," I say. "But he definitely seemed like a shady... a shady..."

"Bastard!" Pinnia cries from the back seat.

"Pinnia!" Mento gasps. "What the...? Don't curse!"

"Yes, but *that*," I say. "He seems like a greedy jerk."

"He was never a good guy," Carver says quietly. I whip around to look at him.

"So you like *really* remember him?" I say. "And you didn't tell me?"

"Your mom and Hurona said he was dead. I thought that was true. It seemed easier for them not to talk about him, so I didn't. The older you got, the less it mattered."

I nod, but the tears sting my eyes again. I wipe them away angrily.

"What do you remember?"

"He was the schoolteacher for a while," Carver says. "He never seemed to care. He was always talking about *industry*." He curls two fingers on each hand. "It's like he thought climate change didn't have anything to do with him? You know? He wanted to talk about business all the time. Stocks and shares of companies and stuff. I was thirteen. I didn't care about that crap."

"Sounds like the governor," Mento says, scowling. I hear him shift the drone in his lap and he pulls out his phone. "Let me see...."

Pinnia leans over.

"What are you looking at?"

"Public record search," he says. "Business permits. Hmm. Erie, looks like your dad and the governor are both on the board of FOL-ROY. Shareholders."

"What's that mean?"

"It means since Arlo Kylak has been in Petrichor, he's been trying to get rich. He owns part of FOLROY, basically. Majority shareholder as of last year, it looks like."

"And what's *that* mean?" I sigh, feeling stupid.

"So basically a board is like a group of people who make decisions about what a company does. Like if the company was a plane, the board is the pilot. And shareholders are people whose money is connected to how well a company does. A company has a certain number of shares, and since Arlo is a "majority shareholder," that means like it sounds: He has more shares than everyone else. It means he has power. If the board ever took a vote on what happens to the company, Arlo's decision as a majority shareholder could tip the scale. He might even have the power to do other things, like pick board members who could make decisions that agree with his. So if there are things he personally wants, he can steer the whole plane toward it."

"Okay, so..."

"Okay, so he's a businessman," Zizi interrupts. "Which doesn't necessarily mean he's *evil* evil. But that remains to be seen. I'm honestly thinking more about the governor. If Dolosalvus isn't actually something to help ag workers, then the odds are it's just a ploy for him to get rich. If so...then you better roast him in the footage, Mento."

"I have a feeling the flames will be hot," Mento answers.

"Dolosalvus uses public funds from the citizens, from people like us. So, if the governor is putting it toward a project that will make him richer? Yikes."

"And my dad is probably doing it with him," I say through gritted teeth.

Zizi makes a sympathetic face but shakes her head. "Who steals his wife's invention, and then runs off and marries a celebrity? He lives in a fancy house while his own kids are barely getting by? What a *bum*."

"He *is* a bum," I cry. "Ugh!"

This all feels like I'm living in an alternate reality. Like going from a universe where my family's secrets are dust bunnies swept under a rug, to a universe where the rug is whipped up and thrown out into the yard. It's like broad noon with no sunglasses. So bright you have to squint. But the sunshine also feels good.

"Now about this girlfriend of Hurona's," Zizi says. We're getting off the speedway now; the van is slowing. "Can you trust her?"

I look out the window. We're on the outskirts of Petrichor. I can see a river, lit up by streetlights along a walkway. But there are hardly any cars. It feels lonely, empty.

"No," I admit. "No, I don't trust her at all. She left us high and dry on the way to Petrichor. So we have to be careful."

"What is even out here?" Zizi goes on, squinting through the windshield. "I don't think I've ever been this far north. The signal keeps getting jumbled."

"I thought these phones had great signals?" I say. "Like two hundred miles or something?!"

"Yeah, this is weird," she agrees.

"Could be they have a scrambler," Mento says from the back. "They started doing that for protest sites a long time ago. Mess up your signal so people can't organize."

"So do we just drive around until we see something?" Pinnia cries. "What do we do?"

"Wait!" I cry, and Zizi jumps. "I have a map!"

I yank it from my bag and open it on my lap, scanning it. Zizi glances over.

"That looks old," she says doubtfully.

"It's the bastard's," I answer.

"Don't say bastard!" Mento cries from the back seat. "Dios mio, you two! Los bebés!"

"Ay!" Pinnia cries. "Cállate!"

But I'm looking at the map.

"We're up there," Zizi says, glancing away from the road to point toward the top. "North. Do you see the river on there? Or the land bridge?"

"I see it," I say, squinting. "But it doesn't say there's anything up here. No buildings. Just looks like forest. And then the wall. And a big conservancy, it looks like."

Zizi frowns, then looks up at Mento in the mirror.

"You know of any conservancies up here?" she says. "We do all kinds of bug tours for the Buzz Yard pollination efforts, and I've never been up here. What's it called, Erie?"

I squint down at the page.

"Bongran? Bongrant? It's kinda faded."

Mento says a word in Spanish that makes Pinnia gasp.

"And you talk about *me*!" she cries.

He ignores her.

"The governor diverted funding from that conservancy a year ago," he says grimly. "I remember covering a protest for it. But then it fell off the radar. I never heard what they turned it into instead."

"I guess we're about to find out," Zizi says. "Look."

We all look out at the road, which had been dark as ink. There's a glow up ahead, though. I imagine it's what fire would look like before it's gone wild. It makes me shiver.

"I think I see something," Pinnia says from the back seat. She sticks her head between my and Zizi's seats. She squints through the windshield. "It's blocked by those big trees right now.... When we go around this corner, we should be able to..."

The Buzz Yard truck goes around the corner, and what lies ahead makes us all gasp.

"...see it," Pinnia finishes, her voice full of wonder.

It's a greenhouse. It makes the one in Dr. Elemnieri's yard look like a shed. It's massive, rearing up into the sky like a crystal globe. It catches moonlight, glowing like a comet. And inside, through the sparking glass, I can see the shadows of something I know very well.

"Lockwood," I murmur.

"This must be their growing lab," Zizi breathes, her neck bent so she can see the top of it. "Geez, it's huge."

"They've got Hurona in there," I whisper. "But why would they bring her here?"

"Maybe just to hide her," Carver says. "Like I said, they're probably looking for you. God, if Arlo and Dr. Elemnieri ordered this…"

"Who else would it be?" I cry. "They're the only ones. Unless…" I freeze.

"What?" Pinnia says. She shakes my shoulder. "What is it?"

"Urtica," I say. "Dr. Elemnieri's assistant. She was behind me and Hurona in the office, and I'm pretty sure she heard at least some of what we said."

"About the lockwood? And what FOLROY is doing?" Mento says.

"And she's the one who picked you up, right?" Pinnia presses. "That was her? The skinny white lady with the blond hair?"

"Yes, her," I say. I feel angry again. "She was supposed to be working for Dr. Elemnieri, but when I asked who she worked for she said the governor…."

"At this point, it sounds like FOLROY and the governor are the same thing," Zizi says quietly. She has parked the truck on the side of the road and we sit in stillness under the trees. I can hear the sound of night bugs buzzing and humming in the leaves. It offers a little comfort.

"At this point," I say slowly, thinking, "it doesn't matter. Whoever's fault it was, whatever's going on, Hurona is here. And now I have to go in there and get her."

"*We* have to go in there and get her," Pinnia says.

"You're staying in the car, Pin," Mento says, and they start to argue about it, but I'm looking at my phone, looking at Iva's last message: *She's here.* I stare at it for a second, and then I send a reply, wondering if the signal will work.

Get in?

She replies almost immediately.

South door. Hurry.

39

"**IF THIS IS** a trap...," Mento mutters for the third time.

"Stop being a punk," Zizi whispers.

We left the Buzz Yard truck, and the five of us creep in the shadows toward the greenhouse. There's a big dark parking lot, and the road that leads to the greenhouse like an artery to a heart. The closer we get, the bigger it seems. It's lit from the inside with soft lights that spill outside. The glass inside is fogged with the breath of plants.

"Which side is the south?" I say.

"The river is west, so that side," Zizi says, pointing.

"Stay in the shadows," Carver says, and we do. He glances at me as we jog. "You should've left your bag."

It bumps against my hip—I'm so used to it, I'd almost forgotten I'd worn it. I shrug.

The greenhouse seems to absorb all the light. It feels like something from another planet. Like we're about to enter an alien spaceship. Except what I can see inside toward the top of the greenhouse isn't alien to me.

Lockwood. Tangled arms of lockwood reaching up to the ceiling.

Then I see the door. It stands out from the greenhouse not just because it's not glass, but because it's open.

"If this is a trap," Zizi says. "It's a good one."

I turn around quickly to face the group.

"Mento, you have to stay out here," I say. "Use your drone and fly it over the greenhouse. Whatever happens, you need to film it."

"Already on it," he says, hefting the drone. But his eyebrows are low. "I can't let you go in there alone, though."

"I'm going with her," Carver says. "She's right about filming. If something happens, somebody needs to stay out here so we don't just disappear."

"I'll stay with Mento," Zizi says. "Nobody should be by themselves right now."

"Good idea," I say. I start to feel like I'm filled with bees. "Honestly, though, I'm the only one who should go in. It's my sister and..."

"Stop," Carver says, putting up his hand. "Stop. You're twelve. And I know you're brilliant and brave, just like Hurona and your mama, but I'm going with you."

"Me too," Pinnia says, and as Mento starts to argue, she reaches over and pinches his arm.

"Ow!" he cries, swatting her hand.

"Go film!" she snaps. "I'm going with Erie. She might need me. And if there's something iffy about Dolosalvus, I'm going to see it up close. I am not moving from Petrichor to some new city that may not even have a tamale cart or pizza or anything."

We're all silent for a minute and then Mento reaches over and pinches Pinnia back, hard, and then he takes off jogging before she can slap him.

"Be careful," Zizi says, glaring at us. She bumps her phone against Hurona's, clutched in my hand. "There's my number. Call me if you need me."

Then she jogs off behind Mento. They stay to the shadows. They melt into the night.

"Ready?" Carver says. His bushy eyebrows and sharp cheekbones remind me so much of Banneker. With the lockwood through the glass and something like my best friend's face in front of me, it's like being in an alternate version of Prine. My heart hums like a grasshopper's wings.

"I guess," I say.

And we enter the greenhouse.

40

THE SMELL OF green fills my nose. It almost makes me dizzy. But aside from the smell, there isn't much actual green. It's a greenhouse, but the lockwood is the closest thing to that color, with its dolphin-gray skin.

Everything else is a dizzying red.

"What is *this*?" Carver says softly. He sounds nervous, and I understand why.

The plants all look like blood. They spread throughout the entire globe of the greenhouse like a red ocean, rearing up in columns in some places. The lockwood shoots up from them in irregular patterns. They're not planted close together in a fire wall like in Prine—they're just scattered, like they've been allowed to grow naturally.

"These must be something new they've made," Pinnia whispers, bending to examine the red blossoms. They even grow from red stalks. "It doesn't look like any flower I've ever seen."

"We should keep moving," Carver mutters. "Stay close to the wall. Keep your eyes open for Hurona."

He doesn't need to tell me that, of course. My eyes are already prying the leaves for her. It feels like when we were little, playing hide-and-seek in the woods. Except back then, my heart wasn't pounding. Not like this. I'd always found Hurona when we'd played—like she always says, I don't miss a thing. I pray I don't miss anything now either. I imagine walking right past her, hidden behind leaves. It makes my chest hurt.

"I hear someone," Pinnia hisses, and she grabs my shirt and Carver's arm, tugging us behind the nearest lockwood. We press against its warm trunk, holding our breath.

"The south door was cracked," someone says. "It looks like maybe there was a solar short and it just wasn't triggered to lock. Looks fine now."

I can't see them, but they walk by a moment later, one set of footsteps. They must be talking into a device. A guard roaming the greenhouse. How many more are there? The angry part of me wants to leap out and grab them, demand to know where my sister is. The bees inside me feel like they're swarming up my throat. But the voice fades away.

"It's quiet now," Carver says, and we keep moving. We try to stay inside the trees, in case someone who works for FOLROY—or the governor?—walks by outside. They could easily see us through the glass unless we're hidden by trunks and leaves. I hope that Mento's drone can do the same.

"How are we supposed to find her in all this?" I say. I start to realize that things are more complicated than I thought. The greenhouse looked like a jungle in a jar from outside. Now we're in that jungle, and it seems even bigger. I look down at Hurona's phone.

Where is she? I type to Iva.

But she doesn't respond. I stare at the screen, willing her to write me back. But the screen stays blank.

"Voices," Carver hisses, and this time we're a little farther from a lockwood. We crouch even lower, hustling over to it, the red flowers brushing our thighs. Some of them, I notice, grow into towering clusters of red. We dive behind a lockwood trunk just in time.

"The bosses have us all on patrol schedule," one says in a complainy voice. "But the bugs still haven't eaten."

"Half of them are going to die," the other says. "And it will be their fault. I don't know why they brought the flies in if they don't know what they're going to do with them."

"They said it was for testing," the first one says, as they move past. "Let them eat in controlled areas, then see how much grows back and how fast."

"I just feed the bugs." The other sighs. "I'll leave the science to the scientists. But all the bugs are gonna be dead if we don't give them the eat frequency."

At first it seems like they're going to continue past, but they stop.

"Did you hear that?"

Pinnia makes big eyes next to me. None of us had moved a muscle. It's like the guards can sense us. I want one of them to talk about my sister. I realize we don't even know for sure that she's actually here. I'd come here trusting Iva again. Iva, who had proved herself to be untrustworthy.

"I don't hear anything," the second guard says. They sound bored, and their partner sighs.

"You'll be hearing *something* if the governor arrives and we don't have this site locked down," they warn.

"Is he actually coming?"

"No choice. There was a leak. He said he wanted this airtight so I know heads are going to roll, and it won't be mine!"

The guards finally move off, their voices fading. When they're gone, Carver shakes his head.

"I think there's a lot more to this than we know," he mutters. "What have you two heard about Dolosalvus?"

"Next to nothing," Pinnia whispers. "I just know they're recruiting like crazy. Including my mom. They're making all kinds of promises."

"Urtica didn't say anything extra about it," I add. "When me and Hurona got in the car, the driver just said *Dolosalvus*, like he was asking if that's where we were going. But this isn't Dolosalvus. Is it?"

I shake my head. I don't get it. I can tell Pinnia is wondering the same thing.

"So what do we do now?" she whispers. "This place is huge."

"Maybe she's not in the greenhouse at all," I answer, looking around. "Maybe they have her in a building behind it or something...."

"We need to get up high so we can look around," Pinnia says. She cranes her neck back, looking up toward the tops of the lockwood. "Can you climb up there?"

I peer upward with her. When they're not planted as a fire wall, the lockwood branches aren't quite the knot of iron wool that they are in Prine. Still, they're tall, and Pinnia has a point. If we could see all of the greenhouse at once, we might be able to find Hurona. I glance at Carver.

"We always had the crane to take us to the top," he says, squinting up doubtfully.

"I climbed it once by myself," I say. "Without the crane."

He raises his eyebrows.

"You did?"

"The night I saw the FOLROY drone," I say, considering. I'm still wearing my climbing shoes. They're the only shoes I have. "I can do it again."

"Let me hold your bag," Pinnia says, reaching, but I shake my head.

"No," I say, thinking. "My hatchet is in there. If I have to cut back branches, I'll need it."

I grab hold of the trunk. It's as warm and strange as ever. But after everything that has happened . . . it feels almost comforting. I hold tight and find footholds, gazing upward to plot a course up the trunk toward where the vines first begin. Hurona always said to look at the lockwood like a puzzle. If I put the pieces together correctly, my sister has to be at the other end of this maze.

"Up we go," I whisper.

Up I go.

It's actually easier without a headlamp on. I can move my head more freely and see more easily. Plus I don't have to focus on following Banneker's pod path, even if I do wish they were here climbing beside me. That's when I notice though—there are no pods. As I climb higher into the vines, gripping and pushing and pulling, still nothing. The vines don't even look like they've already been harvested—there are usually little knots of gray-green where the pods have been pulled. That's how I know Banneker is done with a branch. But this lockwood doesn't look like it's grown any at all. Weird.

"See anything?" I hear Pinnia call, trying to sound hushed.

I don't answer. I'm not high enough yet. A few more feet. I almost slip once, but I freeze the way Mx. Amur always tells us. There's no net here, I remind myself. But there's more light. The moon is bright, and the greenhouse ceiling is lit with a soft golden glow. Grow lights, probably. I'm almost there.

I wrap my legs around a vine, and hold on tight with both hands. In Prine, I would use an anchor strap to secure myself. But there's no anchor here, just my own strength. Adrenaline is buzzing in my ears. At home when I first started going up, I was nervous every day. It wore off eventually. Now the newness is back. The stakes are higher. I feel like a ten-year-old again. But I'm not. I'm older now, and my sister is counting on me.

From here, I can see the whole greenhouse, just as Pinnia thought. I can see the edges of the dome, and illuminated doors here and there that connect to a square white building to the east. I sweep my eyes over the greenhouse: just lockwood and the endless blood-red flowers. I scan the bases of lockwood trunks, hoping to find my sister leaning against one. I don't know what I'm going to do if she's surrounded by guards. Distract them? Demand they let her go? Call the police unit? They'd have to believe me first.

But then I see something else.

A bug tank.

Three of them actually, arranged in a triangle. They're almost as large as the ones at the Buzz Yard, and are set up right at the middle of the greenhouse. Even from here I can see the swarms of insects inside, rising and falling and swirling. Hungry, like the guards said. I'm so busy studying them that I don't notice the small figure curled up between the tanks right away. A girl, sitting with her back to a control panel and its pole.

Hurona.

My heart leaps, but just as I'm about to call down to Pinnia and Carver to tell them what I see, I hear shouting. Without thinking, I tighten my grip on the lockwood, and hug my chest close to the vine. With my face pressed against it, I'm looking right at the ground. I can barely see through the vines and waxy leaves, but I see gray uniforms running up to where I know Pinnia and Carver had been standing.

"Let go!" I hear Pinnia scream.

"You're trespassing," a guard shouts. "This is private FOLROY property and—"

"Leave her alone!" Carver shouts.

"We're taking you both into custody!"

I cling even tighter to the lockwood. I can feel my heart slamming against the limb. I squeeze my eyes shut. What happens if they see me? With my eyes closed, everything sounds louder. The sound of Pinnia yelling at the guards, Carver cursing at them. But neither of them gives me away. They both pretend they are here alone, and that they're not here because of me. The guilt is so heavy I almost fall out of the tree. But I remember what my mom said: Guilt is useless unless you change something with it.

I catch glimpses of the guards walking Pinnia and Carver through the greenhouse. They're headed straight toward the bug tanks. As they get closer, I see a guard pop out from where they'd been leaning against one of the tanks. From here it's impossible to hear what they're saying, but they're all talking, and a moment later they're shoving Pinnia and Carver into the same area as Hurona. I watch Hurona's head jerk up. Even from this far away, I can see how tense she is. She's confused that I'm not with them. She's scared.

"I'm right here," I whisper.

There's no way to get to them on the ground—the guards are hanging around the outsides of the bug tanks, leaving my sister and my friends in the center alone. I can tell their wrists are tied from the way they're sitting. The anger wells up inside me again. This huge building exists because of the work me and Hurona do in the lockwood. And they think they can just tie us up. Shut us up.

I'm gripping the vines so hard my hands start to ache. I look down, taking in how far the vine stretches. It goes on and on, disappearing under other vines, twisting and turning, joining with the outstretched vines from other lockwoods. The trees aren't planted as close as in Prine, but it's like the branches are always seeking each other. High above the greenhouse floor, carpeted with the intense red flowers, the lockwood vines make something like a blanket. A labyrinth of pathways, if someone knows where—and how—to put their feet. Everywhere there are the hanging vines fallen loose from the tangle. Like any forest, they dangle throughout the greenhouse like ropes.

And that's when I start to smile.

I keep my feet planted on the branch, hands down and gripping, and stick my butt up into the air. I monkey-walk, switching my eyes from the vine I'm on to the vines ahead. *Like a puzzle*, I hear Hurona's voice saying. The guards will never see me coming because I'm going to come a way they never expected.

From above.

This blanket of vines is how it had looked the night I climbed up and saw the drone, but it was thicker at home. With the lockwood planted farther apart here, sometimes there are big gaps between vines. You wouldn't need to be a skinny kid from Prine to fit between them. But I don't need to fit anyway: I'm walking on top of them, not squeezing through. I'm almost to the bug tanks—I can hear the humming and buzzing of the insects getting louder and stronger. My heart is buzzing too. I can see my sister. I can't look at her too long and risk falling. But I'm almost there. I just can't . . . fall.

I slip.

I bite back the scream just in time—this close to the guards they would even hear me sneeze. The lockwood is tight enough in this section that I don't fall straight down. If I was in Prine, I'd probably be dead, or at least with a broken spine. In Prine, Banneker and I would have already carved a hole through the knots by the time we got this high. But here, the knots are what catch me.

I'm wedged between two vines, and I'm so grateful I could cry. But I have a problem.

I can't get out. No matter how much I wiggle. In fact, wiggling sticks me tighter in the small opening. In that moment, a thought burns me like the tip of my mom's soldering pin.

Too big.

I'm too big. Survival in Prine means being small. Not just my survival, but my whole town's. Everyone I know. Kids, but especially girls, being told to think small thoughts so they can fit between the knots that FOLROY grows every single night.

But that's when I realize.

I'm not too big. Everything else is just too small. The town, the trees. Maybe even the whole world.

I'm not too big. I just have to make more space.

I reach my hand down between the vines, fumbling for my bag, which had been riding along easily until I fell. It's part of what's making me stuck, I realize, wedged against the vine on one side. I struggle with the flap, yanking it free, then reach inside. The vine is in my way so I can't see inside—I fumble sightlessly until my fingers find the handle I know so well.

My hatchet.

It slices through the lockwood as easily as ever—even though the greenhouse's trees don't have pods, it's still the same stuff. Impossibly hard on the outside, and the strange, moist inside cutting away like cake. I feel the vine start to loosen, and I pause, making sure my feet are braced on another bough, before I cut. Mx. Amur taught me well.

When the vine falls away, I just catch it before it crashes down to the ground. I lift it carefully, my muscles aching, and wedge it in another gap nearby. Free. My ribs can expand all the way now. I take a big, deep breath. I'm almost directly above the bug tanks. I see the vine I'm going to use to climb down. I just have to put my hatchet back in my bag.

I reach down to slip it in. But the handle catches on the edge of my bag. I twist it, trying to get it out so I can try again. But without the guard, the hatchet has hooked onto something inside the bag. I shove my mother's glowing sparrow out of the way, still milky white after Pinnia figured out how to charge it. There's something else in the way. I yank the hatchet one more time. *The Encyclopedia of Entomology.* It's the palest green out of everything in the greenhouse. I watch the green as it goes spinning out into space, pages flapping like wings.

All.

The way.

Down.

It slams onto the ground, and I wince like its leg is broken. I don't even want to look at the guards. But I do. And they're already rushing over to where the book fell, trying to see where the noise came from. There are three of them and they gather near the book. They're confused. Until one realizes, and then slowly, slowly looks up.

"Up there!" they shout, and I feel my heart exploding at the same moment that something explodes through the wall of the greenhouse.

41

MY FIRST THOUGHT is that it's Mento's drone making a crash landing. But it's not up high. The crash is down below, along the ground. The shattering of glass makes me wince, and I cling to the vines again so I don't fall.

"What the—!" one of the guards shouts, and they're running. Not toward the book, but toward where the glass of the greenhouse has been smashed by—I peer through the vines—a teal van?

The van has driven straight through one of the panels of the greenhouse. The plants near the jagged hole wave back and forth in the wind that comes in. Their first taste of free air. I'm so busy watching the plants that it takes me a second to notice the two people leaping out of the car. A short person with masses of black hair piled high on her head, a yellow coat. Then a tall, broad woman. Her hair gold-brown like Hurona's. Like mine. Like my mom's.

It's my mother.

And Mx. Amur. They stand shouting at the guards, who are raising weapons—glowing batons. Things that break you and shock you at the same time. I want to scream, but someone else is screaming. They're saying my name.

Hurona. She sees me. She's tied up, but she has spotted me through the vines and is yelling my name. And I don't have time to wonder what my mother is doing here or how someone convinced her to leave the safety of Prine, or how Mx. Amur got her old van running after all these years. My big sister needs me.

I monkey-walk the rest of the way until I am straight over the bug tanks. Carver, Pinnia, and Hurona are all watching me. I know they're praying I don't fall. So am I. But I know I won't. Not now. I lower myself down vine by vine until I come to one swinging like a rope. I pause, unwinding my bag from my shoulders. I drop it straight down. I've never done this before. Through the lockwood and the blood-red plants, I hear my mother's voice:

"No, you will *not!*" she shouts at a guard. Someone else yells.

I slide down. The lockwood feels like skin under my hands. It's almost strange enough to make me let go, but I hold on tight until I reach the bottom.

"Erie, what's happening?" Hurona says as soon as I land on my feet. "What was that smash?"

"Mom's here," I say and snatch up my bag. As I hoped, the hatchet works quickly on the ties the guards had used on her wrists. I do the same for Pinnia and Carver. Carver has a bloody lip. I fish a shirt out of my bag and give it to him.

"Your mom is here?" Pinnia says. "All the way from Prine? How did she know you were here?"

"I have no idea," I say. "But those guards have weapons. We have to do something."

"What you have to *do*," a new voice says, "is sit back down."

I know before I even look that it's Urtica. She's standing between two of the bug tanks, her white-silver hair looking reddish with the flowers all around her. I expect her to carry a weapon like the guards, but her hands are empty. It's her eyes that are like knives.

"You kidnapped us," Hurona yells at her. "You think we're going to do what you say?"

"Yes," Urtica says. "If you want your town to survive, you will do what I say."

"What are you talking about?" I say. I stand shoulder to shoulder with my sister, Pinnia and Carver on Hurona's other side.

"What you do here tonight will affect what happens to the place where you live and the people you live with," she says.

"You're threatening them?" Pinnia cries, her voice shrill.

Just like that, more guards appear. At least six or seven of them. They stream around behind us and to the sides. Some of them have gray uniforms, some white. It's just like on Tuesdays in Prine, except this time they're not here for pods—they're here for us. I want to run, but there's nowhere to go. We press up against one of the bug tanks instead. And that's when I look at my sister.

Her eyes don't know if they want to be fire or water. She stares without blinking. Then I see why.

Iva.

She's one of the FOLROY guards who stand blocking our way.

None of them have weapons, but I know they're not going to let us leave. Unlike the other guards, though, Iva looks like my sister. Eyes shining. Her jaw isn't made of steel. But I can't look at her, because I realize I don't hear my mom shouting anymore, or Mx. Amur. What happened? Are they okay?

"I am here as a representative of FOLROY," Urtica says calmly. "All I am telling you is that Prine is what we call a single-resource economy. All of you rely on the same thing for a living. And FOLROY owns that thing. So your future is therefore up to FOLROY."

"You think we don't *know* that?" Carver snaps. "We've spent our lives with the lockwood dictating everything we can do and be. And now you stand in front of us acting like you're the master of our destiny?"

"Not me," Urtica says. One bony hand points up, and we all look. High up above the lockwood, where the greenhouse connects to the white building I'd seen from the top, there is a window. From this far down, there are no faces. Just faceless people. All in a row. Watching. "Them."

"The board," Pinnia says. I know she's thinking about what Mento had told us in the car. I am too.

"Let me guess," Carver snarls. "One of them is the governor."

Urtica makes an irritated face.

"Of course he is," she says. "That's a matter of public record, and he isn't breaking any laws by having interest in a company."

"My brother has helped bust people like you," Pinnia shouts. "The governor may not be breaking any laws by being on a board, but if he influences laws that help the company he gets money from so that he can get richer, then that *is* illegal!"

I stand there feeling small and helpless. Pinnia and Mento are both so much smarter than me—they know so much. All I know is what I've been told in Prine, and it doesn't even feel like enough to fill up a teaspoon. Boards and company interest...all I can think about is what Mento said about the man who is supposed to be my father and his votes. Is *this* what Arlo Kylak voted for? Is he up in that window?

That's when it sinks in. That I was right. My whole life, feeling like the trees were watching me...it wasn't the lockwood. There were no monsters in the branches. It was these people. Not watching with their eyes, not even seeing me at all. But measuring. Everything that goes into Prine, and everything that goes out.

"All I'm asking," Urtica says, as calm as ever, "is that you consider: What happens to your town if FOLROY decides to change our minds? What if we decide to get those pods somewhere else?"

"You're lying," Iva says. She speaks so suddenly that even Urtica looks startled. Hurona's eyes are huge. We all stare at Iva.

"Excuse me...?" Urtica says.

"You're *lying*," Iva says again. Her voice is stronger this time, even if it still shakes a little. "Prine is the only place where the pods grow."

"You—" Urtica starts, but Iva keeps going, louder now.

"Prine was the first planting. Something in the soil, or a mistake in the seed sequence. You can't get them anywhere else. And you're hiding it. That's why you're growing all this." She gestures at the greenhouse we stand in, all the lockwood and the red flowers. "But you can't get the pods to grow anywhere but Prine. That's why you're trying to grow the blood flowers. Something new. Something else you can plant in a new town. And start all over."

Pinnia gasps, her hand flying to her mouth. She puts the pieces together at the same time as I do.

"Dolosalvus," she whispers. Then she raises her voice: "You're basically just building a new Prine with a new product!"

"You heard us," I say to Urtica. Her thin mouth is twitching. "You heard us tell Dr. Elemnieri what we saw, what we knew."

"So you kidnapped Hurona and Erie to get them out of the way?" Pinnia says, looking disgusted. "For *what*? Money?"

Around us, the guards are shifting. But Urtica looks up toward the window, the faceless people, and seems to steady herself.

"This is about the survival of a town," Urtica says. "The blood flowers will be even more valuable. This is what I wanted to explain to you tonight. That Prine will have another way to earn money and not rely solely on the lockwood..."

"Let me guess," Carver shouts, his fists balled up. "FOLROY would own that too. So we would still be, like you said, *relying* on FOLROY. How does any of this help us if we can't *own* it?"

"Prine should feel lucky," Urtica says. This is the first time she's raised her voice. "Not all townlands have an opportunity like this. FOLROY is—"

"FOLROY FOLROY FOLROY," Pinnia yells. "That's all you

ever say. I thought you were supposed to work for Dr. Elemnieri. Does she know you work for *them* too?"

Pinnia's finger arrows up at the window of faceless watchers, just as the guards across from me, down here on the ground, shuffle to make room for a new face.

Dr. Elemnieri herself.

42

"I DO NOW," Dr. Elemnieri says.

Urtica was already pale, but now she looks paler.

"What are you doing here?" Urtica says.

"I followed you," Dr. Elemnieri replies. She looks at me, her eyebrows sinking lower. "I saw you when you jumped out of the car, Erie. I tried to follow you and help, but I think you thought I was...them." She aims this last word at Urtica. Urtica's frown looks like broken glass.

"By the time I got back on the road," Dr. Elemnieri goes on, "I was behind. It took me a while to find my way here. I didn't even know this place existed. Beautiful, really. Although I didn't expect to see my new specimen here. Blood flowers, you call them, Urtica? A little reductive. I'm guessing you brought them here, as I don't seem to recall giving permission for them to be grown anywhere but my *own* greenhouse."

Urtica doesn't answer. Her eyes are narrowed into two snakish slits.

"The board gave me permission to use force," Urtica says. She doesn't need to point at the faceless people in the window.

"And you'll use it," Carver says evenly. "Because you want to."

Then Iva punches the guard next to her.

It seems like it happens in slow motion because it kind of does. Her arm pulls back, then pauses, like her body and her brain are fighting. But whichever one wins, it wins hard. Iva isn't skinny like a Prinian. She's strong from lifting pods and lockwood sacks, and her fist makes a pulpy sound when it connects with the other guard's jaw.

Then everything is pandemonium. Another guard has grabbed Iva by the hair, and her scream is electric in the greenhouse. And just like that, Hurona is leaping to her defense. Hurona is too big for the lockwood, but she's not too big here. She swings a guard against a bug tank so hard it cracks.

Carver circles me and Pinnia with his arm, and he already has hold of Dr. Elemnieri's wrist. He yanks us all closer to the tank nearest to us, sheltering us, face grim. Carver is not a fighter, and he's trying to protect us. But I want to protect him too.

"Oh my god," Dr. Elemnieri cries when someone in a gray uniform punches Hurona in the back of her head. Hurona staggers, then turns around and swings back. Her punch isn't great, but when she grabs their arm, Iva grabs the other one. Together, they push the guard into two others. All three fall against a bug tank. Inside, the insects swirl and hum. At my back, the bug tank I lean against almost vibrates with the energy of the flies inside.

"We need to get out of here," Carver yells, and he's right, but how? They won't let us leave and there are more of them than us. I have no idea where my mom is. No idea what's going to happen.

The lockwood towers over us like it's watching, no pods on any of the branches. I hate the sight of it, wish I could make it all disappear. Because if we couldn't pick the pods back in Prine, we'd be even more poor—but at least FOLROY wouldn't be rich. And now the red flowers. FOLROY's next plan to plant something but not do the labor of harvesting it. I imagine Pinnia's mom tricked into living in Dolosalvus, which is nothing but a copy of Prine, and paid in tokens, red flowers pretty and ugly at the same time. She would spend her life picking red flowers that made the governor—and my father—rich, while she got paid in fake money. I wish I could uproot every blossom and watch it wilt in the sun.

At my back, the flies are buzzing. But now something else is buzzing too, this time inside my head. An idea.

I spin around, staring wildly in at the flies in the tank. They rise and fall in black clouds, swarming the walls. I shove my face against the glass, studying them. Not black after all—reddish brown. Slightly different: a green dot on their shell. A new breed maybe. But I recognize the antennae, the six legs like bent wire. FOLROY had given them wings, but I've read *The Encyclopedia of Entomology* enough times to know them when I see them.

I grab Pinnia, pointing.

"Do you know what those are?!" I shout over the noise. At some point an alarm started going off, braying from a nearby control tower, and when I look up at the window where Urtica's faceless bosses were, it's empty.

"What?" she cries, confused. "They're *bugs*!"

"They're dustnose beetles," I yell, staring intently. "They bred them differently, but that's what they are. Pinnia, these eat the lockwood!"

Her eyes widen, then she flinches as a guard slams against the glass. Insects flicker away. We look at the fight—some of the guards are fighting the other guards now. It's not just Iva who made a choice.

Pinnia looks at the bugs, and then she looks at me. I watch her eyes change as she realizes what I'm saying.

"Crop clearers. If we can't burn it all down," she says, "maybe we just eat it."

"Well, not *us*," I say.

"Do it."

My hatchet is in my hand a second later, and I see Dr. Elemnieri's look of horror as I raise it. I don't know if she thinks I'm about to attack someone or what—more guards are coming—but instead I stab it into the side of the tank.

"Wait, that won't . . . ," Pinnia starts, but I know it will. I remember what Zizi said: They make bug tanks out of lockwood. These trees make so many things, but only one thing unmakes them. This knife.

The hatchet cuts through the tank like dough. It's like slicing soft bread in my mother's kitchen.

"What are you—" Dr. Elemnieri says, but then the buzzing of the flies is so loud that she doesn't even bother to finish. I cut and cut until there's a huge hole, but none of the flies are flying out. They spin and circle, billowing but not escaping.

"Hey! What are you doing?" a guard says, and then Carver is grabbing my arm, pulling me away.

"Sorry, Erie, it's time to run," he says, and Dr. Elemnieri is shouting at the guard, but everything is noise and Pinnia is pulling me too. We run, and I see Hurona shove another guard, and I think I hear her screaming at me to keep going. But where are we supposed to go?

Carver drags us to the nearest lockwood, and we take shelter behind it. Dr. Elemnieri is with us.

"Aren't you going to do something?" I shout at her.

"Such as?" she snaps, but her eyes look how I feel: afraid. "They've done all this without my knowledge or consent. I don't think they'll suddenly take an interest in my authority."

I look up at the window far above one more time. Empty. Whoever they were, they left at the first sign of trouble.

"The police will be here soon," Carver says. His voice is shaking. "They're going to book us all for trespassing and property damage. I'll never see Banneker again."

"Why did you break the bug case?" Dr. Elemnieri says. She sounds the way she sounded in her office—curious.

"We heard the guards talking! They breed those bugs to eat the crop," I say. "So they can test how fast they grow back."

"It's faster to let the bugs do it than paying harvesters," Pinnia adds.

"And your plan was what exactly?" Dr. Elemnieri says.

"I was trying to get the flies to just…eat it all," I say. I can feel tears burning. "I heard one of the guards say they hadn't been fed yet. I just figured they'd…eat."

I shove my fists against my eyes, trying not to cry. But then Pinnia's grabbing my face, her hands squishing my cheeks. I'm so surprised I don't even pull away.

"They *are* hungry," Pinnia whispers. "They just haven't been given the eat frequency. Remember what Zizi said? That places like FOLROY use frequencies to train bugs?"

I grab her hands and hold her wrists. We stare at each other.

"The guard said...," I whisper.

We say it together:

"The eat frequency."

"They need to be signaled to eat," Dr. Elemnieri says. She's nodding quickly, catching up. "So we need to give them a signal."

Me and Pinnia look at her, astonished.

"You...you don't care?" I say. "If the bugs eat it all? These are your creations."

"They are certainly *not*," she says, scowling. "I didn't make these things to own them. I made them to help people. And obviously my intention and the reality are no longer in sync. So let the insects eat it all. Every leaf."

"Okay," I say, trying to think. My heartrate is climbing. "We need something that gives a frequency. But what?"

Pinnia is grinning, burying her arm in my bag. When she pulls it out, something in her hand is glowing.

"Luckily," she says, "I know just the thing."

"My mom's sparrow," I breathe.

"Aren't you glad you know me?" She beams. "You're truly blessed."

And then she's running over to the control tower nearby, where the alarm pulses like an ambulance. She carries the sparrow and the other thing she'd pulled from my bag. A tiny tin.

"She has Puttia!" I crow, and Dr. Elemnieri and Carver both look confused.

"She has *what*?"

"Get away from there!" a guard shouts—they're running straight toward Pinnia. I'm too far to stop them, but I run toward her anyway...just as something soars down out of the sky and crashes into the guard. It's a blur of red and black and it's not big, but it's big enough to send the guard spinning backward.

Mento's drone.

I sprint over to where Pinnia is, Carver on my heels. He kneels to pick up the drone, but it's already rising shakily back into the air. It wobbles a little and then circles higher and higher. Back to watching. Somewhere outside, Mento had done what big brothers do: protected his little sister.

By the time I look at Pinnia, she already has the control tower open, and my mom's sparrow too, a bobby pin between her teeth. She's using the Puttia to connect something inside the sparrow to something inside the tower, one long white strand. A moment later, an earsplitting screech fills the greenhouse. Shouts go up from all over, including me, everyone shielding their ears.

"Ay," Pinnia mumbles. "Whoops. Let me just try..."

Guards are gathering by the bug tents, trying to figure out what's happening. No one else notices us yet. But it won't be long.

"All we need is one short signal," she mutters. "One frequency..."

The sound changes, then changes again. Nothing happens. Mento's drone zooms overhead and crashes into another guard who gets too close. It has a harder time rising off the ground this time.

"What about...*this*," Pinnia says. A new sound emerges, so high I can barely hear it. She jerks her head to look at the bug tanks.

At first I think nothing is happening. The bugs still spin and swirl. But with the alarm off, replaced with the frequency, their buzzing sounds even louder. It rises like a chant.

Then, like a bolt of humming lightning, the bugs are out of the tank. From where we stand at the control tower, I can see them clotting around the hole I made, crowding their way out. The guards are all starting to shout.

"Hurona!" I scream. "Hurona! Break the glass!"

She hears me. I can see a line of blood on her cheek. She turns in a full circle, looking around, before she understands. She shouts something to Iva, and then they're picking up loose batons and slamming them against the bug tanks. A moment later, Dr. Elemnieri and Carver are running over and doing the same thing.

And then all the bugs are loose.

Guards are running and shouting, shielding their heads. A woman in a gray uniform runs by, trapped in a cloud of them. These people work for FOLROY and they know what the bugs do—they don't eat people. I think they're used to everything being under control. And right now, nothing is.

43

THE INSECTS SWEEP through the greenhouse in roaring black clouds. Their millions of wings are like thunder and lightning all at once—when they're not contained in the tanks, they block the light. It flashes like a strobe. Whole sections of red flowers disappear at a time.

"They're out!" Urtica is screaming into a device. She's crouched, shielding her head from flying bugs. "They're going to destroy the whole crop!"

I'm forced to crouch now too. There are way more than I could have imagined. In the encyclopedia, I had learned that there are two hundred million insects for every human on Earth. Right now it feels like they're all in this building. They swarm the lockwood, so fully that it looks like entire trees are alive, the bark shivering under millions of hungry mouths.

Urtica screams at me from where she's crouched.

"Do you know what you've done?" she screeches. "The specimens in this greenhouse took two years to cultivate!"

"I've been in the lockwood for two years!" I scream back, and I don't even know if it makes sense, but I don't care. The air is thick with insects, and I'm starting to think I may not have thought this through. What if the bugs *do* decide to eat us? What if we suffocate?

Then a van is screeching up beside us and the doors swing open. My mother leaps out, next to Mx. Amur. They both shield their faces from the clouds of feasting insects.

"In!" my mother shouts, and Mx. Amur leans in and honks the horn. Hurona comes running, towing Iva behind her. Carver and Dr. Elemnieri sprint toward us, ducking. Carver is coughing. An insect flew into his mouth.

I throw myself in the van and everyone else piles in around me. Dr. Elemnieri is last and she's the one who slides the door closed. As soon as it slams, Mx. Amur puts it into drive, roaring through the storm of bugs back toward the hole she'd made in the side of the greenhouse. No one even chases us. The guards are gone, and Urtica crouches alone by the bug tents, still screaming. At whom, I don't really know.

Mx. Amur can barely see, and she leans hard over the steering wheel. The bodies of bugs sound like hail striking a tin roof. We don't even smash them—they bounce off like rubber bullets.

But the moment we hurtle through the hole in the glass, the silence is almost total. All I hear is the heaving breath of everyone in the van. The hum of insects softens as Mx. Amur drives us far out into the parking lot, into the deep dark. But my ears still ring with billions of wings.

When she stops the car, no one has to decide. We all get out again, and everyone turns to stare at the greenhouse. My mom is

313

standing between me and Hurona, her strong arms curled around us both, squeezing tighter than she ever has. We just stare.

Even from here, I can easily make out the swarms of insects. We all watch as they fell first one, then another, then another, of the lockwoods. We all stare silently until the greenhouse is just a big empty crystal ball. A jar that's been poured out. Eventually I can make out white-suited and masked workers running across the greenhouse floor to the control tower, where they finally shut off the sparrow and its frequency. We hear another frequency then, calling the insects back to their tanks. But by then it's too late. There's not a leaf left to save. And we all just stand watching.

We're still there when the media cars pull up. I'm trembling, trying to figure out what we're going to say, how we're going to explain this, when Mento comes running up, holding Zizi's hand. In his other hand is the red-and-black drone.

"Welcome!" he shouts before any of the people with cameras and drones has even said a word. "I recorded everything."

44

WE'VE ONLY BEEN at Pinnia's house for five minutes when her mother gets home from work.

"What are all these cars?" we hear Ms. Mari shout from outside.

There's Mx. Amur's van, the yellow Buzz Yard truck, and Dr. Elemnieri's sleek red Sunflare. Then there's Carver's solarbike. I went from going most of my life never having ridden in a car to riding in several, plus the bike and the bus.

Dr. Elemnieri is outside having back-to-back phone calls. I can almost imagine Ms. Mari's face warping with shock.

"Aren't you famous?" I hear her cry. "What are you doing outside my house in the middle of the night?!"

Then Ms. Mari steps inside.

"And who are all these people?!"

"Let me fill you in real quick, Ma," Mento says, leaping up, and he and Pinnia lead her into the kitchen.

"How did you find us?" I say to my mother. I'm squished between her and Hurona on the couch I'd slept on my first day in Petrichor. It seems like forever ago.

Mom takes a deep breath. This is the first time we've actually been able to talk. One of the journalists who showed up first had hologrammed Mento's recordings into the night sky, and the media units seemed to go from five to twenty in a matter of minutes, questions and our answers whizzing through the night, while over in the greenhouse everything was as silent and still as a graveyard. They didn't even send security out.

"You took a sparrow from my workshop," my mom says. She rests one hand on each of our knees. "After I got Hurona's note, I just sat in my workshop, waiting and waiting to hear from you. To decide what to do. I was losing my mind. And then, like a miracle... one of the sparrow trackers pinged on. I hadn't even noticed you took it. And then suddenly it was telling me exactly where you were. I knew it had to be you. So I deintegrated the solar pack from our house and rigged it to Mx. Amur's van."

"And it got you all the way here," I say.

"It's not so far," she says. "It was harder once we got to the city. The signal kept traveling. And then once we got to the greenhouse, we ran into your friends outside—Mento and Zizi. They told us what was going on. Amur decided it would be best if we...well..."

"Crashed through the glass?" Hurona says, smiling.

"It was the most direct route," Mx. Amur says defensively.

There's a long moment of silence. Zizi and Carver glance at each other uneasily, then slowly stand and join Pinnia and Mento with their mom in the kitchen, where I keep hearing her shout, "You did *what*?" at different parts of the story. Mx. Amur and Iva follow quietly.

316

That leaves me and Hurona and Mom alone.

We sit in silence, and I wait for the storm to break. But instead I hear the softest voice I've ever heard come from my mother's lips.

"Where did you get that jacket?" she says.

It takes me a long second to realize she's, of course, talking to me.

"It was waiting for me," I say. "At Aunt Josie's conservancy."

"You went to Eccles-Tillery?" she breathes.

"Y-yes," I whisper. "I . . . I just wanted to know more."

I can see the storm in her eyes. The clouds and all their thunder swelling. But this time, instead of lightning, there's just rain. A tear finds its way out of one eye and moves slowly down her face.

"And I should've told you," she says. "But I was so angry for so long. I was so mad at her for things that weren't . . . that weren't her fault. She told me the truth and I didn't want to hear it. But she was right. And now it's too late. Every word she's ever said, I wasted."

"That's not true," Hurona says. "You've . . . you've been doing the best you can."

"I haven't, Hurona," Mom says. She squeezes her eyes shut tight. "I've been selfish and bitter, and for a long time I thought if it only hurt me, then it was okay. That I deserved it for not listening to my sister. But now I see that the hurt . . . the hurt has affected more than just me."

All the buzzing from FOLROY's greenhouse feels like it's still locked in my head, in my ears. I feel a swarm of it all rising to my mouth. In Prine, I would've swallowed it down, but we're not in

Prine anymore. Maybe we never will be again. And that thought makes me sadder than I ever thought it would.

"Can we just tell the truth for once?" I cry. Both Hurona and Mom snap their heads to look at me. "Don't you see that you're still doing it? You two are talking in a code that only you understand. Both of you have the same information, and I don't know what you're talking about, and you think you're protecting me but you're *not*."

My fists ball up tight. I can feel the threat of tears and fight them off.

"You're not," I repeat.

Mom stares at me like she's seeing me for the first time. Her eyes are round, the clouds gone.

"Your Aunt Josie warned me about your father," she says suddenly. "She always had a bad feeling about him. She told me so, so many times. But I was...I wasn't well. He was an aspiring businessman—he made me feel like I knew nothing. That all my tinkering was just a silly hobby. I was afraid of the fires. I had nightmares. I obsessed over them. He moved us to Prine. My sister warned me and warned me and I"—she pauses, shaking her head—"I thought...I thought she was jealous."

Hurona is staring at her open-mouthed. So am I. Hurona has always known more than me, but I remember our days in the lockwood, when we were little. Both guessing about the past, making up fairy tales to fill in the gaps. Now Mom is doing it for us with the truth, for the first time.

"As it turns out, Josephine was right," she says softly. "Hurona knows what Arlo did, and I assume you do too now, Erie. When I first told him about what I found inside the lockwood pods, he was excited for me. Told me to keep looking. So I did. I learned what the heartpod could do. The next thing I knew, he left for Petrichor and never came back. Saw him on the Newscast. And I could never prove a thing."

"So you just buried yourself in work," Mx. Amur says from the kitchen doorway. Everyone is listening: Pinnia and her family, Iva, Carver, Zizi. "While he took all the credit."

My mother nods silently.

"I just wanted to forget everything," she says. "I always have. Josephine was all about remembering. When species would go extinct, it would paralyze me. But Jo wanted to remember them. Wanted to talk about them. It just made me sad. Then it felt like something in my life went extinct—one thing after another. Josie. The man I loved. The biggest discovery of my career. Remembering felt like..."

"Like work," Ms. Mari says from the kitchen. She nods sadly. "Remembering is hard work. Sad work sometimes."

"Excuse me," Carver says quietly. "Ms. Nadine, you know I don't mean any disrespect. But..."

He stops, but Mom nods, encouraging him.

"But... this isn't just about you. You knew what the pods could do all this time?"

"Not exactly," Mom says slowly. "But I had a feeling that when FOLROY began paying Prinians for harvesting them... I had a feeling that Arlo had found his intended audience."

"Then you could've stopped this at any time," Carver says.

"Do you know how different things could have been if Prine knew the value of what we were harvesting? We could've... we could've demanded more wages! We could have... we could have..."

"Gone on strike," Zizi says softly from behind him. "Gotten shares."

The storm in my mother's eyes swells, and I tense, but it dies again. Like she's all out of lightning.

"I know," she says. "I know. This is why I've been trying to make something new! To undo it all!"

"But you could've—" Carver argues, but Mom cuts him off.

"I have no proof!" she cries. "His word against mine. By the time I realized what he'd done, he owned half of the town. He's on FOLROY's board, from what I hear! I'm a single mother in the townlands who everybody thinks is the village loony!"

The room descends into silence again. The night is catching up with us. The fear, the excitement of escape. Mento's face on every Newscaster's screen, holding up his battered drone. But the uncertainty has drifted in through the screen door. What happens next? How does anything ever change?

"I have no proof," my mother repeats quietly. And then the realization sails in and sinks its talons into me.

"Proof," I whisper. Then louder. "Proof! Wait. Wait..."

I leap up, grabbing my bag off the floor.

"Erie, what the...?"

But I'm digging around in the bag. We'd left the sparrow far behind in the greenhouse along with the encyclopedia. But please... please... I can't have lost this too....

But I find it. My fingers close around the envelope containing Aunt Josie's letter and the tiny chip.

I turn back to Mom, and avoid Hurona's eyes. This is what it feels like to have a secret. A real one. A heavy one. It doesn't feel good to have kept this from her. But now it's time to bring it into the light.

"Ma," I say. "Aunt Josie left this for you."

45

EYA GETS HOME from ag work just in time to help us with the old projector. The chip that Aunt Josie had left in the box at Eccles-Tillery is out of date and needs an adapter. By the time it's all figured out, everyone but Dr. Elemnieri is in the living room, perched on various sofas and stools.

Mom doesn't seem to mind that our family business has become public. I don't mind either. It kind of feels like *everyone's* business at this point. Pinnia's squishy dogs Head and Tail come and settle near our feet. I squish them nervously while the footage starts.

It's a little fuzzy and jerky, but clear enough to make out the woman with dark gold hair and deeply tanned skin. Her nose bumpy, her eyes brown.

"Josephine," Mom whispers beside me. Her hands clench together in her lap.

I can't focus on anything but the woman's face for a moment. That's her. That's Aunt Josie. I have her smile.

"That's Eccles-Tillery!" Pinnia cries. "We were standing right there talking to Arturo!"

She's right. It's the very same visitor's center. Aunt Josie is all alone, fiddling with things at the desk, humming to herself. The camera is in constant motion, but always focused on Aunt Josie. Even though Arturo had told us about Samantha, it still takes a moment to sink in.

"The camera is on the eagle," I say, and Pinnia nods eagerly. "It's recording from Samantha's collar."

"Samantha," my mom says softly. I can tell she recognizes the name and my heart squeezes.

But the camera jerks toward the entrance and I hear a squawk from Samantha as the door to the visitor's center bangs open. And there, standing in the very doorway me and Pinnia had walked through, is Arlo Kylak. My dad.

Everyone in the room breathes a little quicker. Even Head and Tail.

"Josephine," he says. "Nice to see you again!"

He has that same lullaby voice. But it doesn't mask the unpleasantness of his tone. I can tell Aunt Josie hears it too—now at the corner of the frame, she frowns.

"What are you doing here?" she says.

"I've been told you stopped by my office a number of times," he says. "I figured we kept missing each other so I would come to you."

"Missing each other," she snaps. "I know you were there when I stopped by. You just wouldn't see me."

"Which is my choice," he says evenly. "Coming to my place of business isn't the appropriate place to discuss family matters."

"This is both a family matter and a business matter," Aunt Josie says. It's so strange seeing her face. For the first time, seeing her speak the words in the voice I've come to know so well. "This is a *patent* matter."

"As I'm sure you're aware," Arlo says, striding across the room. The sharp eye of Samantha follows him the whole way. "There is no patent. All records indicate that the heartpod is my discovery, my invention, *my* product. I encourage you to stop this constant barrage or I'll get the authorities involved. It's harassment."

"Authorities." Aunt Josie scowls. "Harassment isn't the crime here. It's *theft*. And abandonment."

Arlo's face shifts.

"I have not abandoned my children," he says. "Their needs are being met. I send a check every month."

"Yes, and *that's* enough," Aunt Josie says. Her sarcasm stings like Hurona's.

"What did you expect me to do?" Arlo cries. His eyes seem suddenly very blue on the footage. "Stay in Prine forever? That was never supposed to be a permanent move. But Nadine wanted to stay! So worried about the fires—"

"As she should be!" Aunt Josie interjects, but he presses on.

"Money can protect us from those problems! Money can solve all problems."

"For those who have it," she says coldly.

"Nadine doesn't care about money." He shrugs, calmer again. "But I do. So yes, I took the heartpod. It would've wasted away otherwise, and so would I. I am making the most of it, and my children get the benefits. Everyone wins."

Aunt Josie calls him a name that makes Ms. Mari gasp, and Mento laughs.

"Jo always had a foul mouth," Mom says, shaking her head.

"A truly bizarre logic, Arlo," Aunt Josie says. "Even for you."

"What would you have me do?" he says. I watch—all of us watch—his face change then. The shiny smile looks weaker. "Stay there forever? Be afraid of the world? Your sister has chosen a lonely path and I'm not required to walk it with her."

At that, Aunt Josie jumps up, and she stands there trembling. I keep waiting for her to speak, hoping that whatever she says makes the lump in my throat smaller. I want to look at Mom but I can't. I'm afraid of what I'll see in her face. This whole recording feels like watching the beginning of a wildfire. The first sparks.

But Aunt Josie doesn't speak. She just screams, and it's loud enough at first until it gets suddenly louder, and the camera jerks, and Arlo Kylak runs for the door. It's as if the camera chases him.

It's not until the camera follows his retreating back out into the open air outside the visitor's center, and then swings up into the sky, that it hits me. Samantha the golden eagle is chasing Arlo.

She screeches again and circles the air over his head, diving every so often to swoop over him and send him ducking toward his car. He throws himself inside. The car has no roof. He presses buttons frantically to get it closed before Samantha strikes again.

Then I hear Aunt Josie calling her back, and the camera swoops back toward her, alighting on my aunt's arm, which is now wrapped in a thick glove. They both watch Arlo Kylak pull off, dust flying.

The last thing I hear before the recording ends is Aunt Josie whispering, "Good girl."

Everyone in Pinnia's house sits in stunned silence. Only when someone clears their throat do I dare to look at Mom.

But there's no storm. No wildfire. She looks as smooth and placid as one of the lakes she named me and Hurona for. She's almost...smiling. Then there's a sound near the front door, and everyone looks.

It's Dr. Elemnieri, and she stands leaning against the wall where she cleared her throat. I can tell by her face, by her posture, that she'd seen everything. I feel the bees inside me again, wondering how she must feel. When I'd met my father at her house, it was like filling in all the gaps for a person I didn't know. But for Dr. Elemnieri, it must be like gaps being created for the person she *thought* she knew. Unless she did know. I hold my breath, waiting for her to speak.

She and my mother stare at each other across the room, and Hurona tilts her head—I wonder what feeling she's getting. My eyes pierce down at the floor. I think of *The Encyclopedia of Entomology*, which is now somewhere on the ground of FOLROY's greenhouse. Maybe the bugs ate it too. But somewhere in its pages, I had learned about a stickbug, which looks so much like a real stick when it holds still that sometimes other bugs will land on it. Predators ignore it. Right now I imagine myself as a couchbug. I think if I sit as still as possible, I can just pretend I am part of the couch, and the awkwardness in this room will just pass me by.

"So," Hurona says. I let her be the big sister. Right now, I really just want to be the little sister.

I'm expecting stony silence. Or maybe even the storm that I keep expecting to break in my mother.

Then Dr. Elemnieri takes a long, deep breath.

"Hello," she says to my mom. She crosses the room and extends her hand. "I'm Dr. Lunata Elemnieri."

My mother stares at Dr. Elemnieri's hand for a moment. Then, like a miracle, her hand reaches out and clasps it in her own.

"Nadine Neaux."

"I understand...," Dr. Elemnieri says. She pauses, then begins again. "I understand that you are also an inventor. And that you're responsible for discovering the heartpod."

My mom stares at her for a long, long time. Maybe it just feels like a long time. I'm half girl, half couchbug.

"Yes," my mom says. And now she's definitely smiling. "Yes, I am."

46

WE GO TO Lunata Elemnieri's house at noon as planned.

Except Urtica isn't with us. And Dr. Elemnieri is.

And Mom.

And Mx. Amur.

And Zizi.

And Pinnia and Mento.

And Eya and Ms. Mari.

And Carver.

And eight lawyers who all say "yes, ma'am" when they talk to Dr. Elemnieri, who all carry briefcases and look very serious.

When Arlo Kylak steps out onto the porch, he looks annoyed at first to find so many people outside his house. Then the annoyance melts into shock, and the shock hardens into something I don't recognize when he realizes he knows some of the faces. When he sees Mom.

Then all the hardness crumbles when he sees his wife, Dr. Elemnieri, standing with us.

"Arlo," she says. "We need to talk."

47

IN MX. AMUR'S teal van, everyone is silent, lulled by the long drive. I sit in the middle row, Pinnia napping against my shoulder, my mom looking out the window on my other side. I hold Mom's old phone in my lap, looking at the list of voice messages from Aunt Josie.

There's only one left.

I shouldn't be surprised when Mom leans over and whispers, "Can I listen too?" but I am. I hold the phone up between our ears and we both lean in.

> *Nadine, it's me. This won't be long. I'm on my way south to what I hear they're calling the Arborklept. I know I've given you a hard time about huddling up in Prine, but I tell you... the sky looks like it's been swallowed, and I'm glad you're there in your little tree cave and not out here. But promise me you won't stay there, Dina. Those girls need to see the sky. They need the stars to dream. I'll tell them myself when I*

finish here. But for now, stay safe. I want you to know
that you're still my sister. And I'm yours. Nothing will
change that. I'll see you. Soon.

My tears swallow the whole sky. But instead of retreating into silence, Mom presses her head against mine.

"We always think we have more time," she says. "And sometimes we don't."

I nod, trying to stop crying.

"You're so much like her," she whispers. "I promise I'll share her with you. It may take some time but...I promise."

We pass the marker that says we're five miles from Prine just as Iva holds her phone above her head in the front row with Hurona.

"It's on!" she cries, and Pinnia immediately sits upright. Everyone stirs, listening.

Iva turns up the volume and then projects onto the van's ceiling. We all stare up at the image of Dr. Lunata Elemnieri, who has just walked up to the mic at the press conference she told us she'd be hosting today. She stands alone, wearing a yellow shirt tucked into blue pants. Her curly hair is loose around her face. Her ears glimmer with gemstones, but her ring finger is empty. Arlo Kylak is nowhere to be seen.

"By now, the events that unfolded on FOLROY property have been made public," she says, scanning the crowd with her eyes. She's the scientist who saved us all from wildfires, so I know whatever room she's in is packed full. "The footage captured—and I'm so grateful it was captured—is on every Newscast for everyone to see.

Now I am here today to share the facts with you, as well as some announcements.

"First," she goes on, "my assistant Urtica Gerund has been released from my employment for contract violations. The facts are this: Urtica Gerund cooperated with the FOLROY corporation to spy on and steal my work and research. At this time, we can confirm that she and FOLROY were responsible for spraying a serum causing unnatural, increased lockwood growth on the area surrounding the town of Prine without the knowledge or consent of its residents. The investigation into the different kinds of harm this activity caused is ongoing. Urtica Gerund has also been charged with kidnapping and other charges, which the investigator will discuss after I'm finished here."

The camera cuts away to show footage of FOLROY's headquarters—not the greenhouse, but their major building downtown—with yellow tape over the doors.

"In the aftermath of last night, community investigators have demanded that the FOLROY board immediately expel board members who were complicit in the Dolosalvus plot, including the governor and"—she pauses, just half an instant—"my husband, Arlo Kylak. Both agreed to sign over their shares to community oversight. That paperwork was completed at noon today."

She rustles some notes on the podium. Through the van's windshield, I can see the circled clump of lockwood that marks Prine. It's the end of the day, the sun almost setting. But I can see everything: the flat empty landscape beyond my town, still recovering after years of wildfires. And the circle of trees that has protected us, but also hurt us. When I'd climbed in Iva's truck, it was my first time leaving. This is my first time coming back.

"Today I am announcing that, thanks to a few brave young people, FOLROY will now be a company owned by the community that powers it, overseen by board members selected by that community. Dolosalvus was thought up with the intention of exploiting the workers who keep our city green and our tables filled with food; that project is now dead. I will work with FOLROY's new board to make amends for my role in this suffering. Harm inflicted unintentionally is still harm."

I replay those words in my head as she goes on talking. I think of what Pinnia had said—how everything I think I know about justice is like a pair of boots, broken in. I reach my arm around Pinnia and squeeze her. She grins, because we both know what Dr. Elemnieri is about to say next.

"Finally," she says from the ceiling of Mx. Amur's van, "today I am officially announcing the opening of a new center for the study of environmental science, open to young people starting at age four. Our survival on this planet means learning to become partners with the land, including insects and plants. But we can't forget each other. In the last twenty-four hours, I was reminded of this. Pinnia and Mento Kip, Erie and Hurona Neaux, Iva Lovelock, Carver Copeny…thank you for—"

The screen goes black. We have entered the tunnel.

"We always lose signal right here," Iva groans. "Even the fancy phones. The lockwood is just too thick in the tunnel."

"That's okay." I grin. "We got to hear the best part."

The rest we already know—that the citizens of Prine will now be paid fairly for the pods that only Prine can grow.

"She said our names on TV!" Pinnia crows. "How does it feel to be a board member, Ms. Neaux?"

My mother lets her hand trail out the open window, smiling.

"I'm excited to be in the same room with your parents, Pinnia," she answers.

When we enter the tunnel, Pinnia sits forward to peer through the van windows.

"Is this it?" she breathes.

"This is it," I say softly.

The van trundles through, and I remember how I felt just last week: like Prine was in the belly of a monster that had taken a bite and swallowed us. It feels different now. Last night, while my sister and I were being kidnapped, the FOLROY drone had flown over the lockwood and made all the vines grow for the last time. Now, whatever grows in Prine will grow because we watered it. Not with some special serum made in a lab, but with water. In Prine, we're named for dead and almost-dead things, but we are also named for dreamers.

I can see the light up ahead. We're almost home. It feels like we've been gone a year. I wonder if I will even recognize it. Behind me, Hurona leans forward and wraps her arms around my neck. She hasn't hugged me since she started going into the trees.

"What are you going to do?" she whispers in my ear. "Now that you can?"

Maybe she thinks I haven't thought about it. Maybe she thinks

I'll have to rack my brains. But I don't. Outside this ring of trees, I've seen what's possible.

"I'm going to start a Buzz Yard," I reply. "Here."

"Perfect," she says. "Perfect."

Mx. Amur's van breaks out of the tunnel and into the circle where FOLROY's trucks usually park. The circle is empty. I hear the whine of the pulper before we even open the door. But once we do, I hear the machine slowly, slowly die. When is the last time a car drove out of FOLROY, and when is the last time someone who left came home? When the van comes to a stop, a beetle lands on the window, green and smooth. It wanders for a second before I give the glass a tap. Up it goes.

We pile out of the car, Pinnia looking around in wonder, at our town like a fossil clenched in stone. The lockwood kids have carved the sky open. Everyone is making the most of what they think will be a short day of sun. All around us, Prinians are wandering over from workstations, from the store, from the schoolhouse. This place is so small and word travels so fast. Soon the streets are as full as they ever get, but I don't see who I'm looking for until I hear someone shout my name.

Banneker.

I see them coming down the Spine, and I want to shout too, but I'm a brimming jar, and if I open my mouth, I might spill. I want to introduce them to Pinnia. I want to tell them about Mento and Zizi and every part of Petrichor. Instead I just run toward them, and I realize in that moment how scared I had been. To be gone. To be away. Afraid that while I was gone, Banneker would fall before I had time to figure out how to make us birds. It turns out we don't need to be birds, and I don't want to be one. I just want to be.

When me and Banneker hug, I feel the humming of a million bees deep in my heart. It's getting dark, but I don't care. I point up at the sky, unable to speak. Because tomorrow the sun is going to rise, and we are going to see it.

ACKNOWLEDGMENTS

I wrote this book on Earth, and you're probably reading it on Earth too. (If not... wow!) This planet is home to life. How could I ever thank it enough? Bugs and birds and volcanoes and the most incredible sky. Dinosaur bones and geodes and coral. Horses. *(Horses!)* Canyons and cliffs and goldfinches. All of this stuff, right here. I'm amazed by it. I am in awe of this place.

I want to save this place.

And so I thank, in addition to Earth, my agent, Patrice Caldwell, and my editor, Alexandra Hightower, who read this book and said, "We need more climate-hopeful fiction. Especially for young people." Yes, especially for young people, who are inheriting a hurt world they didn't injure, a broken climate they didn't ruin. I thank these young people, too, for continuing to imagine something beautiful as the people in charge hold up their own hands and claim they're tied.

Those hands are not tied: They are simply too full of money. With that, thank you to Stuart Cipinko—may he rest—for, when I was in tenth grade, being the first educator to instruct me to look at any suffering in the world and ask, "Who is getting rich from this?" I also thank Frank X Walker and the Affrilachian Poets for teaching me much earlier to respect the people of Appalachia and the people of Kentucky, even if my own self-hatred kept it from sinking in for a while. There is a unique history of struggle in this state. No, I am not "just" from Louisville. I am from Kentucky. This book is for Harlan County. This book is for the mining towns. This book is for the warehouses pushing to unionize in spite of threats and ruin.

Is this too heavy for the acknowledgments in a book for children this age? I don't think so. (Young readers: We saddle you with much heavier, don't we?) Our planet is indeed dying, but defeatism isn't how we prolong its life, or our own. Thank you, Octavia Butler, for *Parable of the Sower*. Thank you, Sherri L. Smith, for *Orleans*. Thank you Nnedi Okorafor. Thank you, Rebecca Roanhorse. Thank you to everyone who looks forward and grits their teeth but keeps moving and imagining.

We have lost so much. But we don't have to lose everything. We can learn from this place that we love. We can change the way we live. Did you know there is fungus that can replace plastic? Did you know there are people all around the world inventing and dreaming their way into a future where Earth survives? You can join them. This isn't over yet.

And I am grateful.

Aisha Asad

OLIVIA A. COLE

is a writer from Kentucky. She
writes books for young people
and adults, and her works
include *The Truth About White
Lies*, *Cloud Parliament*, and
Dear Medusa.